INESCAPABLE

A NOVEL

BY

WB HENLEY

This book is dedicated to Shelia, who has been my wife and best friend for over 48 years. Shelia, you have always encouraged me to pursue my dreams and supported me in every way imaginable through thick and thin, good times and hard times, but always loving times. You are the best and I love you with all my heart.

Acknowledgements

If it takes a village to raise a child, then it takes a lifetime and all the people in it to make a book. For a writer, every experience, every relationship, and every emotion become part of a story. Sooner or later it comes out on paper. But not to worry. This is a work of fiction so what should stay anonymous, will stay anonymous.

That's not to say that there aren't many people who contributed directly to this effort. To my sister and favorite writer, Terry Woosley, who without her confidence, encouragement, and many edits, I would have never had the courage to put pen to paper or to finish once I began. To my sister and favorite artist, Sioux Henley Campbell, who designed the haunting cover art for the book and has inspired me with her creativity since she was a child. To my fabulous editor/book coach, NancyKay Wessman, who kept pointing me in the right direction, even when I was determined to not learn from my mistakes.

To my beta readers who slogged through the early drafts and offered constructive criticism and support: Andrew Paradis, who taught me details about firearms I never knew before; Carolyn Ezell, who caught my many inconsistencies and offered much better suggestions for describing a scene; Donna Thomas, who provided invaluable advice on imagery and character development; Jesse Woosley, who helped me sort out a tangled plot and list of characters; Marina Reznor, who kept my chronology straight and offered so much good advice; Tk Cassidy, who prevented a pending death by a thousand "it"s and greatly livened up the story with suggestions of active verbs; and finally to Cheyenne

Henley and Alya Fawal, who sat through a late Waffle House night helping to shape the story and the characters. Thank you all from the bottom of my heart.

Finally, to the best writers' groups that a fellow could ever hope to belong to: the Tuscaloosa Writers and Illustrators Guild (TWIG) and the Write Club of the Hoover Library. I have learned so much from the wonderful and creative artists in our community. You are incredibly patient, helpful, loving, and talented people. Thank you for accepting me and teaching me what support is all about.

BUCK

One

*E**verything happens for a reason.*
That's what the preacher said at Mama's funeral. The kind of thing a preacher says at any funeral, I suppose.

I remember the sun shining on her through this clear glass halo around a cross in the window. Her body looked fake, like a plastic mannequin with Mama's face painted on. My stepfather Leon stood to the side of the casket. Teresa hid against the back of his shoulder. Before the doors opened for visitors, Leon told me it was best if I stayed in the pew.

The grieving widower smiled each time someone offered respects. I pictured him counting the hugs and the handshakes like tickets to the show. Once they paid their admission, the good folks lingered for a long time at the casket, examining the body and looking for marks. Finally, they slow-walked past me, the suspected mother-murderer sitting stone-faced in the shadows. I kept my eyes on the halo in the window to avoid their looks. When the time came, Leon led Teresa to the aisle end of our pew. My half-sister was only eleven, but she held up till her last walk past her mama. When they closed the lid, she yelped and reached out an arm towards me. Leon pulled her back.

When the preacher began his sermon, an angry jaybird hit the window behind the pulpit, like it wanted to break the glass and kill its own reflection. While the preacher quoted his verses, the bird attacked again and again. The slams grew louder.

Everything happens for a reason.

Then the bird threw its full force at the window. Everybody stared, waiting on what might happen and trying to figure out if it was a message of some kind. Maybe from God? Maybe from the grave? Even the preacher turned to watch, but the bird never returned, either too stunned or too dead to keep up the fight.

Evil things happen. Bad things that sometimes...

The preacher paused before saying it again, just to make sure he was clear.

Sometimes... we don't understand.

I felt the stares. Cold eyes that had already decided. Cold minds that wouldn't change.

I had grown used to it, the cold. At the time, I even preferred it. It made me numb, and anything that numbed the beast was fine with me. I wanted the cold, I needed the cold, to keep the heat damped down. Because that's what I was afraid of. The beast. The crazy anger. The madness. The heat that chased everybody from my life.

Three weeks before, Teresa found us in the snow. Her scream didn't even move me at first. Just another blast of winter wind. We looked frozen, she said, my head down on Mama's chest. Neither one of us moving. My eyes closed. Mama's eyes open—pale, empty, still staring at what came for her and left her dead.

Teresa kept screaming, wouldn't stop screaming—shrill, harsh, accusing. The sound finally cut through the fog. I looked up towards her but kept my head down like I was caught in some howling windstorm. Teresa's face was all contorted, and it jerked me back to reality. It was pure fear, and fear meant hot-blooded life. But at that moment, I didn't want life. All I wanted was to die and leave all the heat behind. I wanted to join my mother. Maybe find some peace in cold, empty death.

When Teresa's words fully formed in my brain, they filled all the empty spaces and swelled so fast, I could almost feel the blood trickling from my ears. The fear crept back inside me.

"Buck," she screamed, "what did you do?"

Two

I don't think it rained a drop for months after Mama died, like God forgot how to cry, if He ever knew how. I don't know, maybe He was waiting on me to cry first.

Leon cleared the new field that summer, just to give me something to build a fence around, I guess. I didn't mind the work. It kept me busy, kept me from thinking too hard, kept me in shape for football, the only place where I could let the beast out. It was the only place I could hit people and be rewarded for it. The only place it felt good to be angry.

He laid out the little orange flags like tiny soldiers. Perfectly spaced at 6-foot intervals. I imagined them on a parade ground. Leon ordered them to advance to the end of the field, execute a perfect column left, march on for another eighth of a mile, and then stand at attention waiting on their fate. My orders were simple. Join them, post-hole diggers at the ready, and bury them where they were placed. Fate.

Leon Bustard is a small man, even though he does his best to look bigger—feet apart and shoulders back, crisp khaki shirt tucked neatly into a pair of creased denim jeans, which are always tucked into a polished pair of leather boots. He wasn't in the military, although he does sport a skull tattoo wearing a sergeant's hat. On his own head, he wears a nice clean Stetson, so everybody knows who owns the "ranch." Only two of the five steers he bought at auction have survived the summer so far. The other three he shot when they didn't get on their feet quick enough. Yet, here I am building another fence around another pasture.

On the day it hit 100, Leon came to inspect his troops.

"Not even halfway finished. Let's pick it up, Buck." His voice always had this hint of satisfaction when he was giving me orders.

"Go a lot faster with the tractor," I said.

Leon pulled a water cooler from the truck bed and glared at me from under his hat.

"See that fence?" He motioned to the other side of the road and spit the words out through his teeth. "Nearly a mile of it, and every damn post I put in by hand."

"Yeah," I mumbled, "you told me."

"Brought you water 'cause of the heat. Didn't affect your attitude any." Leon dropped the cooler back in the truck. "I'll send your sister to check on you later."

His spinning tires wrapped me up in brown dust, and I hid out for a few seconds till the hot wind brushed it away.

A couple of hours later, Teresa puttered up on her four-wheeler. Strapped behind her was the water cooler Leon had left in the kitchen. A small bouquet of red flowers cradled in her lap.

"Daddy said you might need this," she said, thumbing at the cooler.

"The little man taketh, the little man giveth."

She looked at me like she didn't hear.

At least God hadn't taken everybody away. Not yet.

"Thanks," I said. My face was streaked with dirt and I lifted the cooler to drink straight from the tap.

Teresa had fallen in love with Robinson Crusoe a few months before. She laughed. "You look like a washed-up castaway."

"Oh, I'm not the castaway," I said in my deepest voice. I aimed an imaginary spear at my kid half-sister. "I'm the head-hunter."

Before she could start up the ATV, I grabbed her by the shoulders. "But first I gotta boil ya."

She giggled but slipped out of my hands. The flowers spilled out into little splatters of red on the dead grass.

"Stop," she yelled. "Now look what you made me do."

I knelt down and picked them up, twelve of them, two for each month since Mama passed. "Ah, they're all right," I said. "Just need a little water, that's all."

I rinsed each flower in the cooler, then soaked my sweaty T-shirt and squeezed out the salt.

Teresa looked at the brown water. "Eww, you're gonna drink that?"

"No, I'm gonna throw it on you," I said and faked like I was going to catch her again. She grinned. I wrapped the flowers in the wet shirt and handed her the bundle. "Here," I said, "say hello to Mama for me."

I watched her disappear past the scrub trees at the edge of the field, headed to the bottom where the creek used to run, until it dried up like everything else. The engine died in the distance, and I remembered when I found Mama, six months ago to the day, face down in the water. I shook the vision out of my head and looked down the line of flags marking my path. If this was my fate, then let's get to it. I pounded on the clay till I dug another hole and set another post, poured another bag of concrete and sealed one more poor soldier in his place.

Three

∞

Six dry months, the last few hot. What's the word the people around town use for me? Pitiless.

Sheriff Jefferson stopped his Bronco up by the row of wooden posts I had planted along the roadside. He had been sheriff for as long as I could remember, but I still knew him as Coach Ben from Dixie League days. Guess he knew he'd find Leon's boy out here at the end of the line.

I was sprawled in the dirt, eyes closed. A steel pry rod stood tilted in a half-dug hole. He pulled on the shoulder and rolled down his window. His radio crackled.

"Still haven't found that missing cow yet, Coach?"

He ignored the remark and waded through the briars, swearing that they must be the only things still alive in this damned heat. Coach Ben looked so much older than baseball days, since his hair had gone mostly gray, along with the moustache. He was a big man, still in good shape for his age. I guess he had to stay in shape to keep all the people in line who didn't like dealing with a Black sheriff in a small Alabama town. Even I knew there were a lot of those people.

"Buck," he said.

"Better get back at it. You got a cow to find. I got a rock to dig out."

I grabbed for the rod and drove it back into the hole. The rod bounced and a few sparks flew out of the darkness.

"Thought I'd come by and tell you personally. The coroner returned the autopsy findings. He won't sign off on homicide."

The steel bar landed with a crack, and the rocks flew out, burying themselves in the dust.

"But he won't say it was an accident, either."

"Leon and the DA go way back. Figured he'd keep pushing you and the coroner to stick me with it." The bar landed with another crack.

"I don't know who did it, Buck. That don't mean I won't still be looking."

"Just not at anybody else, right?" I picked up the broken pieces.

"As far as anybody knows, she slipped, hit her head on something, and drowned. Maybe God did it."

I stood with a chunk of jagged quartz in my hand and glared at him. "You know who did it, and you know me and my sister are still living with him."

"Put the rock down, son, and count yourself lucky. You're off the hook for now."

He kicked at a briar in his way and covered his boots in powder.

"Goddammit," he said.

When he got in his car, the sheriff turned his radio to the classical music station. Sounded like a funeral song. I imagined some old dude pining over a lost lover, tears falling on the piano keys. Sad stuff. Beautiful stuff. Coach Ben turned it up and kept still for a long time. I heard the dispatcher say a cow was found wandering along the highway.

Four

After the sheriff left, Leon came back to check on me. One post to go to the corner, but a long, long way to the end of the flags.

"Two weeks left. You gonna make it, boy?" said Leon. He always seemed more chipper when the prospects of my failing seemed high.

"I'll make it."

"Got a lot on it. No fence, no driving. I'm gonna check on the bus sign-up. Bet ol' Miz Simpson's missed you."

"I been thinking. Why you suppose Mama was out here by the creek?"

"You still got your panties in a wad?" Leon shook his head. "Your mother was drunk. She was always drunk in case you don't remember. Maybe she went looking for her missing dog in the middle of the fucking night."

"How come you didn't go look for her?"

"Don't cotton to your attitude, boy. If I chased her every time she left the goddamn house…" Leon didn't like the way the talk was headed, and he cut it off. "You made it to the woods, but you still got another line to go. You're wastin' daylight."

He left, frowning. I watched him go, set the corner post, fastened the two angle-posts to hold the strain of the barbed wire. The sky got dark quicker than usual. I felt a low rumble, coming through the ground more than the clouds. I still had an hour of daylight left, enough to get a good start down the next line. Instead, I just sat in the dirt and stared at the woods.

This was as close as I had been since the day I found Mama. Honestly, I couldn't say to the sheriff or to Leon or to Teresa or even to myself what had happened before I came across her. But finding her, that I could picture every time I closed my eyes.

There's the big oak tree I spent so many nights under, including that night. Its branches are covered in white. Little clumps of snow slide off, and they make a little shush sound each time one hits the ground.

Down the hill, through the small trees, I can see where the creek runs. I can hear the water splashing. I shiver.

Something calls me. Maybe something in the creek or maybe something in my mind, I can't tell. Each time I take a step, the snow melts under my feet leaving a dark spot on the ground. The call gets louder.

Patches of white dot the rocks in the stream. Little rays of sunlight make their way through the tree branches. It's almost peaceful. Except something is wrong.

Something dark lay in the creek. Gold grass floats on the water. I know it's out of place, but I can't figure out why. Something juts from the shadows, maybe a broken tree limb. My heart beats out of rhythm. I can't catch my breath. In the water, the broken limb bounces in the water in the same uneven beat. I can't look away. It looks... like a body. A human body.

I inch into the creek until my feet hit bottom. I lean over to touch the limb. It's a leg! The foot bounces against my hand, and I scramble backwards, soaking myself. Something holds my eyelids open. I can't close them. I can't look away. I can't leave. I reach down and turn it over with a grunt.

The rest was a rush of images—Teresa finding me holding the body, yelling at my sister to go get help, the interrogation.

After the sheriff let me go, Leon wasn't there and he wouldn't answer the phone. So I called Mandalee. She was my girl then, until I hurt her like I seem to hurt everybody I know. Only two people in this world really meant anything to me after Mama died—her and Teresa. Mandalee's father believed in his daughter, so he agreed to let me stay with them for a few days. When Leon finally let me come home, he never asked what the sheriff said. Never asked about their suspicions or their accusations. Hardly mentioned the death of his own daughter's mother. Until the funeral.

"Everything happens for a reason," said the preacher, while an angry bird crashed into the window.

People talk if you don't cry at your mother's funeral. I had been found with the body.

People talked.

Five

Wasted time, trying to change the past. Out here at the edge of the new pasture, I felt completely alone. Even this late, the heat was thick, like a heavy wool blanket you can't throw off. A cloud rumbled threats, and a hot wind rustled through the trees. I caught a glimpse of something moving in the shadows where Teresa traveled every day to the bottoms, the place I had avoided for half a year.

"Hey," I called. A pale shape faded into the trees. I followed, slipping into the woods and down the long hill. Under the canopy of the large water oak, I could see the dry creek bed in the gloom. A figure sat on the bank, feet dangling where the cool water used to run. A soft female voice hummed a low melody, a lonesome Hank Williams tune I hadn't heard since…Oh, how she loved sad old country songs.

"Mama?"

The song grew louder, and a few words reached my ears. "Who is that?"

The last rays of the sunset penetrated the shadows for just a second, glinting off a tall amber bottle in my sister's hands. The glare threw a streak across her face.

"Teresa? Why are you out here so late?"

"Daddy thinks you killed her," she said. "He says angry can't help itself." She lifted the bottle and sucked down a gulp, making an ugly face.

"Leon hates me. Of course, he'd say that." The sky flashed above the treetops, and a loud crack echoed from deep in the woods. Dead leaves fell from the oak. Dry leaves. The wind swept them into the creek bed, out of the way—where things and people go to die. I sat down beside her, and in my mind, my mother's body lay a few feet away.

"What the hell are you doing with that shit?" I said, reaching for the bottle.

"Good enough for you, then good enough for me," said Teresa. She yanked it away and took another gulp. The liquid dribbled from her chin.

"Give me the goddamn bottle, Teresa." This time, she didn't resist.

"When you and Daddy were yelling that night, Mama left—said she couldn't stand it anymore."

"Mama did crap like that all the time."

I reached out to pull her to my shoulder, but she yanked away. "She never said goodbye."

"I know, it's been tough. You could've talked to me."

"You never asked about anybody else. You just sulled up," she said. "You know, Daddy doesn't hate you. He just doesn't understand you. You're always angry."

"I can't stand to be around him. He's mean. Mean enough to hurt Mama."

The wind moaned through the oak branches. The sturdy trunk swayed but held its ground.

"Take it back," she cried.

"You know he likes to hurt things."

"He wouldn't do that to Mama. You just hate him."

"He didn't love her. He fucking called her a drunk. What do you want me to do? Hug the guy?"

"I want you to be part of the family," she screamed. "You've been tearing us apart as long as I can remember. I know you lost your real dad, but why can't you accept mine?"

"I tried. Hell, when I found Mama, he didn't even go with me to the sheriff's office. He ain't ever liked me."

"You don't remember what you said that night, do you? You were the reason she left. You said she always took Daddy's side and you hated her as much as him."

"Why would I say that?"

"'Cause you were mad. You've been mad for years."

I didn't have an answer. Anger is so much a part of me, I don't care anymore who it hurts.

"Everybody thinks you did it," she finally said. "I didn't wanna believe 'em till today. You killed her. Didn't you?"

The accusation slapped me hard, and I leaned backward from the blow. Even if I thought I could have done it, I didn't think Teresa believed it.

She slid off the bank and stepped through the dead leaves to the spot where our lives changed. On the other bank stood a little stone altar where Teresa had placed all her offerings. The sky lit up, cracking from one end to the other.

I could clearly see what she had put there. The wilting flowers. My crusty T-shirt. A small animal's skull.

I blinked.

"It's Scout. I found it today," she said softly, picking up the skull and turning it in her hands. "There's a bullet hole in it."

The wind howled, still as hot and dry as it had been before the lightning strike.

I went to her and took the skull. The hole passed clear through, shattering the opposite side, taking brain and bone.

Her voice came stronger now, with the dry eyes that come when you're certain you're right. "When I found you with Mama, you had your gun."

"Yeah, but I didn't . . ." She thought I shot Scout. "No, it musta been Leon. He shot her dog. Maybe she tried to stop him, and he hurt her, too."

She rained both fists down on my chest. "No! You shot Scout. Then you killed Mama. Why didn't you just leave like you said you would? I hate you!"

And then she ran. Ran till the dark swallowed her up, back to the only person she had left. I watched her run, and for the life of me, I couldn't blame her.

Six

When the storm passed, I felt like it had broken me open and bled out any last bit of goodness I had left. I dropped the skull and reached for the bottle. It was still almost full. Next to the skull, next to the altar, I wondered again what dying would be like. Would it stop the feeling? I looked at the bottle. It had been my friend long before my mother died. Since then, I kept it close, trying to drown something in me that wouldn't die. What was inside the bottle didn't matter, as long as the liquid numbed the pain. It was as close to dying as I could bring myself.

The night was deep when I woke up. For a moment, I didn't know where I was, until my hand brushed the skull. I scrambled to my feet, stumbling over roots and branches until I clawed out of the creek bed. The moon peered through the branches and left a ghost-like glow on the path that led toward the house. I wandered into the light and stopped in my tracks, like a rabbit exposed.

"Did you do it?" a slender girl in a long white gown asked from the shadows.

I stared into the dark. Her face was mostly hidden, but I could see a bottle raised high like she was offering it to me. All the time her eyes stayed fixed on me. I couldn't make out the face, but her eyes shone clear. They were the same pale eyes I remembered from six months ago.

"Who are you? Are you real?" I asked.

"Of course I'm real. You're talking to me, aren't you?" Her voice was sweet, in a black licorice kind of way.

"Then, why are you out here in the middle of the night?" I asked. I still couldn't see her face, but she had to be young from her voice and her build. "Do I know you?"

"I come down here often," she said. "I've seen you around, but first time here since…" her voice trailed off. She tipped the bottle for a long swallow. "Must be difficult," she said and held up the bottle again. "I don't mind sharing."

A soft wind left over from the storm whispered through the branches, rustling their leaves and disorienting me. I felt the panic rising.

"Maybe I shouldn't have come here," I said. My voice echoed in my ears, like the thump of a heartbeat.

"Had to do it sooner or later," she answered. "It's as good a time as any." Her voice was quiet and measured.

I can't explain it, but I felt drawn to her, even as my heart beat faster, like when you creep toward the edge of a cliff. She was the only still thing around me, and stillness was all I had wanted for months. I held onto a sapling and slid to the ground a few feet away, staying in the moonlight. She leaned towards me and held out her arm. I took the bottle, and it felt cold and real. I leaned back and slugged down a swallow. The sting was real.

The light was faint, but I studied her face as best I could. She looked to be about my age, maybe a little younger. Skinny, too skinny. Fair skin stretched over her cheekbones. Skin so pale it almost shined in the dark. She had stringy blonde hair, messy and a bit greasy. Wayward strands stuck to her head as if she had been sweating. Her eyes were strong, though, and clear and piercing in that way only pale eyes can be. Eyes like Mama's, except alive. I took another drink and decided to stay a while longer. To face this place with someone else felt reassuring, even if I didn't know her. Maybe better I didn't know her. Most everybody I knew had already decided I was a bad seed, the kind that couldn't be trusted.

"Did you know my mother?" I asked. I handed the bottle back to her. She took a sip before answering.

"I came to know her well." She handed the bottle back. "You didn't answer my question."

"What?"

"Did you do it? Most everybody seems to think you did."

The question didn't insult me. "It's just that I don't . . ." I drained the rest of the bottle.

"Don't what?"

"I gotta piss," I said and lurched to my feet, dropping the bottle and leaning against a tree.

"Do you mind?" I motioned at her to turn around.

"I don't mind. Everybody's got to pee." She didn't turn her head.

"Okay," I mumbled. "I'm just gonna go over here a bit." I weaved from tree to tree until I found a suitable place out of her sight.

I stood there a long while letting the poisons flow out. My thoughts tumbled in my head, and I felt an overwhelming need to relieve them, too.

"It's just I don't remember," I slurred over the splash of piss on dead leaves. "I honest to God don't remember."

The sheriff kept asking me at the station that day, over and over. Why was I out there that morning? I lied. Made up a crazy story about checking out the deer stand. That was the only explanation I could think of, but I hung onto it. In desperation, I guess. Because the real reason was buried somewhere deep inside, where even I couldn't reach it.

"There, I said it," I called as the last few drops dribbled onto my boots. I tucked myself in and headed back to my confessor. A few vines grabbed at me, tried to slow me down, maybe even stop me, but I shrugged them off.

When I emerged into the moonlight, the wind had died and taken everything with it. The girl was gone.

"Why can't I remember?" I yelled. Nobody answered.

Seven

Where's a body go when home's no longer an option? Teresa knew I had the rifle. She was the one who found me and our mother that morning. Now she had found Scout, or what was left of him. I must have shot Scout. What else was there to think? What kind of person would do something like that? What else would a person like that do? I couldn't go home. Not anymore.

So I picked a direction, any direction as long as it was away. The darkness didn't stop me because I didn't need to see where I was going. I didn't want to see where I had been. I just walked. For hours. Branches clawed at me. Insisted I go home. Roots tangled up my feet, crashed me to the ground, but I got up and kept walking. Wild voices kept crying out, telling me to stay away. Still, I kept walking.

A faint rippling noise wormed into my head. I followed, more out of instinct than will. The sound grew louder, pulling me towards it. A wall of briars grabbed at me. Through the tangle, I could see light, an opening. I recognized the murmuring rush for what it was—water—and for a moment my thirst overcame everything. I grabbed at the vines. Pulled them off, leaving torn skin and dripping blood. Stumbled into the open. Fell on my knees. The water called me, and I followed. I found a pool and lay down, submerged my face, drank deep. Suddenly, I could see myself from above, watching this figure laying still, face down in the water, not moving, just like my mother.

What does it take? Letting go isn't difficult.

Relax, I thought. *Let everything go.*

I drifted up in the black sky, and my body grew smaller. My head was invisible beneath the dark surface. Lifeless. Still. Just another corpse of another rotten tree slowly fading back into the Earth. As... if... I... never... was.

Something strong pulled me up, and I tried to scream as I fell out of the sky.

I sputtered, trying to cough out the water that had seeped into my throat. When I could finally lift my head, I heard nothing. I called out. No one there. I stumbled to the edge of the woods, and searched for broken branches, disturbed ground, anything to tell me I wasn't alone. I fell to my knees, rocked in the sand, and cried. Every creature in the night waited in silence for the second storm of the night to pass.

I don't remember lying down. I don't remember closing my eyes. I just knew I was tired of running. Tired of holding back the beast. Tired.

When I opened my eyes, morning had come, the sun bringing its daily misery. I watched a mosquito drink its fill until I slapped the blood out of it. I shaded my eyes and sat up. Still alone.

Eight

∞

The river. By the end of the summer, it had dwindled to a few shallow pools with a thin trickle connecting them all like tiny spider web strings. Our little farm was on the terrace surrounding the Tierney River flood plain, where the wildlife refuge and the swamp kept out most people except for the poachers and the bootleggers and the few campers on the other side of the swamp near the state park.

A long time ago, as I was just growing out of childhood, I convinced my girl Mandalee to explore the river bottoms with me. Even then, I knew she was mine and I was hers. We planned the expedition with the zeal of Hernando de Soto, who claimed the wilderness for the White man. De Soto was the one we learned about in school even though the Red man had known these woods for thousands of years before he got here. Together, Mandalee and I lay in the back yard for hours with a flashlight studying the map I copied at the library, picking out a five-mile path to the river. Now, I struggled to remember the map. All I could think of was the girl, my girl.

Mandalee St. James was my best friend since kindergarten, ever since the day she found me in the hall shrunk in a corner in a puddle of piss. Though she was no older than me, she took me by the hand and led me to the bathroom. She told me to take off my wet pants and stay in the stall. She said she would take care of it. A few minutes later she came back with the teacher, Mrs. Richards, who brought an extra pair of pants, ones she always kept for emergencies just like this one.

Together we came back to the classroom and took our seats, and Mrs. Richards thanked the both of us real loud for helping her move the stuff she needed out of the other classroom. Nobody else in the class ever knew. Mandalee never told another soul and never brought up the incident again.

For over a hundred years, the woods of Alabama were the hiding places for stills and the men that ran them, out of the way of nosy revenue officers and strong-armed competitors. Nowadays, legal alcohol was easy to get, and moonshiners were a thing of the past. That didn't mean bootlegging disappeared. Now they peddled a different product. Here in the buckle of the Bible belt, the pot they raised in bigger and bigger patches in the refuge was not likely to become legal anytime soon. The trade was safe as long as thieves, snitches, and crusading lawmen were kept out. The refuge wasn't a safe place for exploring kids. When my mother overheard us making childhood travel plans to the river, she smiled at our adventurous spirit. She didn't know I dreamed that one day, just like old Huck Finn, me and Mandalee would pack all our belongings in little sacks to carry over our shoulders and disappear into the woods, never to be seen again. Mandalee and I never made the expedition. I wish to God we had.

Until a few years ago, Mandalee was a wisp of a girl with a slight build and long honey-brown hair that she kept in a ponytail. She blossomed in her teen years, developing from a waif to a woman almost overnight. Every boy in our class wanted a date with her, but she ignored them, always content to hang out with me. We went everywhere together until the talk got too loud after Mama's death, and Mandalee's parents tried to keep her away from the turmoil. For a while, she resisted their wishes, until our relationship exploded along with everything else.

That morning on the river, Mandalee St. James was almost all I could think about. Until I stood up.

My head pounded from dehydration. I was weak from the work and the emotion and the drinking and walking all night. My muscles, used to running sprints and digging holes for fence posts, trembled like a weakling. I drank from the river the night before even though I knew it wasn't safe. Bad water could put a man down as surely as a knife in the gut. I had been lucky. Now, as the sun chased the desolation just enough to let me move, I knew I had to find food and safe water somewhere.

About a mile east of the river, a county road ran along the top of the terrace. The river wasn't hard to cross right now, as low as the water was. But the woods on the other side were every bit as dense as on this side. I could wander forever trying to get through, and if I got lost and turned around, I would wind up right back where I was. I decided to follow the riverbed.

Few bridges cross the river. Three in the whole county that I could think of. The road we lived on crossed it a few miles east of the farm. If I went that way, I would surely run into my stepfather or one of the neighbors who would call him. The falls were north, and another highway crossed a mile farther upstream. The park had numerous campsites. One or two stores were located just outside. Someone would let me use a phone. I'd call Mandalee. Maybe she had forgiven me. Maybe everything would be all right.

I walked upstream, wading through mud and stepping over rotting logs for maybe a mile or so. On the east bank, a clearing came into view, and I decided to walk through the small field instead of the muddy trek along the riverbed. I pulled myself up the bank and caught a glimpse of red in the brush. When I took another step, the color disappeared. I stepped back and saw it again—just a small patch of red hidden behind the broken branches near the ground. I realized the branches were covered with Spanish moss, except it looked out of place. We were too far north of where the plant was usually found. I moved closer and found a netting of some kind, camouflaged to look like Spanish moss—a hiding place.

"What you doing here?" A female voice called gruffly behind me.

As I turned, I lost my balance and slid down the bank, tumbling over a clump of roots near the bottom. I landed on my face at a woman's feet. She never moved except to poke a stick in my back.

"Why you here?" she asked and poked me hard, twice.

I rolled fast and tried to spring to my feet. She was faster and thumped me over the head. I blacked out briefly and went down, again on my face. The stick was poking in my back again.

"Answer me," she demanded.

"Can I at least sit up so I can see you?" I held the back of my head where a knot was rising.

She pulled the stick away but didn't back up. I slowly rolled over and sat up, still rubbing my head.

"I'm just walking," I said.

The woman looked old, but she hadn't moved like she was old.

"Long way from home, ain't you?"

"Don't got one anymore," I said, shaking my head to clear my senses. "That hurt. Who are you anyway?"

She studied my face. "Been a long time since I seen you close. But you're him alright."

She dropped the stick and squatted in front of me. She reached out a calloused hand to touch my face. When I drew back, she reluctantly withdrew her hand.

"What do they call you nowadays?" she asked.

"What's it to you?" I said. "You gonna hit me again if I don't tell you?" I rubbed my head and glared at her from under my arm.

"You don't gotta tell me. I already know it," she said. "Jamie. Oh, it's so good to say it out loud. Praise God!"

"Lady, you're crazy," I said, backing away. "I don't know who you are, and I don't know who you think I am. But I'm leaving."

"Why, it's your name. You just ain't heard it in so long." She touched my chin and raised my face to study me even closer. "Jamie. You're my son."

Nine

The letter came addressed to the Tierney County Sheriff's Department, Stewarton, Alabama. The address was written in delicate cursive on a pink envelope. Inside was a note in dainty block letters on light pink stationery with an image of a red rose at the bottom of the page. The first line read, "I know who killed Eva Bustard." The note ended six lines later with an explosive accusation.

This message could be a crank. Lord knows, he had plenty of those seeking notoriety or revenge. The communication was one of the first breaks he had in the case, though. Ben Jefferson turned it over, looking for more.

The paper was matte, the kind that's hard to lift fingerprints from. The rose was distinctive, but he had seen similar designs before. Probably a fairly common stock item that could be ordered online. Might be worth checking out the local card store and drug stores, though. The envelope had self-sticking adhesive that didn't require wetting. Probably no DNA, if it ever came to that. No return address. The postmark was local but the letter could have come from anybody in the county. He held the paper to his nose and detected a faint smell of perfume. With no guarantee, the writer of this note was likely female. At least that eliminated half the county's population.

The only real thing he had, for now, was the message itself.

"Eva was Ray Thompson's wife. Ray's law partner, Richard Morrison, had an affair with her. The day before she died, Eva was at

MacInnelly's sitting with Richard. I have to tell somebody. He said if she ever told anybody about how she got her son, she was dead. I think Richard killed her."

Dick Morrison. Everybody in Tierney County knew the man. Judge Richard Morrison was the title he held for about twenty years or so. He was the man who pronounced final decrees on child custody, signed off on financial arrangements in bitter divorces, made life miserable on deadbeat dads and negligent mothers. He was the arbiter of moral values in Tierney County, the final judge of who were the good families—and who were the bad ones. If he was a potential suspect, he would have to be questioned with utmost discretion.

Still, the questioning had to be done. A lead like this, even if it was frivolous, couldn't be ignored. Especially because of the one other thing that tied the great judge to the case. Richard Morrison was married to Eva Bustard's sister.

Jefferson called to his deputy, who was working up complaint reports on the computer outside his office door. "Tom, get in here. I need you to find me some pink stationery. Then you need to head over to Roseboro and talk to Joe MacInnelly."

When Monday came, and Judge Morrison was in his chambers getting ready for another week's cases, Ben figured it was as good a time as any to drop in on the great man.

For the sheriff to come by family court wasn't that unusual. The Sheriff's Office and county jail occupied most of the block next to the Tierney County Courthouse. Ben often visited the court on official business. Morrison's clerk, Sarah, waved him in, and Jefferson knocked on the half-closed mahogany door. He got a mumbled "yeah" in return and pushed it open.

"You got a minute, Judge?"

Dick Morrison looked over the reading glasses perched on his nose and smiled in recognition.

"Ben," he said loudly as he was accustomed, "what can I do for you today, son? Chasing another worthless sperm donor skipping out on his child support?"

"Judge," said Ben with a half-hearted smile, "I got twenty years on you. Wish I were young enough to be your son." Not the best way to begin the conversation, but he couldn't ever get used to the patronizing attitude of the old guard.

"Still a little thin-skinned after all these years? Nobody's questioning your manhood, Ben. Just being friendly."

Jefferson ignored the response. "Judge, you got a minute to talk about something personal? You might be able to help me with something."

"Always happy to help the law. Shut the door, would you?"

Ben pushed the door closed and reached in his shirt pocket for the baggy holding the letter. He thought better and decided to hold onto the note for a while.

He settled in the dark leather chair in front of the massive desk and felt himself sinking several inches below the judge's level. Dick Morrison was the kind of man who used all the tricks of displaying superiority: dismissing appellations, hand on the shoulder, extra firm handshakes that pulled you into his space. Jefferson leaned back and gazed up at the ceiling for a second.

"I gotta tell you, Judge. You have the best chairs in the courthouse. I believe I could fall asleep in one of these." He propped one of his legs on the other knee, and pulled his toes back, showing the sole of his dusty boot. He knew a few of the tricks, too.

"You didn't come here to take a nap. What can I help you with?"

Time to be polite again. He sat up straight and looked the man across the desk directly in the eye. "I'm tying up loose ends on the Eva Bustard case."

"I heard you closed that thing. An accident, wasn't it?"

"No, not closed. Just shelved until something new comes up."

"What came up?"

Jefferson ignored the question. "You knew her pretty well, right? I mean, she was your sister-in-law. You and her first husband were law partners at one time, weren't you?"

"We didn't socialize, if that's what you're asking. Eva and my wife barely spoke, especially after she moved in with Leon."

"I'm more interested in the early years. What was she like back then? How was her marriage to Ray Thompson?"

"Ray Thompson's been dead way over ten years," said the judge. "Why on Earth are you asking about him? I doubt he had anything to do with her death, unless you believe in ghosts. Do you? Believe in ghosts?"

"I believe the past can come back to haunt us. You would have known about the state of her marriage, wouldn't you? Didn't Ray ever talk about it?"

"Let's say it was rocky from time to time. But whose marriage isn't? We all go through rough patches."

"Any indiscretions you hear of? I mean, rough patches happen when one person steps out on the other."

"What are you insinuating, Sheriff? Just come out and say it if you think you know something."

"I'm not insinuating anything. Just running down the facts."

"Gossip. You're running after gossip. You should be ashamed of yourself. *He who spreads slander is a fool.* Look it up. Proverbs."

"Who am I slandering, Judge? I'm just doing my job, asking questions."

"Leave the dead alone and let them rest in peace. Whatever happened in Eva's marriage is long past, deader than she is. Go do your job, Sheriff. I've got a court to run." The judge rose, grabbed his files, and left the room, his black robe stirring the papers on his desk and pulling them onto the floor in his wake.

Ben Jefferson pulled out the pink letter and held it in front of him.

"You're right about something, guilty conscience lady," he said softly. "The good judge knows something he ain't telling."

TOM WALTERS

Ten

In the rural South, titles for ladies by polite folk, emphasis on polite, are still somewhat codified. "Miz," much more drawn out than the Northern equivalent of "Ms.," is for business or as respect for their elders or if they are unsure of a woman's marital status. The old-fashioned, old-moneyed, or one-time-moneyed married ladies still prefer "Mrs." The third choice can be a term of endearment for any woman. But when used by a young man to address an unattached young lady, it's because he either doesn't know her well enough or isn't interested.

"Miss Cheryl," said Tom, "I don't suppose you have any pink letter paper with roses, do you?" Tom called out. He kept thumbing through the stationery display. He had searched three other drug stores and card shops before this one and the phrase "wild goose chase" kept running through his mind.

Cheryl Moon stepped from behind the register, pulled her hair back behind her shoulders and tugged her collar open with both hands.

"Sorry about the AC. It can't keep up with the heat these days." She unfastened a button near the top of her blouse and fanned herself across her chest. She leaned in front of the deputy and reached her hand to the lower shelf.

"Lord, I think I'm gonna melt if it stays this hot," she said.

Tom turned and began riffling through the boxes on the other side of the aisle.

"Pink stationery, huh? You looking for something for a special lady?"

"Nope. Ben sent me to look for some, but I'm beginning to believe I'm wasting my time."

"I would have thought a big tough guy like you would be out catching criminals."

Tom grunted something.

Cheryl unfastened another button and pulled her shirt open a little wider, thankful she had put on the low-cut bra that morning. She grabbed Tom by the hand and pulled him to the end of the aisle. Kneeling down she pointed to the row of boxes near the floor so that Tom could only see by peering over her shoulder.

"I believe these have flowers on them. See anything you like?"

"Maybe," said Tom, his voice betraying a little more interest now. "Anything pink?"

"Well, maybe if we looked a little harder, we could find you something pink." She flapped her collar to move the air and her other assets.

"Those two," he said. "Those two right there." He reached over her shoulder, and she leaned her head back against him. "I'm sorry," he said. "Can you pull them out for me?"

Cheryl tumbled over on one leg and sat on the floor, smiling up at him. He leaned in further and grabbed two boxes off the shelf. He pulled out his phone and studied a picture for a second or two.

"I'll be damned," he said. "Do me a favor, Miss Cheryl? Can you tell me who might have bought this paper anytime lately?"

"Thomas Walters, you're a blind fool." She scrambled to her feet and stalked up to the front. "Give me the box. If we sold any, 'Miss Cheryl' can tell you when. Not sure 'Miss Cheryl' can tell you who."

"I'd be much obliged," he said. "Maybe if you're free this weekend, you might like to go up to the falls. Get you out of this hot store for a while. Whadya say?"

"Well, Tom, maybe you aren't so blind after all. Let's see what I can do."

An hour later, Deputy Walters laid his hat on the bar at MacInnelly's Grill.

"You off-duty already, Tom? Looks like you could use a beer." Joe MacInnelly had run the bar for years. Best grilled cheese around in the daytime. Coldest beer in four counties at night. MacInnelly's thrived in Roseboro, which was more than four times larger than the county seat of Stewarton. Roseboro was the only wet town in the otherwise bone-dry Tierney County.

A wet town, where alcohol sales were legal, beckoned the thirsty citizens of the county like an oasis in the desert. So Tom knew MacInnelly's well, not because he was a regular, but because a big part of his job was trying to keep the drunks off the roads between Roseboro and Stewarton, some 25 miles away.

"I could always use a cold beer, especially in this heat. On official business this time, though." He looked around, but the only business in the bar at 3 p.m. was chunking change into the jukebox. "Ever see Judge Morrison in here?"

"Dick Morrison? Yeah, only once lately. He's not the kind to hang out in bars, at least not anymore."

"What, he used to be a regular?"

"Used to see him years ago until he got all his hound-dogging out of his system and became the staid old judge."

"That's hard to imagine. Old Bible-thumping Dick hoisting a few."

Joe put away a few glasses and mused, "Yeah, he's pretty much a righteous asshole these days. I lost a few dollars to my ex 'cause of him. But I don't hold grudges. When he came in here, he was just another customer. None of my business why."

"How about Sarah Covington? Know her?" asked the deputy.

"Good old Sarah? Now, she's a regular. Everybody loves her."

"Sarah Covington. The lady from Judge Morrison's court. We're talking about the same Sarah, right?

Sarah's like a grandmother. Listens to everybody's problems. Pats 'em on the head. Sends 'em home. But not before they get their fill. Hell, if she didn't work for the judge, I'd hire her. She'd be the best bartender I ever had."

"One more question. You said the judge came in only one time recently. When was that?"

"You know, I guess it was about the time Miz Bustard got killed. In fact, now I think about it, that's who he was with. Eva Bustard."

In a small town, everything is timed by the few big events everybody remembers. The death of Eva Bustard was such a marker. The whole town talked about the woman who, a lot of people said, was killed by her own son. Just nobody had the proof.

"You saying Eva and the judge were here together the night before she died?" asked Tom. "Why didn't you tell somebody?"

"What for, Tom? Everybody knows the boy did it."

Tom was back in Ben Jefferson's office filling him in when Leon Bustard came through the front door carrying a dog's skull. The desk deputy was threatening to cuff him if he didn't shut up when Ben stepped out to see what the commotion was about.

"The boy did do it, Jefferson."

"What are you talking about, Leon?"

"Look at this here. It's the skull of our old dog, the one went missing the day before Eva died. My daughter tells me she heard a shot that morning. And the dog turns up with a bullet hole in his head. You know Buck had his rifle with him the morning Eva died. Teresa says she found the dog's skull yesterday. He's done run off now, Sheriff." Leon paused to let the news sink into the sheriff's thick head.

"I didn't want to believe it about my stepson," he continued without a hint of regret. "I thought for sure it was an accident—that you was after the wrong guy. But now, he's been found out and then he up and runs away. I think Buck really might have done it."

"What you want me to do, Leon? Arrest your boy for shooting a dog?"

"He musta shot that dog in anger. If he did that to his mother's pet, what kind of hate did he have for her? His steam's been building for a long time."

"If you want to report a missing person, I'll look into his whereabouts. I can't arrest anybody because of a dog's skull."

"You're a goddamn hard-head. The murderer been right in front of you for months, and you won't do a damn thing about it. You're a pitiful excuse for a lawman." Leon spit on the floor, speckling Jefferson's boots in the process. Leaving the skull, he stalked out, slamming the door behind him.

Tom let out a low whistle.

"Damn, what did you stick up his ass?"

"Leon's boy is missing. He thinks he's on the run."

"For killing his mother? I thought you cleared him."

"I haven't cleared anybody. But I am worried about him. Ask around. See if anybody's seen him since last night. I'm gonna pay Sarah a visit."

Eleven

Dick Morrison liked sitting in judgment. He was a fair man, he thought, and his strong righteous streak kept him from the softness that corrupted people. He usually knew in his heart what was right, and when he wasn't sure, he consulted his Old Testament because the New Testament was too accommodating for his liking. The old prophets knew there was a time for everything, as long as it was righteous. Of course, he always made sure things were legal—he knew how to use the law to his advantage in every decision he made. He was born to be a judge.

Ray, his former law partner, God rest his soul, relied on human kindness, which is quite easily taken advantage of. Tenderness is a sign of weakness in men, especially in lawyers and judges, who cannot afford muddled minds. A kind lawyer is a poor one, and Dick Morrison refused to be poor. Kindness is what cost Ray his life. Ironically, it also made his widow financially comfortable, because she was wise enough to convince her husband, with Dick's help, that a very hefty life insurance policy was prudent for a young family.

Dick had known Eva nearly all her life. She was his wife's younger sister, the prettier of the two but too young when Dick's adolescent urges sent him in search of female companionship. He settled on the older Yvonne, the strong, solid one with good moral sense. She was no Miss America, the looks having gone to Eva, but she was the ballast he needed to keep him steady. He would need a partner of Yvonne's stability to help him navigate the treacherous shoals of propriety and standards. Still, Eva was nice to have around to talk to, she of the soft heart and full figure befitting a woman.

Eva's memory had been nagging on his mind, ever since the sheriff's visit. Now at the end of a long day on the bench, half-listening to disgusting excuses for the dregs of human behavior, Dick finally had time to reflect. He leaned backed in his leather chair, his black robe still on, a trickle of sweat tracing down his chest. He remembered the evening long ago when Eva stopped at the judge's office. He had become a judge by then, chasing the last, black-robed buffoon out in a landslide election after the sitting judge was caught, quite literally, with his pants down in the company of a young man. One thing for a man to carry on dalliances. Hell, that was almost expected. But it goddamn better be with a woman, a pretty young one as long as she was legal. Tierney County voters had little stomach for the kind of man who would lie with another man. That might work in Atlanta, but not in Stewarton, Alabama.

Eva was such a pretty woman, even if she was married. He was happy to lend her an ear whenever she needed one. That night long ago, when Ray was away and Eva was lonely, the talk turned serious. Eva was desperate, and Ray could not help her. In anguish, she broke down in Dick's arms. He knew when to speak, and every now and then, despite his nature, when just to listen. The pregnancy had happened so easily the first time, she admitted, before they were married. But now, several years after they were wed, Eva could not get pregnant again. She had abandoned her birth control soon after the wedding, though she had not told Ray. He was dead-set against a family. Too young, he said. Too poor, he said. Pregnancy was something to think about later when their finances were adequate.

"Oh, you have no idea how much I regret what we did with the first baby," she confided in him. "It was an awful, terrible decision, but Ray told me it would ruin my life."

Dick was stunned at first. Even the vile thought of abortion made him sick. Yet here he was, alone with the woman he had desired for so many years. So, he stood up and paced a while, trying to sort his thoughts. He closed the heavy door to his office and quietly turned the lock. Then he sat by her and let her talk. Even took her hand when the tears cascaded down her face. His blood surged, sweeping away the righteousness and replacing it with something even hotter. He moved closer on the couch and wiped her cheeks gently with the back of his other hand, resting his fingers on her trembling chin.

"I was only fifteen, Dick. I didn't know any better. Why'd he let me do it? Sometimes, I think it may have been my one chance to ever hold my own baby."

She sobbed and he moved closer, putting one arm around her shoulder and pulling her in.

"I was so young I didn't know what to do. He kept saying my family would run me off. God, I knew it was wrong, and I've paid dearly for it ever since. He doesn't care. I don't know if he'll ever want a child. It's hopeless."

She buried her head in his chest, and he wrapped both arms around her. He'd have to be sure to change shirts before he went home, he thought. He didn't speak, rubbing her back to encourage her.

"I'm stuck. Childless, barren for all I know. Married to a man who doesn't give a damn how I feel."

She sat up quickly and stared him in the eyes.

"Retribution. That's what you called it in Sunday School. God's retribution against a sinner. Why can't He forgive me? Will I be punished for the rest of my life? Will I be damned to a fiery hell? That's where sinners go. You preach it every weekend, Dick. I'm doomed to a loveless marriage on Earth and punishment forever after. Oh God, please forgive me. Please…"

Dick grasped her firmly on both sides of her head and pulled her close.

"Listen to me, Eva. Where there's repentance, there's forgiveness. Where there's forgiveness, there's hope. You're a good woman with a good heart. All you want is to love and be loved. In God's eyes, nothing is purer."

Dick wrapped her close again and kissed her on her head. He kissed the tears from her face. He kissed her neck, wet with tears and sweat and emotion. God, how he wanted her. That desire, ever-present since high school, was rising, building. No, this woman was one of God's innocents, too, preyed on by a sick man who had no regret talking a teenaged girl into killing a baby. Yet, she was the one paying while Ray, sweet old Ray, blissfully went about his life like nothing ever happened.

"I will fix this," he breathed heavily. "I will take care of you. Trust me. I know you will have a child in your arms. You just have to trust me."

She leaned back her head and surrendered.

Two months later, Eva was the adoptive mother of a son, a baby just beginning to learn to walk. With Dick's urging, Ray acquiesced, out of weakness, Dick supposed. Ray had always been a reed in the wind. He could talk an innocent girl into murdering a baby, but he had no strength to stand up to a real man. And if Dick hated anything more than a sinful man, it was a weak man.

Dick handled all the details. To Ray and Eva, everything was completely aboveboard. Dick made sure all was legal. He knew Eva would be grateful forever.

Twelve

Dick had solved Eva's problem and his own desires, but three years passed before the opportunity for righteous retribution presented itself.

He vividly remembered how Eva heard of Ray's death. He was just stepping out of the shower when Eva took the call in her bedroom. Her shock was evident, and Dick didn't wait to towel off before he took her in his arms to comfort her, again. She needed so much comfort. Sometimes, though, a little kindness is completely appropriate.

Not that it was a surprise to Dick—Ray's demise, that is. Dick had asked Ray to take on a pro bono client, in the way that public defenders were historically arranged in the county. Dick had looked into the case, another criminal possession charge for the repeat offender, which if convicted, would be his third strike. Under that law, the discretion of the judge was removed. A guilty verdict would send the young man to jail for life. Dick told Ray that he was the best attorney for the job. Every defendant, no matter how lowly, needs good representation. Always mindful of being a faithful public servant and his weak nature seldom allowing him to say no, Ray agreed to take the case. Though a bit out of the usual way of handling things, Dick visited the charged man in the county jail to let him know who would be handling his case.

He had come prepared.

"Kenny," he said with a slight nod of his head to the accused man, who was still trembling from withdrawal. "You know I've tried to work with you over the years. I thought you might stay clean this time."

"I ain't been myself since my boy was took. It's all I can do most days to white-knuckle it and stay clean. I tried. Lord knows, I tried."

"You didn't try hard enough though, did you?"

"I don't care no more, Judge Morrison. I took all I could take. Lost my boy. Lost my woman. Been to jail two times already. I can't fight it no more. Send me off for life. It's better than living out there where there's no pity."

Dick leaned back in the steel chair in the holding room where lawyers usually met their clients. The guards were down the hall, near enough to respond if trouble started but too far to overhear.

"That's your problem, Kenny. You're always looking for pity. Don't you know pity will kill you? Sure as a knife in the heart, it'll kill you dead."

"Not looking for pity no more, Judge. Just looking for peace."

"Peace?" Dick chuckled. "No such thing in this life. You'll be cold in the ground before you find peace."

He leaned into the man and glimpsed a tiny spark still glimmering deep in his otherwise lifeless eyes.

"It's still there, isn't it? That hatred. You've just been too weak to do anything about it, haven't you? Another man takes your boy and treats him like he's his own, right out in front of God and everybody. Your son, with another man's name. That boy's yours, Kenny. No amount of dressing him up in another family's clothes is going to change that. He belonged to you until that man took him away." The judge spoke without a trace of irony, considering Dick had signed the order.

He went on. "I often wondered how a real man could allow something like that. What kind of man are you, Kenny?"

Dick could see the old fire growing in Kenny's eyes.

"Enough of a man to kill the son-of-a-bitch that took everything away."

"Yes, I believe you would, given the chance. Maybe a little something for courage, and a little steel to make sure it's done properly. I believe you have it in you, son."

Kenny shook violently and swayed back and forth in his chair.

"It ain't never left. I hate that man more than I love my own life."

"Peace, Kenny. Once they put you down, you'll find peace then. And you know of one sure way to make them put you down."

Dick pulled a paper from his briefcase. Underneath was a small plastic bag hidden in his palm. He laid the paper with the hidden packet on the table in front of Kenny and leaned over his shoulder in the manner of a kindly lawyer explaining a document written in legal Greek.

"That man. The one you hate. He volunteered to be your attorney. What do you think of that? He doesn't even remember who you are. He'll be here tomorrow to introduce himself and go over your defense. Take this just before they let you in. A little cough with your hands over your mouth, they'll never notice. It'll help you face what you got to do."

Kenny stopped shaking and sat bolt upright in the chair. Dick went on.

"Feel underneath the table, real gentle."

Dick watched Kenny trace his fingers until his eyes lit up.

"I taped it there before you came in," said Dick. "It'll be waiting for you. And he'll be waiting on you unawares. You're so little to him, he took your son and never thought any more about you. And when you're done, Kenny, peace will be waiting on the other side."

Kenny's face flushed red. The prominent vein in his temple pulsed angrily. His fingers moved from side to side, slowly caressing the object. His eyes narrowed into dark slits while the corners of his mouth turned slightly upward. Dick could almost see the image in the man's mind, the moment when Kenny plunged the steel deep into the wicked man's body, over and over again until his urges were satisfied, until the climax was reached, and the guards reacted, and the ultimate surrender took over his body. Dick's loins began to ache in anticipation.

BUCK

Thirteen

I stared at the woman.
Her face was tanned dark with deep lines like a raisin dried in the sun.
Her hair had mostly weathered to gray. She looked old, rough. Yet she
moved like a cat, quiet and almost graceful. She had obviously trailed
me for some ways and put me down so easily there was no doubt about
her agility. From her looks, she could have been sixty or she could have
been forty. I couldn't tell. She wore heavy khakis, long sleeves, and a
camouflage vest to fend off mosquitoes and briars and spying eyes. She
was suited for life in the woods, but other than her weathered skin, she
seemed to take pride in her cleanliness and appearance. She was the
strangest figure I could imagine seeing in the forest.

"Prisoner syndrome. Don't talk till you know what's going on," she
said. "I get it. No need to talk now. We got plenty of time. I heard they
call you Buck, but that ain't your real name. Your given name, the one
I gave you, is James. I always called you Jamie; so, that's what I'm
gonna call you now."

I shook my head slowly.

"I know, it'll take a little getting used to. Hell, I ain't said it out loud
in years myself." She rose and circled me. "Stand up so's I can get a
good look at you."

I stayed in the mud.

"Fine, strong young man. Just like your daddy till they broke him."

"You knew my father?" I asked.

"Well, how else I'm gonna have his baby? Course I knew him."

"I mean my real father. And I'm not your baby."

"No, you ain't a baby no more. I never got to see you grow up. Don't mean I didn't try, Jamie."

"Why do you keep calling me that. I'm not your boy, and nobody calls me Jamie."

"Cause that's your name, like it or not." She stopped for a moment. "I'm sorry. Nobody called you that in seventeen years, how you gonna know? Let's try again. Name's Jeannine. Most folks call me Jeannie. You're Jamie, I'm Jeannie." She extended her hand. I didn't take it.

"I'm leaving," I said. "Call me anything you want, 'cause I won't be here." I struggled to my feet and fell again, almost immediately.

"Tell you what. Stay a while and let me get some food and water in you. Bet you ain't eat or drunk nothin' in a while."

I stayed silent.

"I was sorry to hear about Miss Eva. Terrible thing that, drowning."

I shot her a hard look.

"What do you know about my mother?"

"I'm your..." Jeannie stopped herself as quickly as she started. "Nothing more 'bout her dyin' than the rest of the county," she said. "I know you ain't a boy could do somethin' like that."

"You're the only one thinks that,"

"Come on, Jamie—Buck. Let me help you. You're gonna need some doctoring, too. Briars done tore you up good."

The Spanish moss netting was effective. Unless you had a sharp eye, you would have walked right by. Or when the river was up, you might have paddled by unawares that someone was watching from the bank. She kept the hiding place neat. A tan tarpaulin stretched across a frame of poles to keep out the rain. Shallow trenches to keep the storm water from running underneath. Big enough to stretch out on a bed of pine straw for a night's sleep out of the rain if somebody had to.

Jeannie pulled a flat rock away from the corner. A dug-out underneath held a five-gallon metal can. She opened a box beside the can and pulled out a cup, unscrewed the top of the can and tipped it, filling the cup with clean water.

"Here, drink this. Take as much as you want but go slow. Your body's dry, and you got some making up to do."

Another reach into the hole produced a couple of protein bars and some crackers. I had already sucked down the water. She filled the cup again.

"You live here?" I said after a long while.

"It's one of my places."

"You got more? One of them near my house?"

"I seen you, from a distance."

"Were you watching when my mom got killed?"

"Like I said, I'm sorry what happened to her. She seemed like a good woman. She raised a fine boy—my boy."

"You know something about how she died, don't you?" My voice raised a little. I felt the anger, sure, but something else too. Something I couldn't quite identify. Hope, maybe?

"I'll tell you everything I know," she said. "It ain't gonna be easy—on me or you. But it gotta be told. I tell it from the beginning, though. My terms."

I thought of the last few months, the lost months. The grief, the anger, the suspicion. The broken family. I thought of the loss. My mother. My dreams. Friends who abandoned me or who I had driven away. Then Mandalee. Now Teresa, the only family I had left.

"I'm listening,"

Fourteen

"Ben Jefferson, as I live and breathe. What brings you round here? I didn't take you for a drinking man." Sarah Covington was attractive, one of those women who aged gracefully, and even now in her fifties turned heads much younger. Her hair was bottle-blonde, pulled back to frame an open smile. Her jeans were one size too small, and she filled them with the confidence of a woman who was comfortable in her skin.

Ben tipped the brown ball cap he liked to wear when he was out of uniform. He had been in office for over twenty-five years, and though he sometimes felt his age, he still cut an imposing, authoritative figure. His smile, when he flashed it, was genuine, and people warmed to him quickly. People accepted him as their lawman, for the most part, though many in the county still couldn't stomach a Black man in charge of the jail. A lot of those liked to hang out in places like MacInnelly's. He could feel the eyes on him, even if he wasn't looking back. Subconsciously, he touched the service revolver he always carried on his hip.

"I like a cold one much as the next guy." He waved to Joe, tending the bar, and ordered a light beer. "Got a minute?" he said, turning back to the woman who greeted him.

"You know, Sheriff, I've been hoping you'd ask me that for a long time," she said, wrapping her pink-nailed slender fingers around his wrist and pulling him towards the back of the room. He managed to reach back for the beer Joe held out with a grin.

"Home away from home, Ben. Welcome to my place," she said, pushing him into a dimly lit booth. She slid in next to him and scooted over so their legs rested against each other.

"I believe we've known each other around the courthouse for, what, twenty years or more. You don't get out much do you, Sheriff?"

"Only when there's a fight to break up."

"All business makes for a dull man, Ben. This isn't about business, is it? 'Cause I don't think you're a dull man."

Ben pulled the pink paper from his pocket and held the note close to his nose, registering the scent. Sarah pulled back an inch or two.

"What can you tell me about this?" he said, tucking the note safely away. "You know something about the good judge that I should know?"

"What is that? You got a love letter from someone, and now you're out looking for the culprit?"

"You mind?" Ben took her fingers and pulled her hand to his face as if to kiss it. "I like your perfume," he said. "Smells familiar."

A man with a shaggy black beard slammed down his glass at the table next to them.

"A woman wants to smell good, doesn't she? And men like it that way." She didn't pull her hand back. "It's a pretty popular brand, but I like it."

"If you wanted to stay anonymous, you should have picked something plain to write on. Something the local drug store sells more than once a year." He placed her hand back on the table and picked up his beer for a sip. He studied her eyes, which darted to the note still peeking from his shirt pocket. "Sarah, you know something, and you want to tell it. Otherwise, you wouldn't have sent me this."

"Look, I like you a lot. You're a good man. The judge is a powerful man in this county, and I can't afford to tell stories on a man like that. You know, I file away a lot of records in that courthouse, a lot of records. It's a good job, and I can't afford to lose it." She edged away and slipped out of the booth, but he grabbed her wrist again. "Leave me alone, Sheriff. I got nothing else to say."

The bearded man at the next table stood up, knocking his chair over.

"This goddamn Oreo giving you a hard time, Sarah?" he said, glaring at the sheriff.

"Settle down, Frankie. He's just leaving," she said.

Ben slid out, still holding his beer, and turned his back on the beard. "Think about it, Sarah. If you really want to help, you know where to find me."

"The lady said you're leaving. Better leave now," said Frankie. He grabbed Ben by the shoulder and tried to whirl him around. Ben turned quickly, throwing the beer into the man's face. The mug tumbled to the floor, and the man let go. Ben brought his open hand up and under the man's chin, grasping him with a tight grip under his jaws.

"Best to keep your hands off the sheriff, son. Unless you want to call it an early night."

"You ain't wearing a badge. All I see is an asshole harassing our Sarah. We don't take kindly to that kind of thing."

"To what kind of thing, son? You worried about Sarah? Or you just don't like a Black man talking to a White woman?"

Frankie tried to pull his hand away while his other fist swung wildly toward the sheriff's head. Ben deflected the blow, swung the man around into a headlock, and pulled one arm behind the man, pushing up until he groaned.

"Lucky for you, I'm in a good mood." Ben pulled hard to one side, and the man tumbled to the floor. He started to scramble up but saw the .44 on the sheriff's hip and settled back to the floor. Ben picked up the empty mug and placed it back on the table.

"What a waste," he said. He carefully smoothed his shirt and tipped his cap again to Sarah.

"Be seeing you," he said.

Fifteen

I could fly again.

The trick was easy once you got the hang of it. You just clinched your core muscles and concentrated. If the power was in you, the ground simply fell away. I tested my skills to see what I remembered. It was nothing like the out-of-control, out-of-body experience at the river, but years had passed since I experienced this feeling.

To rise, I leaned my head back and thrust my fist to the sky, just like Superman in the movies, except no lightning speed. Slow and deliberate. I rose up beside the giant water oak, right through the huge branches, touching each of them when I passed by to make sure they were real. When I looked down, I'd start to fall. The trick was to look where you wanted to go. Your body would follow. But if you wanted to stay above it all, you could only take a quick glimpse at the ground, way down below, or you'd come crashing down in the middle of everything.

My eyes stayed up as much as I could. Then I'd glance at the ground. Then the sky again, trying to stay aloft. All the while, my mind put together the jigsaw pieces. I saw a creek bed. Full. The outer cutbank looked dark and deep. The inner point bar, sandy white. Freckles of yellow gravel sparkled under the water. Teresa sat in the sand with a cane pole in her hands. Every few seconds she lifted the line and swung it back out over the water. A dog lay by her side, his head resting in her lap. Scout. I watched and drifted downward, threatening to tumble any moment until I had to look away, straining to stay safely away where I could see everything without becoming a part of anything.

Teresa cast again, and a bare hook whizzed through the air right under my feet, landing in the deep water, and settling to the bottom. Suddenly, the line grew tight and the pole bent double. Teresa rose to the battle, and a small skeleton clattered out of her lap, a dog's skull rolling in the sand. I looked blankly at the bones, bleached white in the sun. I couldn't help but stare, my eyes fixed by the suddenness of the beauty turned to horror, And while I did, I fell, slow at first, then faster. Teresa was too busy with her fight to notice the bones. She pulled at the line, backing away to haul her catch out of the water. Some kind of shapeless mass rose up from the deep and started taking form in front of her. I fell fast now, unable to stop, unable to look away. The mass took form, a face maybe, two arms reaching for him as he fell. Teresa screamed.

"Easy now," said a voice in the dark.

I sat bolt upright, sweating, panting, my eyes wild in fright. They settled on a young woman kneeling next to me, the same woman that had shared the bottle in the woods.

"Shh, shh, shh, shh," she said. "You're okay now. It's gone. Whatever it was, it's over now."

"Don't touch me. Leave me alone."

"I won't touch you, I promise, but I'll stay right here with you. It's over now."

"It's you." My heart skipped a beat while I drew back from the figure. "Who the hell are you?"

"I told you, a friend."

"Are you real? You disappeared. I couldn't find you."

"You see me now, don't you?"

"I don't understand." A part of me wanted her to disappear again, but a bigger part wanted her to stay—something I couldn't explain, even to myself. When she was present, I felt soothed. I couldn't help but relax. I fell back on the bed and stared up.

The girl began humming softly, the same sad country song he had heard Teresa singing in the woods. The tune was comforting, familiar. I closed my eyes and listened until my breathing slowed. Until my heart quit pounding. Until I slipped into the darkness, this time in peace. This time without the ghosts.

When I awoke, I was soaked in sweat. Not that the night had ever really gotten cool, but now the sun was up, it was sweltering again. Just like all the days in the terrible months since...

I looked around the small lean-to. A full bottle of water sat next to me, a note underneath. "Breakfast in the pack hanging from the poplar about fifty feet away. Tied up to keep it from the bears. Be sure you haul it back up when you're done. Be back soon. Stay quiet or you'll attract unwanted company."

A threat? Or a warning? The message had to be from the real woman that took me in, not from the imaginary girl in white that visited him, then disappeared. Because that's what that was, just some crazy game of my imagination. But here I was in the lean-to that the older woman had built and let me stay in. This one was real, and even though I couldn't be sure whose side she was on, she took me in when nobody else would. Crazy or not, she was all I had at the moment. I found the pack and the food.

At twilight, Jeannie returned. I looked up from the cot, and she suddenly appeared like a spirit, kneeling at the opening.

"Damn, don't you knock?"

"I brought supper," she said. "Fried chicken. I'm guessing you like messy food judging by the mess you leave in the woods. Keep the bones. We'll have to bury them away from here if we want to keep the raccoons away."

I didn't ask questions, at least at first, until the grease and French fries quenched my hunger. By then, I was ready.

"Who am I?"

"I don't know who you are, but I know who you used to be," she said. "You're the son of a music man and the woman who loved him. Lord, he could play so the angels themselves would come down to dance."

"Mama liked to dance. After Dad died, she'd put on a CD and pick me up and whirl around the room till I was dizzy."

"That's what music will do. Make you dizzy-happy."

"I can't call the music man Dad. I already got one. What was his name—the music man?"

"Kenny," she said. One tear traced down a deep line in her face and settled by her ear. "The man loved you with all his heart. He sang you to sleep every night."

"Then why'd he leave me? Why'd he leave you? He must have left or we'd still be together, right? Isn't that what happens? A young mother with no way to support a child has to give him up. Kenny, huh? Just another worthless guitar player, wasn't he?"

"No, Oh, no, Jamie. He didn't leave us. They took him away after you was born."

"Who took him away? He got drunk, and they took him off to jail?"

"We wasn't drunk. First time, before you came along, we had a little weed was all. Wasn't much. Nothing nobody gets sent away for."

"Yeah, booze, weed, it's all the same. Like I said, worthless."

"That time, Kenny and me had one joint between us. We was sleeping in the car one night, and the blue lights come up behind us. Made us get out the car. I was six months along with you at the time. They searched the car, threw everything out on the ground like we was criminals till they found that one joint, stuck way down in Kenny's backpack in the backseat. Cuffed him up like a gangbanger and hauled him off. Said I should get my ass to a shelter and clean myself up. But I didn't go. Didn't need some shelter with folks all up in my business. I already had a home on them wheels."

"You were smoking pot with a baby on the way? Sleeping in the back of a car in some dirty out-of-the-way parking lot? They should have thrown you in jail, too."

"We wasn't smoking. Not since we found out you was coming."

"But you said you got picked up again after I was born?"

"They booked him the first time and gave him probation. Kenny found him a job. Found us a little house, too. Wasn't much, but it was ours. Things were good for a while. Then, we got stopped again one weekend, just coming home from the grocery store. Cops always like to stop the junkers like ours. They said they found two grams of coke under the driver's seat."

"So good father gets caught with crack. Yeah, fine man."

"Kenny never touched nothing harder than weed. And nothing at all after you came along. Not till they took him away. Left him rotting in jail. Took the car and left me on the streets with a child and a broken heart."

"How long did they send away a crackhead in those days?"

"They made us a deal. Said they'd let him out after three months if we agreed to leave town and never came back. Only one more thing. I had to give you up."

"You gave me away to keep your precious music man?" I asked. My voice dripped with hatred. "That's rich."

"I would have died to keep you, but they would have taken you away from me anyway. They said as much. The state lady swore she'd find you a good home and somebody that would treat you good so you didn't need anything. I didn't have a choice, Jamie."

"Goddammit, quit calling me that. I'm not Jamie. I haven't been that boy since you sold your own baby."

"It wasn't right, but I did what I had to do to keep you alive. If it kept Kenny and me alive, too, then it was a good deal." She got up and turned her back on me. I wasn't sure she wanted to tell me the rest.

"Except it wasn't," she continued. "It was the worst deal I coulda ever made. I regret what I did to this very day. Kenny got out but he wasn't the same. He blamed me for taking the deal. He blamed God and the world for taking our baby. He said we was set up so they could steal you. He didn't see another sober day for three years until…"

She stopped, apparently thinking that was enough for one night. She was right. The rest would have to wait until I decided whether to stay or to go. I knew there was more to the story, but I was afraid to hear it. I closed my eyes.

"Don't know what you was dreaming last night, Buck, but I hope you sleep a little better tonight," said Jeannie.

She hummed an old gospel song for a while, waiting until I fell asleep. When she stepped out, I registered the movement somewhere deep in my consciousness. I heard a lighter click, a long inhale, and a moment later, a long sighing exhale. I smelled the acrid smoke, and as the darkness grew thicker, I heard her say, "Leave us alone."

Sixteen

"You look like shit, Tom. Didn't see you at MacInnelly's last night. You find a better class of drinking partner somewhere?"

"Sorry, boss. I guess me and Cheryl might have partied a little too much last night." The deputy was nursing a cup of coffee in one hand and propping his head up with the other.

"Look, I don't give a good goddamn about your love life, and I sure don't want to be hearing about it. But I need your head on straight when you come to work."

"Yes sir, I know. I'll be okay after I get some caffeine in me."

Ben read through the note for the hundredth time. "Her story's credible, Tom, even if she won't say it out loud."

"If she don't talk, how we gonna find out what she knows?" said the deputy.

"She talked. Not much, but she talked."

"What'd she tell you? You just said she won't say anything."

"Her note says Judge Morrison was talking about how Eva got her son. Buck's adopted. Gotta be some papers on it somewhere."

"Most adoption papers are sealed."

"Yeah, reluctant mamas don't want their children to come looking for them. But Sarah said her job is to file records. Said it twice. Why would she say that, Tom, if I already knew what her job was?" He tucked the note in his desk drawer. "We'll find a time when the judge isn't at the courthouse. Go through any family court documents you can find about the adoption of Eva and Ray Thompson's son. Sarah won't directly help you, but she might just point you in the right direction."

Tom downed the rest of his coffee.

"While you're at it, see if you can get a copy of Eva's will. Be discrete. Don't want the DA finding out what you're looking at. Not yet anyway. If people won't talk, maybe the records will."

"Got it, boss." The deputy stood, slapped himself across the cheek, and shook his head.

"Not right now, Tom. I don't know how or when. I'm guessing Sarah will let us know."

"Right, boss. I got paperwork to catch up anyhow." Tom trudged back to his desk, rubbing his eyes.

"One more thing, Deputy," Ben called after him. "Stay home tonight, will ya?"

MANDALEE ST. JAMES

Seventeen

Mandalee lay on the floor and listened to the cacophony outside. Every now and then a hoot from a barred owl punctuated the sounds of tree frogs, crickets, and katydids. In the distance, a coyote yipped and barked, and another joined in with a rousing howl. The jumble of sound was soothing, the rhythm of life in the dark, everlasting, ever-unknowable. One could get lost.

She missed Buck with an ache that wouldn't subside. She wondered what he was hearing right now. Could he hear the same night noises? Had he fled the county? Was he even still alive? She didn't know where he was or what he was thinking anymore. The sheriff said he'd run away—wanted to know if she knew where. She didn't. Hadn't seen him in over a month, since she got hurt.

She reached behind her head and felt the bandages on her neck, the misshapen ear, the missing patch of hair. The skin grafts were starting to heal. At first, the pain was unbearable, but the doctors had cut the nerves in the area. Now she didn't feel anything. The hair hadn't grown back yet, but some day it would be long enough to cover the scars. Nobody would notice them except her, and her parents, and her friends who knew what happened.

She stared at the ceiling, feeling the cool surface of the hardwood against her bare back. Reclining on the floor was the only way to escape the heat in the evenings since she had taken to leaving the windows open at night, hoping Buck would come see her one night. Her father scolded her for wasting the AC, demanded that she close the window. But each evening she locked her door, turned out the lights, and slid the window open, listening, yearning, for the sound of Buck's voice among the other night creatures. Short of nailing it shut, her father could do nothing to stop her.

Until Eva Bustard's death, seemed about the only time Buck wasn't angry was when he was with Mandalee. After his mother died, as the stories grew wilder and the pressure mounted and he drank more and more, their relationship grew strained. Mandalee never believed the awful stories flying around town. He was not a violent person. The Buck she knew could never hurt someone, much less someone he loved. But the stories wouldn't stop. The vile gossips wouldn't stop. Finally, after a loud public confrontation with a gang of classmates taunting him as a mother-murderer, his temper boiled over. Name-calling led to pushing, and shoving led to punches. Mandalee tried to intervene but fell down a flight of concrete stairs in the process. The other kids fled. She had nothing broken. But her parents, the ones who had once treated him like a son, wanted nothing more to do with him. They forbid her to see him. Even teachers warned her. Stay away, they all said. If you know what's good for you, give him some space until it all gets cleared up.

Mandalee and Buck spent the next couple of months dancing like tag team wrestling partners in a too-small ring, sneaking back together as often as they could, neither one wanting to throw in the towel. But the taunts and cheap punches they endured from the growing crowd fighting against them had them reeling until all they could do was stand swaying together, arms linked, leaning against the ropes, desperately seeking support from each other.

Several times a year the kids gathered for a huge bash at the Pipeline, the abandoned compressor station in the woods behind old man Haddington's place. The gas field in that part of the county, never much to begin with, had fizzled out years ago. All the facilities, one by one, were abandoned, too. The compressor station was torn down but the old concrete pad and stubs of the steel pipeline remained. Most every weekend, a few kids built a small fire there and drank beer. But on every Fourth of July, Halloween, and New Year's Eve, they strung up lights on a few poles and someone rented a generator; the local rock band wannabes and aspiring country singers would grab an electric guitar and play all night long. The place was a teenager's drunken paradise where anything could happen, and usually did.

The year earlier, before all the trouble, he and Mandalee loaded up a few six-packs into the bed of the old red pickup, covered the cans with a few bales of hay and a tarp, and headed to the Pipeline on the Fourth. As evening came on, the small bonfire grew with the size of the crowd and the pile of beer cans until by midnight it was huge. That night, Mandalee got drunk, she sang in front of a group, and they made love— all for the first time. Taboo. Terrifying. Magical. They were both happy. She wished the night would never end.

A year later, Independence Day came again, but nothing was the same. So much had happened since the previous glorious party, yet the couple desperately still clung to each other, trying to beat back the world. The strain was taking its toll. Buck was sullen and already half-drunk when he picked her up. She insisted she drive. He finally relented but only after pulling another six-pack from the bed to nurse along the way. His mood worsened with each can.

The glow from the fire could be seen from the highway, a good sign that the party was in full swing. Mandalee pulled onto the old gravel road and bumped along the edge of a cornfield for half a mile before turning into the woods. Through the trees, the flames leaped with a bacchanalian fury. A rap beat pounded from the speakers, and a White boy riffed on tailgates, beer, and moonlit nights on a dirt road. Ten girls in oversized cowboy hats and undersized halter tops gyrated and jumped in front of him, their frantic dances generating enough heat, along with the bonfire, to keep themselves and the boys yelling in the crowd stoked for action.

The song ended in cheers and chugs just as Buck and Mandalee walked into the glare.

"What the hell you doing here, killer?" yelled the cowboy rapper into the microphone.

"Come on," said Buck in a low voice. "Don't need to be somewhere I'm not wanted."

"No," said Mandalee, standing her ground. She faced the kid with the microphone and yelled. "Shut the fuck up, Parker. We got as much right to be here as you pretending to be a cowboy Eminem."

"Ohhhh," yelled the crowd, forming a circle around the couple and the rapper and pushing them together for another show in the ring.

"You got some nerve bringing a murderer here. I used to think you had better sense than that," taunted Mandalee's best friend Janet—at least she used to be.

Mandalee grabbed the beer out of Buck's hand and chugged it down. She threw the can at Janet's feet and pushed her. Janet fell on her butt, and Mandalee closed in. But before she could, Buck wrapped his arms around her and pulled her away. In the process, he tripped over Parker's foot, who grinned down on them.

"What the fuck?" he yelled and scrambled up, pushing Mandalee off him. She tumbled sideways and into a log that had fallen from the bonfire.

Buck rushed the boy leering at them and knocked him off his feet, wildly swinging and sometimes connecting. Boys and girls alike crowded around them, urging on the violence. Parker dodged a wild punch and elbowed Buck in the nose. Blood spurted down the front of his shirt, and the crowd crushed in, like piranha in a feeding frenzy.

A shriek stopped them short; they turned to see Mandalee slapping at her hair. The back of her head was on fire, and she flailed away in a panic.

Buck ripped off his shirt and threw it over her head, succeeding in smothering the flames, but not the painful screams. Janet threw herself between them and pushed Buck away.

Parker glared. Twenty teenagers stood behind him.

"What the hell, you sick fuck?" said Parker. "Man, just leave. Nobody wants you here."

"It was an accident," said Buck, his head slumping nearly to the ground. "I didn't mean to hurt her."

"Yeah, I bet that's what you always say," said Parker, stepping closer to Buck as if to kick the boy. He stopped suddenly and grabbed Buck's hair, pulling it off his back. "Dude, that's some ugly scar. What is that, the mark of the devil?"

"Hellboy," said one of the boys just now gaining courage to step forward.

"No, he ain't good enough to be Hellboy," said Parker. "Devil boy, maybe."

"Satan's child," said a girl.

"Demon kid," yelled a boy.

"Devil boy, devil boy, devil boy," chanted Parker. The crowd behind him joined in the chant and began circling him. The bonfire cast dancing shadows that seemed to grab at him, and Buck suddenly charged the cowboy ringleader.

Parker easily stepped aside and pushed Buck back into the dust.

"Begone, Satan!" yelled Parker, laughing. The crowd joined in.

"Begone, Satan; begone, Satan; begone, Satan."

Buck's wild eyes stared at the crowd of contorted faces steeped in the shadows of the fire. "Goddamn you," he yelled. "Leave me alone."

He tried to get to Mandalee again but Janet yelled. "Can't you see what you've done? Get the hell out of here."

They led Mandalee, sobbing, to a car and roared away. Buck stayed on his knees, watching as they disappeared through the cornfield.

BILLY WEISMAN

Eighteen

Tierney Falls dwindled away in the drought, but the crowds of families and couples that used to commune in nature's beauty had been drying up for years. The place had changed. The drought only made things worse. The teens still came to drink and party. They would always come. Since the water dried up to a trickle, there were no more fishermen. Instead, a couple of black SUVs made a drive-through every few evenings. And a small army of traders met them there on their routes on the dirt roads that traced through the woods. Some had cash to give. Some used their bodies as currency, given to another class of customers that especially thrived on young desperation. This place was a marketplace, the freest kind, with no regulation other than pay what you owed or face the consequences. The ones who frequented the marketplace understood the one rule, or they learned it quickly.

Billy Weisman met his customers out the window of the Escalade that his buddy, Patch Wilson, drove. Patch was Stevie Wilson just a little over a year before. He lost an eye after a particularly brutal arrest at the hands of Ben Jefferson. Even with only one eye, Patch saw more than most men could imagine with two. He didn't like to imagine. He liked cold hard facts. He set the meeting places because he had to make sure they were safe. He set the times so he would know who would be around. In his jacket, he carried the semiautomatic piece that would enforce the rule, as well as the long gun he kept on the seat beside him.

He was the driver, the security, the scout. He was everything except the brains. That was Billy's job.

Tonight's meeting wasn't with a customer. Tonight, Billy was on his way to meet a special guest. When Patch pulled the Escalade under a particular tree, at a particular out-of-the-way campsite, the red dually pickup was waiting.

In the unwritten rules about establishing the pecking order in meetings, the most reliable indicator is usually who comes to whose office. Who is the visitor and who is the host? The door of the red pickup opened and a small man in a big hat stepped out. He stood momentarily peering into the headlights until he was satisfied, or at least resolved, to move forward. He walked briskly to the rear passenger door of the SUV, opened the door, and slid in. In a show of bravado, perhaps, he didn't remove his hat.

"*Pinche vaquero*," muttered Billy. Patch nodded in the rearview but didn't turn around.

"Say what you want in Spanish, but I think you want to hear what I have to say."

"Take off your hat," said Patch, still without turning.

"What?"

"Take off your fucking hat," he repeated.

"You're talking to the next sheriff of Tierney County, asshole. The hat stays on."

Patch turned finally and reached into his jacket.

"Fine. Want me to leave? I'll leave, but you should consider if you think your harassment problems are bad now, what will they be with the next sheriff? Wanna talk? The hat stays on."

"He's just fucking with you, Leon. What are you, bald under there? Cowboys and their *jodido* hats."

Patch turned back to the front, but his hand stayed in his jacket.

"Let's quit talking hats and talk facts," said Leon, whose face was a bit redder, unnoticeable in the dark backseat.

"Election's coming, and I'm the odds-on favorite. The current asshole can't solve the biggest murder in the county. People want action. They feel for me, plus they know I'll get results. You'll be dealing with me soon."

"To see a new face, even if it comes with a fucking cowboy hat, will be nice. You know Jefferson's been giving us a hard time. Even messed up Patch here a while back."

"I don't give a good goddamn about Patch's troubles. I'm here to make sure everybody stays in line."

"Mr. Leon, how much money you get for your campaign when your wife was…when your wife passed away?"

"None of your goddamn business. My wife was murdered by her own son. I'll see to it he pays for it. Even if Jefferson can't fucking do it."

"Yet you're here looking for money?" asked Billy. "Sounds like it's my business, too. I don't get it. You got connections. Got the family name. Sheriffing runs in the family, I suppose. Yet you need money?"

"To be clear, in case you're fucking taping me right now, I ain't asking for nothing except your cooperation." The undemanding demand slid glibly from his lips as if he was accustomed to these kind of arrangements.

"Uh-huh. Then, what's all this night-time meeting, cloak-and-dagger stuff about, Mr. Future Sheriff?"

"When I'm in office, things go the way I want them to go. As long as Jefferson's around, who knows what happens? He's old. He's lost a step. And he hasn't done his job. But he's still got a lot of support."

"So you need him removed from contention?"

"Oh, Billy boy, what the hell are you talking about? I'm just saying everybody in this town will be better off when old Ben hangs up his star and rides off into the sunset, like a good boy." Leon smiled but he didn't extend his hand.

"You give me a lot to think about."

"Don't think too hard, Weisman. You ain't really made for it." He opened the door and got out, not even pretending to be concerned about the firepower he knew was in the front seat. Before he closed the door, he leaned back down.

"I believe you called me a fucking cowboy. This one's gonna ride your ass hard if you're not smart, Weisman. What is that—German? A fucking German gangster from Mexico trying to make a living in backwoods Alabama. How 'bout that? Hope it all works out for ya."

Leon slammed the door and strode back to his truck. Sometimes rules are made to be broken. Sometimes the pecking order isn't about whose place the meeting is at. Sometimes, it's how the meeting is conducted. In the glare of Patch's headlights, Leon unzipped his jeans and took a nice long piss. Patch threw the Escalade in gear and spun out of the meeting place, throwing a few rocks and a lot of dust.

Nineteen

Tom and Ben pored through the digital photos of documents he had found at the courthouse. Sarah had come into the office over the weekend to get a little work done. She made sure she stopped at The Coal Fire Café for a coffee before she went in, knowing that Ben took his breakfast there. She made sure she complained loudly to the waitress about having to work on a Saturday, right after she made a point of waving and saying hello to the sheriff. Deputy Walters was at the courthouse within the hour and stopped in to check on Sarah, who ostentatiously placed a key in her desk drawer and excused herself, after noting how hot the file room was on the weekends, especially the back left walk-in closet where the sealed files were kept.

The big closet contained many more sealed files than the deputy expected. The judge had worked to keep a lot of things quiet over the years, most often for the benefit of the parties involved, but as Tom and Ben suspected, maybe for his own benefit, too. Sarah was meticulous, though, one of the reasons she had been around so long. Maybe also because she knew where the skeletons were buried. Before long, the deputy retrieved two files: a thick one filed under adoptions labeled Ray and Eva Thompson, and a thin one containing the Last Will and Testament of Eva Thompson. He snapped a picture of every page.

Later, the deputy sat with the sheriff, whose reading glasses perched on the tip of his nose. A radio on the counter behind them played a

Marvin Gaye song, and Ben sang along under his breath as he read through the documents.

"Says here the adopted boy was a ward of the state," said Ben. "Mighty slim on the details, though. Don't see anything about the natural parents."

"I'd bet the father wasn't in the picture anymore," said Tom. "That seems to be the case when the kid winds up with child services."

"Prob'ly right, but it'd sure be nice to have the name of either one." Ben swiped through the photographed pages. Most of them were about the Thompsons and their suitability as adoptive parents. A medical record listed the boy's blood type, weight, and vaccinations given by DHS. "Huh, according to this, the kid was fostered by the Thompsons just three days after he entered the system. They adopted him less than two months later. Order signed by Judge Morrison."

"Wasn't a planned thing, then. Maybe the parents got killed?"

"Yeah, something like that. Gonna take a subpoena to get records from DHS. Let's check what we have here first. We got car accident deaths in the system for around the time the boy was turned over to DHS?"

"Yep, accident reports are digitized back to two years before then."

Ben went through the adoption papers again, scanning to see if he missed something. On the fourth page, Tom stopped him.

"That's a DHS form," said Tom. "Look, it doesn't have a recorded stamp on it. Why's it in an official court file? Zoom in on the margin there. What is that, phone numbers?"

"Yeah, they're phone numbers all right," said Ben. "One of them's mine."

"You mean the Sheriff's Office?"

"No, I mean mine. That's my old home number. The one I had when me and Laura first got married." Ben leaned back and rubbed his forehead. "I don't remember anything about this case, though."

"One of them's scratched out. Which one's yours?"

"That one."

"So maybe they were looking for somebody else and got your number by mistake," said Tom.

"Or maybe they were trying to get me, but somebody told them to talk to somebody else."

"Why would Laura point them somewhere else?"

"No, not Laura. Maybe the good judge needed someone with a badge. Just not me."

"Lot of maybes, boss."

"Yeah, probably nothing. Still, let's find out who the other number belongs to. Tell you what, Tom, let's check arrest records, too. See if anything interesting comes up around that time."

"On it, Sheriff, but it might take a while. The jail kept the arrest records, and they aren't as computer savvy as we are. I bet their old records are still on paper. Might have to pull the logs from storage."

Tom headed to his desk to start searching, and Ben pulled up the other photos. With only a minute or two of reading, Ben whistled long and low, like he'd just had a revelation.

"Find something else?" Tom called from the next room.

"I'll say. Don't know why I didn't remember this before. Leon told us his wife didn't have a will, yet you found it in the court files. And he said her life insurance was only $10,000. Not enough money to count as motive for murder. That's why we didn't pursue him harder."

"Yeah, that and the DA was pretty clear to keep off Leon unless we had something solid." Tom was leaning on the doorframe now, waiting on the next shoe to drop.

"Over six months and this will isn't probated yet. It's dated almost two years or so before Leon and Eva married. Wonder if Leon even knows about it."

"Not unusual for it not to be probated yet. I mean, these things take time, don't they?" asked Tom.

"It's unusual if it's worth a million dollars," said Ben. "That's what this list of assets says Eva Bustard was worth dead. Is that enough motive for you?"

"I'd say," said Tom, peering over Ben's shoulder. "If Eva wasn't married and her daughter hadn't come along yet, then it stands to reason the beneficiary would be her son, Buck. So you're saying Buck killed his own mother to collect on a million bucks?"

"Not necessarily. Can't keep life insurance money if you murdered for it."

"So if Buck is found guilty of murder, the insurance money goes to whoever else is named in the will."

Ben swiped back through the photos. "The will says nothing about any life insurance in this part or even any name. Just that all her assets not otherwise specified go to her child. If it can't go to Buck, seems it would go to her daughter. Thing is, Eva's daughter isn't but twelve years old. A judge would have to decide, but it sure sounds like Teresa's father would control the money."

"Huh," said Tom. "Pin the murder on Buck and guess who gets the money?"

Ben answered for him. "Yep. Leon."

BUCK

Twenty

"Well, I guess if you're gonna stick around here for a while, you'll have to earn your keep," said Jeannie.

"What, you want me to sweep the dirt floor or something?" Of course, I was glad I had a place to stay although I wouldn't mind some better accommodations. Still, beggars can't be choosers, as they say. And right then, that's all I was.

"Well, you can't stay here. I think it's time I bring you home." Jeannie directed me to retrieve the backpack and bury the trash properly.

"Wait, you got something better than this?"

"Well, what do ya think I am, an animal or somethin'?" she said. "I told you I had a bunch of places, didn't I?"

"Okay. Has it got a shower?"

"Hell, yeah, it's got a shower. Toilet, too. All the modern features of indoor plumbing."

"Why didn't we go there the first night?"

"I had stuff to tend to, if it's any of your beeswax. Didn't that woman teach you any manners, boy? What kinda way is that to talk to your mother? I expect you to be grateful if I'm gonna put a roof over your head."

"By 'that woman' I'm assuming you mean my mother. I don't care what you say, you're not my mother."

"Jesus H. Christ, boy! You got some mouth on you. Just get the backpack and let's get the hell out of here."

"Your business all finished at that pot field through the woods a ways?"

She gave me the side eye and shook her head. "Been spying on me, huh? Well, I guess that's reasonable. Might as well know how your bread is buttered. You got something against pot? Or was you raised a goody-two-shoes."

"I've smoked my share."

"Yeah, I'm sure," she said, a little too sarcastically for my liking. "We don't smoke the shit, we just grow it."

"And sell it?"

"A gal's gotta make a living. Better than what I used to do."

I thought it best not to ask more questions for the time being. I didn't really want to know what Jeannie used to do, although I could guess. Plus, I had to eat. Teresa hated me, now she had found Scout's skull. I couldn't go home again. One thing I knew: I wasn't going to ask Leon Bustard for anything, ever again.

Twenty-One

"It ain't much, but it's home."

The cabin in the woods was built of precut logs and designed to resemble a miniature mountain lodge, emphasis on the miniature.

"You're right about part of it," I said.

"Got a couch you can sleep on. Better than the hard ground."

"Why you letting me stick around? Don't you know what they say I've done?"

"I told you why. You're my boy."

"Bullshit. What's the real reason?"

"You got a lot of anger in you," said Jeannie. "It's no good. Makes you think bad about everybody you meet. Makes you drive off people, even the ones you need."

"Makes you kill people, too. How do you know I'm not a killer?"

"I told you. You're my boy, and I know you ain't no killer."

"I don't know you or anything about you. Which means you don't know anything about me either, except maybe what you've heard."

Jeannie began rattling under the stove until she found the biggest skillet she had. She lit a gas burner and pulled out a glass jar of bacon grease.

"You like eggs?" she asked. Without waiting for an answer, she retrieved a carton from the small fridge along with a pound of bacon. "Tell you what, you get you a nice hot shower. I ain't being rude, but you could really use one. I'll lay out some clothes for you. By the time you're out, I'll have a dozen of 'em whipped up. I'm guessing you're a mite hungry by now."

"Well, anyway, whoever you are, I do appreciate you letting me crash here." I walked to the back of the house. A small bedroom was on the right, the bathroom just across the hall.

Jeannie began cracking eggs and singing a gospel song I had heard on the country station my mother used to listen to.

"Will the circle be unbroken," she sang softly. "By and by, Lord, by and by." She had a sweet low voice with enough gravel to make the song feel even older than I thought it was.

I reached in and turned on the bathroom light. The room was spotless and contained a small white sink set in a worn countertop, a round commode set low to the floor, and a vinyl-sided shower stall. A clean bathmat covered part of the faded linoleum floor. I turned on the shower faucet, waiting on the water to warm up and reached to close the bathroom door. The light shined directly across the hall and into a little bedroom, where a cluster of picture frames sat on a wooden chest of drawers. In the middle, between a picture of a young couple holding hands and one of a man playing a guitar, was an eight-by-ten color photograph of a baby dressed in blue. The baby in the picture was maybe a year old and had a frown; his eyes were narrow and watery in the midst of a good baby tantrum—a funny way to photograph a baby. His eyes looked pale blue but I couldn't quite be sure of their true color because of the puddled up tears. He wore a small baseball cap on his head, and his hand gripped the bill like he wanted to throw it off but couldn't quite manage. Blonde hair curled out from the sides.

The shower felt good, and I let the water pour over me, washing away months and months of tension. It had been so long since I let myself relax, I just stood there until the heat in the water faded away, replaced by stinging cold. Still I stood there, letting the heat seep away, numbing my heart. Besides, I wasn't ready to feel good again. I needed to face it, whatever it was. And I didn't deserve to rest until I could.

"You was in there long enough," called Jeannie when I opened the door. "Guess I'll have to wait till morning to get my shower."

"Yeah, sorry about that. I was pretty dirty. You said you had some clothes I could wear?"

"Yep, I set 'em out on the floor. Look behind you."

I reached down to pick up the clean clothes and thought of peeking in the bedroom again. But the door was closed now. I didn't see any underwear, so I hurried into an old pair of jeans, a little short but not too tight. The long-sleeve flannel shirt, the pocket slightly torn, fit no better.

I rolled up the sleeves, thinking this might be okay tonight but flannel in August isn't going to work.

"I kinda look like Huckleberry Finn in these things," I said, walking in and sitting down at the dinner table.

"They'll do. You growed up some bigger than your daddy was," she said. "Food's ready. Gonna get cold like that shower had to be if we don't eat now. Get your fill."

She ladled out several spoons of eggs and grits and laid out four thick slices of bacon. I dove in.

"Whoa, now. Ain't you learned to say grace first?"

"Sorry, Leon don't say grace."

"Well, God bless you. We gonna see to that. You thank the Lord for what you got, even if it ain't much."

Still holding my fork up, I just looked at her. I didn't remember any blessings except "Good food, good meat, good God, let's eat." So that's what I said.

"Hmmm. I'll teach you somethin' a little more respectful next time. But I guess that gets the point over. I'm sure God's okay with it for tonight."

Nobody spoke another word until the platters were cleaned, and I leaned back. Now seemed a good time to ask questions.

"Is that me in the picture in your room?"

"What you doing in my room, son? Don't you know better than go in somebody else's room without asking?"

"I didn't go in. I saw it from the hall. Sure looks like I was mad at something."

"Well, mind your manners if you going to stay here." I didn't say anything more, and she finally responded. "Yes, that's you when you was less than a year old. Lord, you was a bawlin' all the time it seemed."

"Was that my daddy in the other pictures? You said he liked music, and this one was holding a guitar. I guess people thought he was handsome."

"Kenny was 'bout as handsome as any movie star. Most folks say you shouldn't marry a music man, but he was nothing but good to me and you. He always made me think of Johnny Cash, you know, the man in black. Uh-huh, he was a looker alright."

We talked for an hour or more, me asking questions, and Jeannie reminiscing like it was yesterday that they were all together. All the time, I felt uneasy and disloyal, like I was disrespecting the memory of my mother and father. This woman came out of nowhere and claimed to be my real mother. She claimed the man with the guitar was my real daddy. Why would she make up something like that? What did she have to gain by taking me in and giving me a place to stay? She didn't have to do that. Nobody else was willing to do that. I studied her again while she told stories of the good times when they were all together. I still couldn't tell her age, but that could be explained by a rough life. What I couldn't explain, what I would have to figure out as time went by, was why she was telling such an outrageous lie.

Jeannie stretched and leaned back in her chair, pulling her hair out of the rubber band she used to keep it in a ponytail. When she shook her head and let the locks fall past her shoulders, I thought of the women in the Church of God I visited one time with Mandalee and her evangelical friend. The older women usually kept their long hair all rolled up in a knot on top of their head, hair they refused to cut because it was a woman's glory or some such bullshit. She looked strange, backwoodsy, old-timey, with her long dark hair streaked with gray. Looking at her, I could imagine her when she was young and happy, like in the photograph in the bedroom. Maybe it was the company she had missed for so long. Maybe it was telling all those old stories. Tonight, she was obviously happy, and her bright eyes sparkled.

Twenty-two

Creed National Trust Company was an insurance behemoth with a bureaucracy to match. When the sheriff got through to the vice president of sales for the Southeast Region, he was directed to the legal department, who left a message with a mid-level corporate attorney, who got his secretary to call the sheriff informing him that a subpoena would be required before the company could release anything at all about the policyholder. Convincing a judge in Tierney County to issue a subpoena without the knowledge of the family court judge would be tricky. Thankfully, Ben had treated the son of Judge Neighbors with discretion when he was arrested for DUI. The judge owed him one, and Ben decided this was a good time to collect.

With the paper in hand, Ben took a trip to Atlanta the very next day, where Creed National kept an office on the forty-third floor of Peachtree Plaza. Sheriff Jefferson did not *dis*like Atlanta. The Braves were a favorite of his, and he had spent many summer evenings at the ballpark there. He knew and liked the Fulton County sheriff and many of his deputies. Best of all, this is where he met Laura, the woman he thought he would spend the rest of forever with. He loved Atlanta.

Corporate offices near the top of high-rise glass buildings were not his normal haunt, though. Not that he felt out of his element. He could handle himself well enough in a white-collar world. But the white collars were usually around white necks with white faces that often didn't care what a Black man wanted, even if he wore a badge and carried a piece of paper with the weight of the law.

After being kept waiting in reception for twenty minutes, Ben decided to quit the nice act.

"Catherine is it?" he asked as he stood in front of the mahogany-topped counter where the young woman sat with a phone headpiece and an open game of Candy Crush on her cell phone.

"Yes, can I help you?"

"You can get Mr. Lance Taylor out here to take me to the file room, or I'll find someone else that can help me."

"Officer…"

"Sheriff," he interrupted. "Sheriff Ben Jefferson."

After a short phone call, she looked up and said, "Sheriff, he's tied up for a while. If you will have a seat, I'll get you some coffee. I let him know again that you're waiting."

"Catherine, I've served a lawful subpoena on this business, one that your company required me to get. So, if you can't pull Mr. Taylor out of his meeting in the next minute, I'll go door-to-door through every office until I find him. And if I still don't find him, I'll call up my buddies at the Fulton County Sheriff's Department. You don't want me to do that, do you?"

Ten minutes later, Ben Jefferson sat in a conference room with a stack of papers printed out from the file of Eva Thompson, thumbing through an application, a beneficiary designation form, and a history of previous claims including all investigations related to them.

Ray Thompson had once applied for a life insurance policy in the amount of $500,000. Creed paid off that policy to Eva a few years later, after the murder of her husband. According to the file, an investigation into the death concluded that a disgruntled client took Mr. Thompson's life while he was on a jail visit. Nothing indicated any fraud or involvement by Mrs. Thompson or on her behalf. It was a tragic incident, one of the many violent crimes that plagued the prison system in Alabama or pretty much any state for that matter. All correspondence from Mrs. Thompson was on the letterhead of her late husband's law firm, and they were all signed on her behalf by Judge Richard Morrison, Ray Thompson's former law partner.

Ben pulled out a file on Eva Bustard that he had brought with him. She remarried about two years after Ray died. Her daughter, Teresa, was born only a few months after the marriage. Ben suspected that Leon burned up the life insurance proceeds she received in improvements to the farm. Could be the couple was having financial problems at the time Eva died.

The first policy was paid out several months before the date of Eva's will. The second policy in Creed's files was issued just the week before the date of the will. This one was taken on Mrs. Thompson's life in the year after Ray died, well before she had remarried. Not so unusual by itself. A widow who came into some money could afford a hefty life insurance policy to make sure her heirs were covered in case the first proceeds didn't last. The second policy was in the amount of $1,000,000, and as Ben suspected, Buck Thompson, Eva's only child at the time, was the primary beneficiary.

Ben scanned through the rest of the electronic files, directed the now very cooperative Catherine to copy them all on a thumb drive, gathered up the papers flagged with post-its and marked in red circles, and stuffed them all into his briefcase. Catherine apologized for any inconvenience, whispering that Mr. Taylor is kind of a dick, and she was happy to see how things turned out. She even gave him the coffee she had promised earlier.

Ben settled into his Bronco in the parking garage and pulled out the second policy again. In his mind, that the policy had never been updated after the birth of her second child, the one she had with Leon Bustard, was extraordinary. But something else was even more remarkable. He pulled out of the garage as the radio played a Rachmaninoff symphony. He began to think about his next move. He knew how to play the game, of course. Times when discretion earned a favor, and times when a strong arm got results. But he refused to look the other way. He had sworn to uphold the law thirty years ago, and he wasn't going to stop now. He just had to figure out how he was going to investigate the most powerful man in Tierney County because the secondary beneficiary on Eva Thompson's life insurance policy, the person who would stand to rake in a million dollars if Buck Thompson was no longer around, wasn't Leon Bustard. The secondary was Dick Morrison.

PATCH WILSON

Twenty-three

Patch Wilson didn't care about much of anything really except getting paid, which Billy Weisman had already done, and getting even, which Wilson himself would take care of. After their meeting with Leon Bustard, Billy gave Wilson a special project: meet Ben Jefferson when he came to investigate an anonymous tip of a drug drop and put the fear of God in him. Of course, the sheriff wouldn't know about Patch's appointment with him.

According to the tip, a grocery delivery truck would be meeting a green van in the far south end of the county just off Route 239 at seven a.m. on Wednesday. Wilson knew that Ben Jefferson would get there early in an unmarked car and stake out the place. The sheriff would see the van already parked, nobody visible behind its tinted windows. He'd find a place to park out of sight and watch, maybe from the abandoned farmhouse just up the road, where a strong set of binoculars gave a perfect view of the van. He'd probably have a deputy in place just down the road to spring into action as soon as he was called.

What the sheriff didn't know was that the van belonged to the delivery truck driver. At least until a few days ago when Patch lifted a set of keys from the delivery truck while it was on rounds and then stole the van from the driver's warehouse in the next county. The driver, making his usual Wednesday rounds to Emmett's Grocery farther down County Road 239, would see his van, prominently parked off the road where he couldn't miss it. The driver would stop, of course. He'd cautiously walk over to the van, checking around him to see if anyone was there. He'd call out a couple times. He would be scared, most likely, or he could be brash.

Either way, because the van was his, the owner would eventually check it out. He'd peek inside. Seeing nothing of interest, he might try to call the cops to tell them he found his stolen truck, maybe see if they could come look for clues about who took it. He'd find there's no service on this stretch of County Road 239. He would have become brave by then so he'd try to open the van door, which would be locked. He'd check every door, including the rear one, out of sight of the sheriff's view.

Ben Jefferson, seeing the man looking like he could have taken something out of the back of the van, would make his move. He'd call the deputy, and together the two would converge on the drug deal, sirens blazing and lights flashing. He'd skid to a stop and pull out his gun, ordering the truck driver to the ground. The driver might argue, but eventually he'd go down. The straight-arrow working guys were always compliant, always predictable. The deputy would hold the truck driver while the sheriff checked out the van. Finding the doors locked, he'd pull out the jimmy stick he always kept handy in his car. When he opened it, he'd get a surprise.

Leon wanted the surprise to be big enough to scare the sheriff so that he'd get the message. Patch wanted more. Patch always wanted more. Sheriff Jefferson wouldn't be in any shape to run for another term as sheriff or anything else. The outcome might be more than the pretend cowboy wanted, but then Jefferson shouldn't have taken Wilson's eye. Patch had his own grudge to settle.

Wilson assured himself that all the pieces were in place by two a.m., himself driving the van and checking the triggering device. Then he placed the tip call to the sheriff's office. The night dispatch would call the sheriff, setting everything in motion. Now, just a matter of waiting. A country boy and an ex-logger, Wilson knew the woods. He knew how to climb trees. He found the perfect spot, far enough away to be out of the immediate area but close enough to keep a direct view with the collapsing telescope he always used to check out his drop sites.

At 5:12 a.m., just as the light was rising, a car drove slowly past the green van. The vehicle didn't stop until the farmhouse, where the car lights went out. Patch watched as a Black man with a badge got out and walked up to the sagging front porch. He saw him walk around the house a couple of times and out to the road, just as the sun topped the horizon.

Satisfied he was in a good place, the man got back into his car, parked facing the drop site, and turned off the engine to wait.

At 6:51 a.m., a delivery truck topped the hill about a quarter mile down the road. Apparently, the driver almost missed the van, drawing nearly even with it before he applied the brakes hard and crunched to a stop. The truck backed up slowly and stopped even with the small turnoff, blocking any escape in case the thief was still there. He stepped out and stopped at the back end of the truck. He shouted a couple of times, just as expected. He walked over and tested the driver's door, just as expected, and went back to his truck. Wilson figured he was making the phone call to the police. Just as expected.

Then the driver did something unexpected. He got back out of the truck and strode up to the van, dangling what looked like a set of keys. He appeared to insert them into the van door.

"Shit," cursed the one-eyed man in the tree. "Goddamn spare key. Leave it alone, idiot."

From the farmhouse, a car turned on a set of blue lights and a siren and sped down the road. Patch kept his eye on the truck driver.

"Don't you hear that? Wait on the damn sheriff, fool."

On the other end of the long stretch of open road, another car turned on lights and siren, speeding to the same place. The truck driver turned, seeing the approaching lights, and waited.

"That's right, stay where you are," said Wilson under his breath.

Ben Jefferson jumped out of his car and crouched behind the hood, holding a revolver pointed at the driver. He shouted something. The deputy's car was just coming to a stop.

The driver held up his hands but took a step toward the sheriff.

The sheriff stood, still pointing his pistol and extending his arms full-length as if to get his point across.

The driver dropped his hands and turned, reaching for the door.

The sheriff continued issuing commands. Patch could pick up a few. "Open that door, and I'll shoot. Down on the ground, now," yelled the cop.

The deputy jumped out of his car with his gun drawn. Both law officers advanced toward the driver, who had his back turned to them.

The driver, apparently realizing the seriousness of the situation, finally put up both his hands and turned slowly. The deputy must have spotted something in the man's hands.

"Drop it. Whatever you have, drop it now," the deputy ordered.

Wilson almost chuckled out loud. From his vantage with the looking glass, he could see the object was likely the driver's keys. Why couldn't the deputy see that? "Fucking cops," he said to himself.

The driver's right hand, still holding the keys, came down quickly, and he began to turn his hand over to show them what he had.

Everything happened so quickly, Patch had a hard time processing it. A tongue of fire spit from the end of the deputy's gun just as he lifted the muzzle. An instant later, Patch heard the sheriff yelling something, and almost simultaneously the crack of the report reached his ears. The driver spun around as if he had been kicked by a mule. He fell against the car door, and bounced backwards, grabbing at the handle. The car door swung open with his weight, and an instant later, a ball of fire shot out, blowing the door off the hinges. The shock wave threw the lawmen backwards onto the pavement.

The sheriff wiped his face and looked at the blood on his hand. He crawled to the deputy, whose face was covered with blood. Flames engulfed the vehicle. A body lay crumpled a few feet away. The clothes were on fire, and the sheriff stripped off his shirt to smother the flames. Patch could see through his scope that the body had no head.

"Officer down. Officer down." Wilson could hear the sheriff yelling into his radio at the top of his voice. He repeated the call three times.

Steven "Patch" Wilson, cursing every swear he'd ever learned, slid down the tree and pulled his pistol from his belt holster.

"Goddamn idiot. Wait on the fucking police, asshole. That's all you had to do was wait on the fucking police." He stepped out on the asphalt and marched briskly toward the flames, racking the slide back to chamber a round as he went. When he was fifty feet from Ben's car, a pickup truck topped the hill behind him and rolled toward the scene. The Black farmer driving the truck slowed to figure out what the hell had just happened here. Wilson noticed the truck but kept walking, hell-bent on finishing the job. Rounding the delivery truck, he saw the sheriff and deputy huddled together.

He raised his gun and took aim, the sound of an engine sped up behind him.

"You won't be fucking with me again, asshole," he yelled.

The pickup struck Patch from the side, and he rolled onto the hood. Just before his face smashed into the windshield, Wilson saw his own face staring back at him, an open eye socket gaping like the devil's own visage. He could see the farmer's dark face through his own reflection, as if the two heads had merged. Patch registered the fear, but could not tell which face he could see it in. The windshield cracked into a spider web, and the farmer slammed on his brakes. Patch Wilson's body flew into the weeds and tumbled down the steep shoulder into a ditch. In the distance, a siren wailed.

Twenty-four

Mandalee tried to calm Teresa, who sobbed on the other end of the phone line.

"Now hold on, girl. If you want to talk, you gotta stop bawling so I can understand you. Now tell me again what happened."

"I didn't want him to run away," Teresa sputtered out between gasps. "We had a big fight, and then he just didn't come home."

"Okay, what was the fight about?"

"You know what it was about. It's what everything's about." Teresa sucked in a deep breath and let it out slow, just like Buck had taught her when she was younger and got scared in the middle of the night.

"That's right, take your time," said Mandalee. "What did you say?"

"I told him he killed Mama. I was really mad, and it just came out. I don't really think he did it."

"Of course, he didn't. He's just all mixed up and angry how he's been treated." Mandalee's voice was reassuring, and Teresa calmed herself a little more.

"So, what were you mad about?"

"I found Scout, at least what was left of him, just the bones." Her words poured out and she couldn't stop. "His tag was still on him; so, I knew it was him. And he had a hole on one side of his head like a bullet hole. And I remembered Buck had his gun with him the day I found him with Mama. And I accused him of shooting Scout just to make Mama mad. And that Mama and him got in a big fight and he killed her."

"You don't really think that," said Mandalee as more of a statement than a question.

"No, no, no, he's all bluster and stuff. He acts all angry, but he wouldn't hurt anything. Daddy even made fun of him for not shooting a deer when he had the chance."

"Look, Teresa. You were just upset. We all say crazy stuff when we're upset."

"But I made him run away. I don't want him to go away."

"Okay. It's gonna be alright. We'll find him and let him know we're still on his side. It's gonna be okay. You'll see."

"What if he don't ever come back?"

"Calm down. We'll find him. Tell me about finding Scout. That must have been a shock."

"It was. It was crazy, I mean, I wouldn't have ever found him if it hadn't been for the lady."

"What lady?"

"Well, it was really weird. I mean, I think it was a lady. I didn't really see her. I just saw something way down in the woods. It was all white like a long dress. She must have seen me coming, 'cause she moved away. I yelled that it was okay for her to be there. I thought maybe she was a friend of Mama's. I kept calling and trying to catch up with her but I never could. Then she just disappeared."

"Disappeared?"

"Yeah, went away. I mean, she didn't run away. She just...disappeared."

"You shouldn't have run after her. You don't know who it could have been."

"That's the thing. I wasn't scared. It was more like she was scared of me. When I got to where I last saw her, I couldn't find her. That's when I saw it. Scout's shiny tag poking out of the leaves and stuff. I reached down and pulled on it and..." Teresa stopped, her breaths coming in short gasps.

"Oh God, that must have been awful!"

"Yeah. It was horrible. His skeleton came up when I pulled on the tag and I fell down, just looking at the bones and trying to make sense of everything."

"Buck didn't shoot him."

"I know. He wouldn't do something like that." Teresa was sobbing again. "But that's all I could think of. That, that, that . . . that Buck shot Scout and, and, and...if he would do that, then...then he could have..."

"Buck didn't do it. He didn't kill your mom. You know him better than that."

"I know. But I accused him of it. And he left. And it's all my fault he's gone. "

"Look, we gotta do something. We'll find him, and we'll figure this out."

"No, he won't ever come back."

"We'll figure out what happened first, and then it'll be okay for him to come back." Mandalee thought of all the detective shows she had seen.

"Teresa, do you remember where you found Scout?"

"I don't know. I wasn't thinking straight. Maybe I can."

"So, the police can tell what kind of gun a bullet came from, right? I mean that's what the TV shows say. So, we'll take a metal detector down there, my Dad's got one, and we'll search around where you found Scout. The bullet's still there someplace. We'll find it, and we'll take it to the sheriff, and he'll figure out whose gun it came from. And we'll know who did it."

"What if it proves Buck did it?"

"It won't," said Mandalee. The discussion was over. They'd do their search and find the person who shot Scout, and the sheriff would pick him up, and he'd tell him what he did, and it would all be over.

"That's all I want. Just for it to all be over," said Teresa, though the quaver in her voice betrayed that she didn't really believe it would be that simple.

"Me, too, Teresa. We'll prove Buck didn't do anything, and it'll all be over."

When Mandalee hung up the phone, she hadn't convinced herself, either. Even if they could prove Buck didn't kill Scout, that was no proof he didn't hurt his mother. She shook the thought out of her head and looked out the window. No more sitting around waiting. She hated the waiting. Time to do something, anything. No matter where it led.

Twenty-five

Attempted murder is a huge deal. Attempted murder of a lawman brings all kind of hell down on you. Not long after, authorities identified Patch Wilson. And similarly, not much longer for Billy Weisman to be rounded up. Weisman was cuffed to a table in the interrogation room. Three deputies waited outside the door. Two more were inside with him, hands resting on their guns, hoping for a chance to use them.

"This is my case," Ben said to the federal agents assembled in his office. "I don't care what you think, I'm interrogating this man. You can sit in if you want and take notes."

ATF agent Schuyler Jenkins leaned down and rested his hands on the sheriff's desk.

"Look, I'm all for letting a man do his job if he's capable," Jenkins said.

"What the hell does that mean?"

"It means you probably have a concussion. You nearly got killed; you saw a man blown to shreds; your deputy's in the hospital. You're not in the best shape to conduct interviews."

"I'm just an old Black sheriff in a small county. You wouldn't be saying that to the White sheriff in Jefferson County."

"Don't play the goddamn race card with me, Ben. I've known you for twenty years. You're a good man and a good sheriff." The agent stood back up. "And you just got blown up. Take a step back and let us handle this."

Ben stood up and stepped around the desk, stopping a few inches from the agent. "This is still my county, Schuyler. My deputy remains in that hospital, and one of our citizens is lying in a morgue without a head. I can't step back from this one." He brushed by the man and walked out the door. "One of you can come in with me. The rest stay out here."

"Mule-headed son-of-a-bitch," muttered Jenkins, following the sheriff down the hall.

In the room, Ben motioned for the deputies to remove the cuffs and leave. Weisman rubbed his wrists and stretched, leaning back in the metal chair.

"Go ahead and get comfortable, Billy. Get you something to drink? Maybe a Coke or something?" Ben slid the chair to the side of the young man and leaned in close. Schuyler took the seat across the table.

"This here's Agent Jenkins from Alcohol, Tobacco, and Firearms. Just thought you'd want to know you attracted the big boys to this little shindig."

"Agent, nice to meet you," said Weisman, extending his hand. Jenkins ignored the gesture and stared back into the man's eyes.

"Oh, you're the bad cop. I got it."

"Guess that makes me the good cop," said Ben. "I don't mind; I really am trying to do you a favor, you know."

"Oh yeah? How's that, old man?"

"Well, Jenkins here, he wants to take you into his custody. They got lots of procedures there and backlog like you wouldn't believe. The war on drugs and all that, you know. I figure you go in there, and maybe you come out in a year, if you didn't have anything to do with all this. Maybe never if you did."

"I hear federal prisons are country clubs. Might get a good rest," said Billy.

"I hear that, too. But then I hear there's a lot of skinheads in there, too. Crackers that would like nothing more than get hold of a wannabe Mexican drug kingpin. Don't forget about the Black gangs. I imagine a few of them are Willie Pearson's people. You know Willie, don't you? He's the fellow you've been trying to push out of our little corner of paradise. You're small potatoes to a guy like Willie, but Willie didn't get where he's at by overlooking small potatoes."

"Don't none of them scare me," said Billy. "Patch was prob'ly cousins with some of them crazy ass mother-fuckers." He pulled his arms back in and folded them across his chest.

"Uh-huh," said Ben. "Could be he got some Nazi relatives. I figure they either hated cousin Patch for taking up with the likes of you. Or they were real close and hate you for getting him killed. Either way, they won't look kindly on you, *amigo*."

"Wadn't none of me, Sheriff."

"So let's see. You got Willie Pearson who hates you. You got Patch's kinfolk who hate you. You can probably guess how the law feels about you, trying to kill a lawman. You don't have a lot of friends. Now me, I don't like a skinhead. Guess you can figure out why. I might be able to keep 'em away from you, here in our little jail. And I don't know of any of Willie's people in our custody right now. Besides, I'm the law over here. You go off to some federal lock-up with lots of guards just aching to put a cop-killer in his place—well, I can't help you there."

"Y'all don't got nothin' on me, or you woulda already charged me."

"I have your man's words."

"Patch wasn't my man. He was just an acquaintance. Besides, he's dead. He ain't telling nobody nothin'."

"How do you know he's dead?"

"Word gets around in a small town, Sheriff."

"A dying man's words carry a lot of weight in a court. He told me what you put him up to." Ben leaned in a little closer. "And he told me who put you up to it."

"So why do you need me to say anything?"

"Because a judge will look at you a whole lot more kindly if you're cooperating."

"What if I didn't have nothin' to do with nothin'?"

"Well, then you better tell me who did, or we're going to have to assume it was all you," said Ben. "I got enough to hold you indefinitely right now, or at least Agent Jenkins can hold you. But if you tell me I've got it wrong, maybe we'll listen."

"Maybe I know something. Maybe I tell, it gets me killed."

"Who you scared of? Willie?"

"Willie don't scare me. I know how to deal with people like him."

"You're talking about the man who put you up to this," said Ben. "You help us put him away, and we'll protect you."

"You can't protect shit, Sheriff. Couldn't protect your deputy. You couldn't protect your wife."

"My wife? What do you know about my wife?"

"Look, Patch did a lot of shit on his own. He was a loose cannon. No secret he had a hard-on to kick your ass after you beat his eye out of him and locked him up. No, I didn't tell him to do nothing." Billy smiled and a gold crown glinted on his front teeth. He leaned back. "But Patch liked to brag. He might have talked some smack about last year."

"Keep talking." Ben's jaw tightened and his eyes narrowed. His hands clenched against the back of his chair, fighting the urge to tear this asshole apart.

"Nah, you get my lawyer in here. Maybe I talk through him. Until then, we're done."

Ben and Agent Jenkins got up without talking further. The deputies came in and led their prisoner away. When he was out of sight, Ben slumped against the wall.

"He's bluffing," said Jenkins.

"What if he's not? It took everything I had to keep from beating the shit out of him."

"He's looking for leverage, Ben. He knows he's in big trouble, and he's weaseling a way out of it."

"I've been pressuring those guys for a couple years now. I arrested Wilson on a dealing charge about a month before Laura died. We couldn't make it stick, and the asshole got released the day before Laura's wreck. I know in my bones he had something to do with it."

"Now, see? This is what I'm talking about. You arrested Wilson on a technicality and beat the shit out of him after Laura died. Which case are you investigating now, Ben?"

"The son-of-a-bitch was resisting arrest. He had it coming. Now Weisman dangles that shit in front of me?" Ben's heart pounded in his chest.

Somehow, the sheriff managed to rise to his full six-foot-three-inch height and looked the federal man in the eye. Jenkins didn't back up. Finally, Ben sat back down.

"It's awful personal for me now. I know that," said Ben. He stared at his hands and marveled that he was able to keep them from throttling the cocky Mexican. "Look, he's got to think I'm in charge, that I can help him."

"I should at least be taking him to Birmingham right now."

Ben looked his friend in the eye. "But you won't because I'm asking you not to."

Jenkins liked Ben. He and his wife had spent Christmas with the Jeffersons two years ago at a Coosa River cabin, fishing in the daytime, cooking in the evenings, telling stories and drinking beer and wine around a fire pit at night. They were good people. They were good friends. Ben and Laura were especially supportive when Schuyler and his wife lost their son a few years ago.

"Two weeks. If you got nothing by then, I'm putting him in my custody." Jenkins laid both hands on Ben's shoulders. "Look, Weisman's lawyer won't be here till tomorrow. Go home. Get some rest. You look like hell."

RUSSELL LEE

Twenty-six

"Miss Jeannie, what you doing here?" The wiry and whiskered old man stood in front of a small barn as worn as he was. It hadn't seen a coat of paint in thirty years.

Jeannie closed the door to the white van adorned with magnetic florist signs on both sides and the rear. Buck watched from the passenger seat as she strode confidently down the overgrown dirt road, brushing spider webs away like curtains into another world.

"Whadya mean, why am I here? It's Sunday, ain't it?"

"You didn't hear?"

"Russell Lee, quit messing with me. I ain't got all day. It's a long way to Mobile."

Russell peeked around her shoulder and nodded to the boy in the van. "Who the hell's that? This ain't no time to be fuckin' around, bringin' somebody new in here."

"What's got under your saddle? First of all, you know I don't like you talking to me like that. Second, it's my business who I get to help me. You just do your part."

"I'm sorry, Miss Jeannie. It's just things are kinda messed up right now."

"Tell me what's going on, Russell, or get me loaded up. I can't stand here and swap pleasantries with you all day long."

"Can't move nothin' today. The boss man's in jail."

"Just part of the job. He'll be out soon. In the meantime, I got a delivery to make."

"No, I don't think he'll be out anytime soon this time. Where you been the last few days? Patch done tried to kill the sheriff."

"Stevie done what? Why that crazy backwoods redneck. Ain't he got no sense?"

"Miss Jeannie, he's dead."

"The sheriff?"

"No, Patch is dead. Look, I'm sorry to have to tell you that way. I thought you woulda heard by now."

Jeannie Roberts dropped her head and squeezed her eyes shut. Russell touched her arm, but she jerked away and stumbled to the barn.

"Goddamn you," she whispered.

"I'm sorry, I thought you knew."

"Goddamn you! Goddamn you!" she screamed, tearing into Russell Lee like a mad dog, her eyes still closed.

Russell covered his head with his arms, but he stood still. Buck scrambled out of the van and was at her side, wrapping his arms around her and dragging her off the little man. He knew enough to stay silent.

"The Mexican put him up to it, didn't he?" she asked, wresting her way out of Buck's grasp and wiping her eyes.

"No, ma'am. He went rogue, Miss Jeannie. He wasn't supposed to kill the sheriff, just scare him good. You know how much he hates him."

"Yeah, I know. Stupid son-of-a-bitch couldn't put nothing behind him. I thought he got all that out of his system."

"Yes'm. Me too,'" said Russell.

"How'd he die? Sheriff shoot him?"

"Way I hear it, he tried to blow up the sheriff and his deputy but killed some other guy by mistake. Then he tried to shoot the Black son-of-a-bitch and some damn farmer ran over him."

"Why'd he always take things too far, Russell? He done that our whole life. Even when we was kids, Stevie would get mad at somebody and nearly beat 'em to death. He done it for sure the last time Papa hit Mama."

"An eye for an eye, Miss Jeannie. 'Cept Patch always had to take more than got took from him. I guess he couldn't get over the sheriff beating him till he lost his eye. Jefferson didn't have to do that."

"Now Russell, don't you get all worked up over the same sad stuff. It don't lead nowhere but straight to hell, getting revenge on somebody. Weren't nobody's fault but Stevie's."

"Wait," said Buck, "who's Stevie? Who's Patch?"

"Who the hell are you, kid?" shouted Russell, taking a step toward the teenager. "You ain't got no business here. Get back in the fuckin' van before I drag you out of here."

"No," said Jeannie, "it's alright. 'Bout time you knew. This here's my son, Jamie."

"What the hell?" said Russell.

"It's Buck. She says I'm her son. I say she's crazy."

"Whoo-wee. Ain't that something? You're Jamie? Why I ain't seen you since you was no bigger than a rabbit." Russell eyed him up and down with a squinted eye. "I was your daddy's best buddy. Hell, I'm your goddamn godfather." He slapped Buck on the back and shook his hand. "Proud to know you. I gotta say you don't take after your old man much. I guess I'm s'posed to teach you shit, but from the looks of you, I got my work cut out."

"Russell, we'll catch up later. Right now, this is what we're gonna do." Jeannie hadn't made it this far by being blown around in the wind. "The sheriff's gonna be looking for stuff out here in these woods, and you don't need to be found with it. We're gonna load this van, and me and Buck's gonna drive it to Mobile. I figure it'll take two trips. When we get done, we're gonna go claim Stevie's body and take care of him. It's the least a little sister can do."

A few minutes later, Buck stood at the door to the barn and peered into the gloom at thirty bales of marijuana stacked neatly in the center.

"Just who the hell are you?" he said, as much to himself as to Jeannie who was already pulling out the first bale.

"Come on, son. We don't got forever," she said.

"You're going to load all this in your van and drive it to Mobile," Buck stated rather than asked. "And you expect me to drive you there?"

"Yep, twice, it'll take two trips. Look, I'll drive down while you lay low. No need somebody recognizing you before we get out the county. You can drive back when the van's empty. Anybody stops us, I just gave a hitchhiker a ride, okay?" She shoved the bale in his chest, and he instinctively caught it. "See? Just like loadin' hay."

"Whoa, whoa, whoaaa. This isn't hay. You're a freaking drug mule."

"You been watching too many movies. It's just our little family operation. You're part of the family now, so pitch in." She tossed a second bale into the back of the van, backed up to the door.

"I didn't sign up for dealing drugs," he said.

Jeannie looked exasperated. "First of all, it's pot, not heroin. Second, we don't deal the stuff. We just grow it and take it where it needs to go. Third, you ain't got no place else to go, do you?"

Buck thought for a few seconds until Russell kicked him gently in the butt and chuckled.

"Dammit, boy. You gonna stand there all day wringing your hands like a altar boy or you gonna help out your kinfolks?"

Buck hesitated for a second, like he might tear into the old man. Russell's three-tooth grin, small stature, and good-natured laugh must have disarmed him. Buck visibly relaxed and grabbed a second bale by the strings.

BUCK

Twenty-seven

The next morning, an hour or so before sunrise, I drove the big white florist van past pine plantations and sleeping cows along the backroads of Alabama. Jeannie curled up against her door with a hat pulled low over her face. Even at this time of morning, the air conditioner couldn't keep up with the heat.

The yellow light on the gas gauge flickered on just when we reached the Carrollton town limits. I thought of a ghost story Mama used to tell when we would build a campfire in the backyard. One of the stories was about Henry Wells, whose face was etched by lightning into the attic window of the county courthouse while he stared in terror at the lynch mob in the street below. I felt this overwhelming urge to visit the doomed man and pulled the van over at the edge of the town square. The lights lining the street frosted the windshield through all the smashed bugs and accumulated dust from long hours on the road. I squinted at the courthouse windows but couldn't make out anything spookier than a passing firefly or two. Jeannie snored in the passenger seat; so, I slipped out.

I walked slowly around the square, empty except for a lone police car parked in front of the station across from the courthouse. When I reached the other side, I saw the arrow directing curiosity seekers to a particular dark pane of glass. Nothing. I crossed the street and leaned against a brick column on the sparkling new county building, which was a real contrast to the old ghost-possessed courthouse. I settled to the sidewalk, and waited for Mr. Wells to show himself. In the east, the dark blue sky of predawn dissolved toward another white hot day.

"He doesn't show his face to just anybody," said a woman's voice behind me.

"Oh shit, I'm sorry," said Buck, scrambling to his feet. "I didn't see you there."

She stepped out from the shadows of the columns and lit a cigarette. Her pale face glowed in the matchlight.

"You!" I said, stepping backwards. "What the hell?"

"I come here a lot," she said.

"You following me?"

"Might be the other way around," she said. "Ever thought of that?"

"Are you a fucking ghost or something?"

"Why, you believe in ghosts?"

"No."

"Why you here then?"

"Just stopped to rest a minute."

"Uh huh," she said and pulled a long drag. When she exhaled, three perfect smoke rings floated in front of my face, expanding slowly. "Look again. See his face now?"

I didn't want to look, but I couldn't help myself. My eyes turned toward the courthouse, and I found myself staring through three perfect rings at a ghastly face taking shape in the dark window. His eyes were wide and his mouth contorted like some grotesque frozen scream. I stumbled backwards against the wall and slid to the ground.

"Scary, huh? The face of death, up close and personal."

I shuddered and blinked. The face disappeared, and I sank my head into my open hands, gasping for breath.

"Son, you alright?" A policeman leaned over me.

"I remember," I said.

"You been drinking?" said the cop.

I jerked my head around. "Where'd she go?"

"Come on, son. Get up and go home. You can't be sleeping on the sidewalks in front of the courthouse."

"A woman was here."

"There's always a woman, son. Still can't stay here." said the officer, pulling me to my feet.

The white van pulled up in the street beside us, and Jeannie leaned out the window.

"Come on, Jamie. Let's go home," she said.

"He belong to you?" asked the cop.

"Yeah, he's all mine," she said. "Get in. Let's go home."

I steeled myself, realizing I had only one way to get to the bottom of things. I dusted myself off and drew a deep breath, letting it out slowly.

"You don't look good, son. Drinking don't agree with you. Do what your mama says and go sleep it off." The policeman led me to the passenger side and even opened the door. "I won't be this nice next time. We usually send drunks to the tank till it wears off."

He looked over at Jeannie. "Keep an eye on him. Next time you'll have to pick him up from jail. You don't want that."

"No, sir, we don't want that for sure. He'll be a good boy from now on, officer. I appreciate your kindness."

The policeman noted the tag number as they drove off.

Nobody talked, even after Jeannie stopped for gas and picked up honey buns and coffee for breakfast. On the road again, I turned to the window and stared at the passing pines.

"Were you drinking?" Jeannie finally asked.

I said nothing.

"The man said you were drunk."

"Yeah, I bummed a bottle from a wino in front of the police station at five in the morning."

"Hell, I done that before."

"Well, I didn't."

"Then, why you acting crazy enough to get a policeman talking about jailing you?" she said. "How am I s'posed to trust you delivering our stuff if you can't stay out of trouble?"

"I didn't ask for this shit," I muttered.

"Well, you're in it now. Too late to be complaining."

"I remember," I said.

"Remember what?"

"I saw a woman there." I threw her a side-look to check her reaction.

"What you talking about, boy? I didn't see nobody but you and a cop."

"When Mama died, a woman had her hands around Mama's throat, pushing her under the water."

Jeannie stomped the brakes and pulled on the narrow shoulder. A red pickup swerved around them, leaning on the horn.

"What are you saying, boy? Are you accusing me of something?" she demanded, her eyes growing black with anger.

"I saw it. I was there."

"Did you see me? If you gonna throw around wild statements like that, you better look me in the eye and say it straight up."

"I didn't see her face. She had a hood over her head. But it was a woman. I remember clear as day."

"Say it, damn it. Don't beat around the bush. You got something to say, be a man and say it."

I jerked open the door and slid out. A logging truck roared by, horn blasting.

"You can't say it, can you? 'Cause I wasn't there," she said. "Get in. What are you gonna do, walk home?"

"Who else would it be?" I said. "What other woman would want to kill my mother except the one who lost her baby to her?"

"Yeah, she took you away from me. But if I was gonna kill her, why would I wait seventeen fucking years to do it? Jamie, you ain't thinkin' straight. Get in the van."

"You know something, though. Don't you?"

"Look, I know stuff would make your hair curl. But you ain't ready for it. Not yet."

"What's that supposed to mean? Do you know who killed my mother or not?"

Jeannie sighed and dug in the glove compartment for a stray cigarette. She found one crumpled under the loose papers, a pocketknife, and a packet of Kleenex, but no matter how much she searched, she couldn't find anything to light it with.

"We had a van full of pot and not a damned lighter anywhere." She put the unlit cigarette in her mouth and breathed deeply. Then she rolled down her window and threw it out. Another logging truck passed, sweeping it down the highway.

"Get in and get some sleep. I'll tell you everything I know when you can think straight."

I crawled back in and slammed the door., leaned against the window and half-closed my eyes, but I couldn't sleep. I didn't say another word all the way home.

DICK MORRISON

Twenty-eight

Dick Morrison checked his office voice mail near the end of his usual late summer vacation. His wife wasn't happy when he attended to business on his time off, but he couldn't wait to get back to the Lord's work protecting the families of Tierney County. As soon as he returned the missed phone call from Lance Taylor at Creed National, he canceled the rest of the vacation and headed home.

Who the hell did Judge Neighbors think he was? Up to now, Dick had treated him with the utmost respect, but going behind his back to issue the subpoena of Creed's records was unforgivable. The old man wasn't long for the court. Dick had thought of him as a doddering fool but pleasant enough. More importantly, he was malleable enough. Apparently so malleable, he let another old man, the sheriff, talk him into digging into places he didn't belong. All the incidents of forgetfulness and diminished skills, whether imagined or not, crowded into Dick's mind, and he determined to make sure they were revealed in unsourced flyers and whispers in the next election.

The real problem was Ben Jefferson. Even though Ben had been in office for nearly thirty years, Dick still didn't think he was up to the job. But he could be a thorn in your foot for sure. The law's hands were tied up with this bombing thing right now; so, Dick had a little time to get things straight. Near the top of his to-do list would be a visit to Leon Bustard. Leon was a loud-mouth and crooked as the day is long, but he was not weak. Neither was Jefferson, but at least Dick knew how to handle Bustard. He knew where his interests lay. It was time a Bustard was back in charge of the county jail.

But first things first. Bustard could wait. How else could Jefferson know to go after the insurance policy with Creed unless he knew about the will? And how would he know about the will? Where else would he see a copy of the will except in the secure records room at the courthouse, the room with the key that Sarah Covington kept in her desk?

Sarah had been his court clerk for nearly twenty years. She had always been a loyal and discreet employee. At first thought, he didn't believe she would have anything to do with this. On the other hand, he had heard plenty of stories about Sarah keeping regular hours at the disreputable bar in Roseboro over on the west side of the county, a bar whose reputation he knew from his early wild oats days. Can a drunk really be trusted? Lust wasn't hard to spot in a woman, and she had all the hallmarks in addition to spending too much time at a bar: the dyed blonde hair, the low-cut blouses that he had talked to her about several times, her extra friendly demeanor with men, particularly Black men, as he thought about it.

Specifically, Sarah always perked up whenever Ben Jefferson came into the office. Jefferson was snooping around trying to get information, and she might be more than obliging to him. The more he thought about it, the more morally incensed he became. The idea of any White woman lowering herself to chase after a Black man, any Black man, disgusted him. He had been particularly hard on the women with mixed race babies that came through his courtroom. But he had been too close to see the same nasty behavior in one of his own staff. The thoughts of a slut like Sarah throwing herself at a Black man playing at being a sheriff was too much. Time to pay her a visit. Find out what she knew and why she was willing to sell out her official duties for the chance to lay with a Black son-of-a-bitch. Theirs had to be a private talk. Not one he could handle in the office. That's alright, he told himself. He knew where to find her.

He slipped into his silver Lexus and headed home for a few hours. The timing had to be right. MacInnelly's closed at two a.m. He would be waiting for Sarah when she left.

Twenty-nine

When Deputy Walters was discharged from the hospital, Ben Jefferson and Cheryl Moon were waiting for him. The sheriff told him to take off the rest of the week and not even think about coming into work. He didn't tell him yet that he was on paid leave until the DA finished his investigation of the shooting of the unarmed van driver, an investigation triggered by the coroner finding a bullet lodged in the man's shoulder and one bullet missing from Walters' gun. Plenty of time for that. Cheryl placed him in the passenger side, told the sheriff she would make sure he obeyed orders, and drove him home.

Ever since his encounter with Weisman in the interview room, the sheriff did not feel comfortable at home. He knew he would just sit up all night, again, and listen to Chopin recordings or watch videos of his dead wife playing on stage in Atlanta or just for guests at the Christmas parties she loved to host. No, he couldn't do that anymore. He couldn't handle this alone. He couldn't handle it sober. So, when he pulled into his driveway in the Bronco with the Sheriff's Office logo, he carefully removed his badge, walked inside, and laid it on the kitchen table. He changed into jeans and a clean unmarked shirt, climbed into his old Chevy pickup, and headed toward MacInnelly's to forget about being a widowed lawman for a while.

At six p.m., Sarah Covington walked into the barroom and was immediately greeted with raised glasses and a hearty "Sarah." She ordered her customary Irish Pub Salad and a glass of white wine and settled next to Bob Armstrong at the bar. Bob had recently been divorced and needed an ear. That was Sarah's job, and she did it well. After Bob had downed five more beers, Joe called him an Uber, and Sarah kissed him goodbye at the door.

At seven-thirty, Sarah took her second glass of wine and sidled in beside Teddy Ames, who was still celebrating the final divorce decree he had received in the mail last week. Teddy bought Jack and Cokes for all the surrounding tables, and all the patrons gave him a rousing cheer. When Sarah introduced him to Stacy Pruitt, who had just moved to town to take care of her ailing mother and had an infrequent night off, Sarah slipped back out of the booth and let the two of them get acquainted. Her work done there, she got Joe to pour her a Sprite, and she headed to the back table where Ben Jefferson had been admiring her work for the last couple of hours.

"Mind if I sit here for a while? Looks like Teddy's found a new friend," she said, and sat down beside Ben without waiting for him to respond.

Joe brought another double bourbon and set the glass in front of the man, holding up five fingers where only Sarah could see them.

"What brings you here, Ben? Slumming tonight?" said Sarah.

"People love you, Sarah. Know that?" The words came out slowly, but clearly, not slurred.

"What's not to love?"

"True," he said and hoisted a toast. "Here's to love." He drained the glass and set it precisely back on the table.

"You alright tonight, Ben?" she asked.

"I've been better," he said, leaning in toward her and placing his hand on her arm. "You are a beautiful woman."

"Thank you!" She put her other hand on top of his and squeezed. Sitting this close felt good. She had always been attracted to Ben, more for the way he handled himself, and for the way he treated people, than for his looks, though he was still a fine-looking man. He was still strong at sixty-two, still confident and commanding the way a sheriff had to be, especially one of a different color than the power brokers in a small backwoods Southern town. The situation couldn't have been easy for him, but he never complained, never whined. He just did his job, honestly and fairly. That takes courage and integrity, she thought, the two most attractive qualities in any man. He was a few years older than her, but then she was no longer a beauty queen herself, though she still took pride in her appearance. A little gray had crept into their hair, both of them. She just did a better job of hiding hers.

"Awful thing what happened to your deputy and you," she offered.

"Yeah. We both got lucky, though. I've seen some bad things in my forty years on the force, but I've never seen a man's head blown clean off before. Laura, sometimes seems the world is full of evil."

She lifted her hand to his chin and raised his eyes to meet hers.

"Ben, look at me. I'm Sarah."

"Of course you are, the most beautiful woman I think I've seen in a long time."

"You miss her, don't you?"

"He was right, you know?"

"Who, Ben? Who was right?"

"He said I couldn't protect you, and he was right. I tried. God knows, I tried."

"Everybody knows you did the best you could. That's all anybody can ask of a man."

"My best wasn't good enough. Who the hell did I think I was, marrying you? I was just a stupid ignorant cop. And you? You were too good for the likes of me. You could have gone places, special places. Instead, you wound up dead in Stewarton-fucking-Alabama."

Ben's raised voice caught the attention of Joe, always on the alert for trouble. He wandered toward the table where Ben and Sarah sat. Sarah raised her hand to stop him but kept her eyes on Ben's.

"You know I didn't want to be anywhere except where you were."

"I killed him, Laura," said Ben.

"Who, darling?"

"The man that killed you," Ben mumbled. "I took a rock and bashed in his fucking head. He won't hurt you ever again."

Sarah looked at Joe and back at Ben, whose head slowly dropped to the table.

"Help me get him out of here, Joe. Let's get him in my car, and I'll get him someplace safe. He's out of his mind."

"Why'd he call you Laura?"

"Because that's all he can see. Shit, he said everybody loves me, but I'd give anything for what he had." She sighed, and Joe laid his hand on her shoulder. She pulled on Ben's arm and helped him slide out of the booth. Joe helped her get him out the door and into her car. When she drove out of the parking lot, a silver Lexus pulled out of the pawn shop lot next door, but the car's lights didn't come on until it was a block away and out of sight of prying eyes.

DICK MORRISON

Thirty

Judge Richard Morrison was a man of action. If he wanted something, he took it, and rationalized the morality later. If something, or someone, menaced him or his status, he retaliated with enough force not just to neutralize but to eliminate the threat forever. Two eyes for an eye. A mouthful of teeth for a tooth. Old Testament justice taken to the next level. He was, after all, the dispenser of justice.

Sarah Covington had committed a mortal sin. Dick could overlook all the venial ones that she engaged in every night at MacInnelly's. They didn't affect him one way or the other. But betraying the judge was to betray justice itself. That type of sin required swift retribution.

Keeping a safe distance behind Sarah's car, he thought about his options. He could just fire her, but that wasn't that big of a penalty really. Dismissing her wouldn't drive home the point, which was don't fuck with the judge. He could inflict physical violence, but that would require enlisting another person to inflict the punishment. A judge doesn't get his hands dirty. He wasn't worried, though. God always supplied the opportunities. He would know what to do when the moment came.

Sarah's unassuming five-year-old Buick cruised through the night, unnoticed by everybody except one. The car slowed on the edge of town and turned into an older subdivision filled with small square homes, some still with the original asbestos siding popular when they were built decades ago. The Buick pulled up in the half-dirt front lawn of a yellow-painted house with a single porch light. One streetlight flickered on and off a block further down. The rest of the neighborhood remained in darkness. The silver Lexus turned into the subdivision with the lights off, floating through the night like an elegant ghost, stopping a few doors down as its driver watched, waiting.

Sarah stepped out of her car, and instead of going inside, she opened the passenger door. The interior light backlit the outline of a man inside. Interesting, thought the judge. He had not seen anybody get into the car with Sarah at the bar. He had just seen her drive away and followed. The man slid out and stood, supported by Sarah's strong arms. The judge lowered his window and grabbed his digital camera, the one with the telephoto lens he kept in the glove compartment for special opportunities like this one. The normal cacophony of katydids and crickets was quieted for a moment by the night intruders.

"You're beautiful," said the man, loud enough to wake the neighbors. Dick recognized the voice and zoomed in on the figure.

Sarah said something too softly for Dick to overhear.

Ben wrapped both arms around her and pulled her to his chest. He leaned in for a kiss. She let him.

The judge snapped off a series of shots. He worried they might be too dark.

"I've missed you so much," said Ben, his voice still too loud for the tender moment, and he leaned in again.

This time Sarah pushed him off, but led him to the front door.

"Why did you leave me?" he asked excitedly, as she fumbled for her key.

She pushed the door open. The camera clicked over and over.

Ben shook his head and stared into her eyes. He leaned against the wall under the porch light and closed his eyes. Sarah took his arm and pulled.

When he raised himself up, he swayed backwards and grabbed Sarah's arm to steady himself. The shutter snapped furiously, the scene now well-lit by the bare bulb. He stumbled backwards, and his weight pulled Sarah toward him. Both of them tumbled off the small stoop and into the rose bushes.

"Ben Jefferson, now look what the hell you've done," she cried. Both of them rolled out of the thorn bushes, yelling and laughing hysterically. The telephoto lens automatically adjusted, and the shutter worked feverishly. The porch light on the house where the Lexus was parked snapped on. Sarah glared in its direction.

"Shit, now you've woke up the nosy neighbors," she said and pulled him to his feet. Ben's shirt tail, ripped by the thorns, fluttered outside his pants. Sarah's face was scratched and bloodied. Dick snapped a few more pictures before he decided to leave.

As the Lexus pulled out, Sarah stared after it, wondering why the hell a car would be out this time of night with no headlights. She couldn't tell the make in the dark. The neighbor across the road leaned out of his door and yelled an obscenity voicing his displeasure for being awakened at such an ungodly hour. Sarah raised her middle finger over her head as she dragged Ben inside and closed the door behind her.

Thirty-one

Ben Jefferson was at his desk, nursing a lingering hangover and a large black coffee when Mandalee St. James and Teresa Bustard burst into the sheriff's office. He threw down another two aspirin before he invited them back to explain why they were there.

Mandalee looked at Teresa as she started.

"Sheriff, we brought you something," she said.

"You're Buck Thompson's ex-girlfriend, right?" he asked. "The one he burned." Even though Mandalee took care to hide the scars, the misshapen ear was visible under the thin veneer of hair that would never grow thick on that side anymore.

"That was an accident, Sheriff. Buck's a good guy."

"Okay," he said and nodded. He had seen plenty of beaten women standing up for their abusive boyfriends, even while wearing bandages or trying to cover bruises.

"What can I do for you today?" he asked. He pulled his cap down low to keep the fluorescent light out of his eyes and took another sip from the coffee cup.

"We found this in the woods." She extended her open hand across the desk. A small mangled slug and a spent brass cartridge rolled in her palm.

Ben sat up and pulled his cap back. He took the pieces and inspected them closely.

"So?"

"The bullet was buried in the ground where Teresa found the dog's skull. This is what somebody shot him with."

"And the cartridge? Where'd you find it?"

"Just a foot or two away, under some leaves," she said.

"Okay," he said and looked at Teresa. "So, you're assuming that whoever shot the dog had something to do with your mother's death."

"You can tell what gun it came from, right?" asked Teresa.

"You know your father thinks your brother shot the dog. What do you think?"

"I accused him of it because Buck had his gun with him that day." Teresa's voice wavered a little, but she kept going. "I told Daddy about the skull, and he got real mad. But now, I just can't believe Buck would do something like that."

"We can probably tell its caliber," he said, rolling the slug between his thumb and finger and examining the cartridge. "It's stamped, center-fire, a .25." He looked up and said, "Buck had a rifle, a Marlin."

"You mean Buck did it?" said Mandalee.

"No, Buck used a .35 caliber."

"So Buck didn't do it?" said Teresa, exhaling. "I knew it."

"The .25 caliber is mostly for small handguns. Light weight. Fits easily in a small purse. People used to call them a lady's gun."

"What? A woman shot Scout?" Teresa's voice rose in excitement. "Sheriff, I thought I saw a woman running away from me the day I found Scout's bones."

"Whoa. Might not mean anything. Small ammo, small gun, easy to conceal. But it could be a man. Could be anybody."

"But what about the woman Teresa saw?" asked Mandalee. "Can't you try to find her?"

"Can you tell me what she looked like?"

Teresa looked puzzled and hung her head. "No."

"Did you see her face?"

"No, sir."

"Was she light-skinned or dark-skinned?"

"I don't know."

"Was she tall or short? What was she wearing?"

"I don't know. Something white?"

"Look, Teresa, I know you're upset. That's understandable. Are you sure you saw anybody?"

"I think so. She was far away, and I called after her, but she didn't stop. Then she sorta…disappeared."

Ben looked at Mandalee and back at Teresa.

"But you said the bullet was from a lady's gun," said Mandalee. "You got to look into it, Sheriff. It's all we have." Mandalee had taken Teresa's hand and was squeezing it. Teresa's eyes were brimming with tears.

"I'll see what I can do, girls. I can't promise anything. It's not a whole lot to go on. Even if it is a woman's handgun, a lot of women carry these days. And the dog might not have anything to do with your mother's death. Doesn't prove anything one way or the other."

"But it's a lead, right?" asked Mandalee.

Ben sighed and leaned back in his chair, closing his hand around the bullet and cartridge.

"It's a lead," he said.

After the girls left, Ben put on another pot of coffee and closed his door. He'd send the slug to the state forensics lab in Montgomery to see if the cartridge matched. It was a reach. He wouldn't be able to use them as evidence since the girls had removed the bullet and cartridge from the scene, but maybe it would help. Analysis would take weeks, like everything else in this business. Unless you had connections or it was a high-profile case, you might as well get used to waiting. He had a connection in Montgomery, but this wasn't enough to ask a favor yet. He pulled out an envelope and placed the pieces inside. When he finished the paperwork, he gave it to a deputy to handle. Then he took Eva Bustard's file out of the cabinet and re-acquainted himself with all the women she might have crossed in her last few days.

LEON BUSTARD

Thirty-two

Leon didn't like answering his phone from unknown numbers, but he was expecting a call.

"Yeah," he said. "Who's this?"

"Job's done, *vaquero*," said the voice on the other end with a heavy Latin accent, "but now we need somethin' from you."

"Who is this?"

"A friend of a friend who's tied up for a while."

"I don't know you or what you're talking about. And I sure don't trust friends of supposed friends," said Leon.

"*Jefe* said you'll get the other half of the deal, but you got to help him out first."

"From what I hear, your *jefe* done tried to kill two lawmen. Who the hell told him to do something stupid like that?"

"Yeah, he feels bad about that, but what you gonna do? Can't get good help these days, you know, what with nothing but rednecks to choose from."

"I don't give a shit. A boss is responsible for what his men do. You tell your *jefe* that."

"You want the other part, you gotta show some good faith, you know, *vaquero*? *Jefe*'s lawyer won't see him 'cause things are too hot; so, he's got a fucking public defender. We need you to call off the dogs."

"First of all," said Leon, his voice rising, "I don't know who the hell you are or why you're calling me. Second, I don't have any dog to call off."

"Have it your way. Just so you know, *Jefe* records all his meetings. Think about it, Mr. Leon, maybe some of your friends have dogs. You got a week."

The phone went dead before Leon could answer. Just as well, whoever was listening on the other end wouldn't have wanted to hear his response. He checked again to make sure the call was disconnected, safely tucked his phone back in his pocket, and kicked a plank out of the fence he was standing next to.

Fucking Mexican gangster, he thought. Without a trace of irony crossing his mind, he wondered what the hell happened to the good old days when you could depend on another White man to do your dirty work? He stomped across the dusty yard. Mandalee St. James' car was in the driveway, and Teresa was just getting out.

"If you know where your worthless boyfriend is, you better tell him to come home now," he yelled through the open door. Mandalee stared back at him but didn't answer.

"Daddy, that's what I was going to tell you. Buck didn't do it." Teresa was excited and ran to her father despite his harsh tone.

"Didn't do what?" he asked, his voice still hard-edged.

"He didn't shoot Scout. The sheriff thinks it was a woman." The words came tumbling out in her excitement that her brother was innocent.

"Get in the house, Teresa," he demanded.

"But Daddy, didn't you hear…"

"Get in the goddamn house, girl."

Teresa's face dropped, and she froze for a moment.

"Did you hear me? Get in the house."

Teresa turned and ran, her eyes wide and frightened. Leon watched until the door slammed and then he stalked up to Mandalee's open car door.

"You tell that bastard boy to get his ass home, or I'll find him and drag him home."

"I don't know where Buck's at, Mr. Bustard," she said.

"Don't fuck with me, bitch. I ain't in any mood for any of yours and Buck's shit right now."

Mandalee reached over and slammed the door shut. She threw the car in reverse and stomped the pedal, sending gravel and dust spewing out and tossing an unfortunate wheelbarrow out of the way. She yanked the gearshift back into drive and spun around in the dusty yard. By the time she straightened out the car on the asphalt road, Leon Bustard and his wretched house were covered in a brown haze.

Leon cursed out loud and walked to the road where he pulled out his phone and looked up the district attorney's personal cell phone number. As usual, Frank Stone didn't answer and let the call go to voicemail.

"We need to meet, Frank. Call me back as soon as you get this."

YVONNE MORRISON

Thirty-three

Yvonne Morrison was not usually a quiet woman, except when she was around her husband. In those times, which was most of the time, she bit her tongue, but not because she was too weak to stand up to him. She told herself, being a good Christian, that a woman's place is to be submissive to her husband. To stay quiet was easier if she could believe that she was following God's will. And if God's will was for her to be submissive, then the man she submitted to must be righteous, at least most of the time. Just as God is the head of the Church, Dick is the head of the household. She really believed that.

Yvonne accepted her role with no question. However, as much as Dick liked to think he was God, she knew he was only human, with human frailties. A sinner. Just like everybody else. So Yvonne's mission was to correct his human frailties or at least cover them up, so that their household remained strong in the eyes of the rest of the world.

Women were Dick's sin. They always had been as long as she had known him, ever since she witnessed him lay lustful eyes on her sister, Eva. Lust wasn't his fault really. God created men that way, or at least gave them awareness of those urgings after they were banned from Paradise. Ever since, man has been a lustful being, who is easily led into depravity by his sexual urgings, unless he is constrained by pure women outside his marriage and satisfied by a willing woman inside it. Yvonne's holy calling was, therefore, to make sure he didn't need to look elsewhere. She could be a sexual tigress when she needed to be, or more accurately, when he needed her to be. But she also could use her claws to protect her position, especially when another, not-so-pure woman tried to take her place.

Eva had always been such a woman, casting eyes where they did not belong. Eva did not hesitate to use her attributes to her own benefit, most of the time without even being aware of what she was doing. She was a shapely girl, and she liked when people took notice of her. She would flash her smile, lean into them, laugh a little harder, touch them and herself in suggestive ways. Although she made a point to allow a man to think his actions were his own, you could almost see her grabbing him by the balls and leading him wherever she wanted to go.

Yvonne would have none of it when Dick began dating her. She made sure never to allow Eva and Dick to be by themselves. She made sure to exclude Eva, to poor-mouth her, to put her down whenever she could, and especially to convince the ambitious Dick that Eva would only hold him back. Yvonne won that battle, and once she and Dick were married, and knowing that Eva was a much more alluring female than she could ever be, Yvonne made sure that Eva was seldom in their lives.

That worked until Eva married Ray Thompson, a weak man that Dick despised almost as much as Yvonne. So when Dick asked Ray to be his law partner, Yvonne was surprised. In retrospect, it made sense from Dick's point of view. Ray could be easily led. That's why he married Eva. Dick liked to be in charge so he and Ray fit, at least for a while. Not until Dick began to feel that Ray was not strong enough to pull his weight, did he begin to realize how weak the man was. About the same time, Yvonne became pregnant with her third baby, within two years of bearing her first one. She had her hands full, and motherhood being nearly as important as her wifely duties, she took her eye off the ball. Dick, being a lustful creature, looked elsewhere for his satisfaction and found Eva still there, still as attractive as ever, and looking for her own satisfaction.

Dick got away with the affair for years, even for a while after Ray Thompson was murdered, until Yvonne convinced him to allow their youngest to go to daycare. Always suspicious but always tired, she finally had the time and the energy to keep a close eye on her man. She began to follow him, showing up at the office or at conferences, when Dick didn't expect her. The one-nighters he arranged at out-of-town events didn't bother her that much, as long as he used a condom and stayed disease-free. She knew he would be careful about those things. After all, he couldn't afford to have a bastard child foisted on him one day. But when she walked into Dick's hotel room in Atlanta, bearing a bottle of champagne and wearing nothing under her fur coat, and found Eva going down on him, she threw her sister into the hallway without so much as a towel. Then she poured the entire bottle of champagne over Dick and his little limp self and took a photo of him lying stunned in the wet sheets. That was the only time she had ever physically attacked him. She thought it scared him enough to fly straight for a while.

Yvonne stayed that night, and apparently the evening was successful. Yvonne and Dick left together the next day after getting another room with dry sheets and spending the entire next morning in bed. She never asked Eva how she got home to Stewarton without money or clothes. Eva never offered to tell her the story. They did not speak for years, even after Eva married her newest redneck. But Yvonne never forgot, and she always kept her eye out for signs of Eva's return.

Yvonne figured out an easier way to keep track of her wayward husband's whereabouts after that. Cell phone apps can be amazing, especially the hidden ones. Yvonne rested easy knowing that Dick was never without his phone, the lifeline to his office and his friends. She knew when he was likely indulging a dalliance somewhere. If she found the woman to be someone to fear taking her place, which was seldom the case, Yvonne was sure to directly confront her and warn her away. She was never shy in staking her claim to Dick—and backing it up with unequivocal physical threats. In those encounters, if her foe tried to laugh her off, Yvonne didn't mind grabbing a handful of hair and giving her opponent a peek at the steel enforcer concealed in her purse. Afterwards, none of the bitches ever thought Dick was worth the trouble anymore.

One woman drew Yvonne's suspicions for years. Sarah Covington. The woman was attractive in a trashy kind of way. Dick liked trashy as long as he could benefit or if he could make an example of the woman. Yvonne knew that Dick would like Sarah in a bedroom, but Yvonne had not discovered anything to tie the two together outside of the courthouse offices. So several months ago, Yvonne was surprised when she got a phone notification telling her the judge was at MacInnelly's Bar, where he had spent a good bit of time in his youth. His position did not allow him to spend time there anymore, and Yvonne's previous investigations had told her that the bar was Sarah's home away from home. So with great wariness, Yvonne loaded herself into her black Volvo and took off for MacInnelly's. Sure enough, Dick's Lexus was there, though he had made sure he parked his car around the side. Yvonne patrolled the block a few times until she pulled into the pawnshop lot next door, where she could see the Lexus taillights.

Dick came out a few minutes later, alone. He got into his car and drove away, as if he had just quenched his thirst and was done for the evening. Yvonne carefully watched the blue dot on her phone screen representing Dick's location and was surprised to see it stop about two blocks away. Her mind worked out the possibilities. Was he waiting for someone? Was he looking up directions? Should she wait until he moved before she followed?

The next moment decided for her. A blonde woman walked out of MacInnelly's, and stopped for a moment, looking up at the sky. Fat snowflakes drifted down like confetti, changing colors as they passed through the glare of the yellow parking lot lights, flashing red bar sign, and blue neon beer bottles in the window. The woman leaned back even further and opened her fur-lined jacket, letting the snow settle on her chest and her outstretched tongue. In open-mouthed astonishment, reality hit Yvonne like a two-ton block of ice falling from the heavens. Eva, goddammit. How did she miss that? Here she thought Sarah Covington was her new rival. Instead, she had underestimated her skank of a sister. Eva slid into a low-slung, red BMW rag-top and glided out of the parking lot, moving toward Dick's location. Yvonne pulled out a hundred yards behind her and kept pace, all the while keeping an eye on Dick's location on the phone and mumbling every curse word she had learned. When Eva drove up next to Dick, Yvonne quickly pulled into a driveway and shut off her lights. From her vantage, she could see the light come on inside the BMW, and a figure struggling into the tiny passenger seat. The light went off and the car drove off. Yvonne watched her phone. Dick's little blue dot moved away. The silver Lexus stayed right where it was parked.

The porch light came on, and Yvonne yanked the car into reverse, sliding the car backwards onto the asphalt, lights still off. When she looked in the rearview, the fast-approaching headlights nearly blinded her. A car horn sounded like it was coming through her rear windshield, and the sound of tires sliding sideways roared in her ears. The car's back right quarter panel made contact with Yvonne's car, and the skidding vehicle instantly spun like a billiard ball with extra English. Yvonne's car spun around too, still in the road but facing the other way. She could see lights wildly flashing through the sky and heard the sound of crunching metal. Yvonne slammed the Volvo into drive and stomped the pedal. Only after two blocks did she turn the lights on.

"Shit, shit, shit! Fucking whore!" she shouted.

Thirty-four

Yvonne drove for fifteen minutes before stopping, finally assuring herself that no one was following her. She got out and surveyed the damage. The rear corner on the driver's side was crumpled inward but had not impinged on the tire. Nothing was leaking. Remarkably, the high-mounted taillight on the banged-up side still worked though the bumper-mounted fog light was broken. In the dark, a cop might notice, but maybe not enough to warrant a traffic stop. She was, after all, a White woman in a White woman's car. The biggest problem was the swath of white paint the other car had left on the Volvo that stood out like a beacon light.

So far she had not attracted any attention. If she drove carefully, as if she was just another passerby, nobody would give her a second glance, especially in the night. She retrieved her phone from the floorboard and pulled up the tracking app again. Her husband was still on the move, driving back to Stewarton. Were they headed to her house? Was Eva's husband out of town? The risk of being stopped didn't matter anymore. She had to know. She took four or five deep breaths, shook her arms to ease the tension, and turned the car back in the direction she had come.

Blue lights were everywhere when she approached MacInnelly's, even though it was almost two a.m. The patrons who had remained until last call rubber-necked from the bar parking lot, drinks still in hand. You could almost hear the comments about how bad the wreck might be judging by the number of emergency lights. Nobody looked her way as she crept by in the barely moving line of traffic. Once she traveled even with the accident scene, she couldn't help but glance in the direction of the wreck. In the surreal white haze, a car lay upside down, an ambulance pulled up in the yard next to it. A policeman in front of her whistled and banged on her hood, snapping her out of the trance. His other hand was thrust out to halt her. She reacted quickly and hit the brakes. The cop cursed, but he had bigger issues. He motioned the ambulance out of the yard, leaving black tracks in the accumulating snow pointing right at her. The siren screamed away in front of her, and she felt her chest thumping hard. Her breath came out in shallow wheezes, and she fumbled in her purse for an inhaler. A black pistol tumbled onto the floor at the same time the policeman knocked on her window. She sucked on the inhaler before looking at him, convinced she would just quit breathing if she turned. He shouted at her to move, and she nodded, still not turning his way.

The cop had to have seen the damage to the rear end. He had to know she was involved. He would be jumping in his car any moment and pursuing her. A flash of a high-speed chase jumped into her consciousness. She quickly dismissed the fear, but not before her speed had crept up to fifty. She tapped the brakes and looked in her mirror. A steady stream of cars was behind her, but none had flashing lights. No siren was closing in. She cruised slowly out of Roseboro, leading a parade of impatient cars that had backed up in her wake.

Get it together, she thought. You couldn't do anything more to call attention to yourself if you wanted to. The number of streetlamps dwindled and so did the cars, each turning off toward their own homes, their own beds, where they would talk about the cop cars and the wrecked car and the fresh snow that probably caused it all. Nobody would think anything about a slow-moving black Volvo, even one with a splotch of white. By the time she neared Stewarton, her pulse had steadied though her breaths were shallow. The highway ahead cut a dark ribbon through the snow still falling hard.

Eva's house was a couple miles away from the county road coming up on the left. She glanced down at her phone and pecked a few times to pull up the app again. Dick's phone was no longer moving. He appeared to be at Eva's place. Yvonne turned into an abandoned gas station and turned off the engine. She shivered. She got out of the car and sat on the wet ground. She put her head between her knees and tried to swallow her heart that had risen with the bile in her throat. She stood and immediately threw up, retching until her stomach ached and her throat blazed with the strong acid she couldn't hold back. She speculated who was in the upside-down car, who was raced to the emergency room. Someone innocent, she wondered? The only thing open that time of night was the bar. She remembered her mother telling her a long time ago that nothing good happened after midnight. No, she decided, the ambulance was not speeding off to save some innocent person. It was probably a drunk, who simply didn't react in time.

She pulled on the sweatshirt she had thrown in the back of the car and walked in the cold darkness to clear her head, happy to be away from prying policemen. Yes, a stupid drunk driving too fast. He got what he deserved.

A car drove by, either a late-night partier coming home or an early riser up for work already. The automobile slowed slightly. She reached in the car and retrieved the pistol off the floor, but the lights passed and disappeared over the next hill. She walked around the lot, leaned on the signpost that still displayed the price of gas from ten years ago, calmed her breathing, and worked things out in her mind. Her heart slowed as she talked to herself. She realized the pistol was still in her hand, and she slid it into her pocket. The anger she had felt towards Dick earlier gave way to cold, logical thoughts that matched the weather. She planned her next moves.

Dick wouldn't come home at this time of night. He would phone in the morning and say he was called out of town to consult on an emergency case, probably knowing but not caring that Yvonne knew a family court judge doesn't need to go out of town on an emergency. If someone needed a ruling in the middle of the night, they would come to him—late night visits from an investigator or a lawyer, pleadings for restraining orders. The judge loved those calls. They made him feel important. Her, too, if truth be told. She served up sandwiches and coffee, talked up the visitors, found out what was going on. But when he called to say he was going out of town, it meant he was shacked up screwing another slut. This time, after so many years, she knew the slut was her sister.

Yvonne studied the phone app. She called up the satellite view and saw the phone appeared to be a few hundred feet away from Eva's house. He was fucking her in the goddamn car. No, the damn thing was too small, and he was too fat. More likely Eva was making him happy in another way. Yvonne fumed as the image pushed its way into her head. This time she had gone too far. Eva needed another lesson. She would wait until Dick was almost ready to leave. Probably just before daylight. He wouldn't want to be there if Eva's husband came looking for them when the sun came up.

The night was frigid, and the snow fell in waves of thick fluffy flakes that quickly covered her windshield. She waited until four o'clock and cranked up the car. She pulled onto the county road and slowed to a near crawl. When she got within a quarter mile, she turned off the headlights, peering through the darkness using only her yellow fog lamps to light the way. She cruised along the dark strip of asphalt between the white shoulders, thinking the road to sin is damned easy to follow. A single streetlamp illuminated the pavement a few hundred yards ahead. Eva's place. Yvonne turned off the lights completely. Even in the blackness, she could still make out the edges of the road.

By the time she saw Eva's car, it was almost too late. The rear end of the BMW protruded slightly into the road. Startled, Yvonne swerved as a faint white shape emerged from the other side and onto the pavement. The thump sounded sickening and the bile in her throat rose again. She stamped on the brake pedal and another thump sounded through the darkness, this time like the sound of a slab of meat slapping the floor. She waited for a second, listening for another sound. Hearing none, she opened the door and stepped into the cold.

She retrieved her phone and fumbled until the flashlight came on. Eva lay on the asphalt, her shirt partially open. Her head rolled from side to side, and she moaned softly, almost inaudibly. Yvonne knelt over her sister and shook her slightly.

"Eva? Are you okay?"

A man's voice surprised her from behind. Yvonne had completely forgotten that Dick was still here. He must have been in the woods relieving himself.

"What the hell? Yvonne? What did you do?" Dick stood behind Yvonne but didn't check any closer on Eva.

"What did I do?" she said, her voice betraying that she had abandoned her traditional role. "What did I do?" she asked again.

"Jesus, did you kill her?" he said.

"She's not dead, you fucking pig. Get your dick back in your pants and help me get her off the road. Some farmer's going to wander by any minute."

He looked down at his zipped-up pants. A shirttail hung out. He tucked it in.

"We weren't messing around. We were just driving around and talking. Why do you always go off the rails?"

"We can talk about your skirt-chasing later on. Right now, we need to take care of this."

"Alright, let's think about this."

"Jesus, Dick, there's nothing to think about. We're going to make it look like an accident and then we're going to get out of here." Yvonne's voice slowed as she spoke. The wheels were turning smoothly now, as she methodically worked through the options open to them. "She's out of it now. We'll get her in the woods and leave her there, next to a tree. She stumbled in the woods and hit her head. She couldn't see anything in the dark. She doesn't know anything."

"We should get her to the house," he said.

"No," she said calmly. "Help me move her," she commanded.

"What about her car?" he asked.

Yvonne silently rolled her eyes. For all his machismo, Dick was not the boss in emergencies.

"We'll get her in the woods, and then you'll push it down the road and into the driveway with the lights off. She got out for a walk, slipped on the icy road, hit her head, and stumbled into the woods. Simple as that."

"When she wakes up, she'll remember I was there," he said.

"She's not going to tell anybody you were there, especially Leon. She's got more reasons to make up a story than we do. Come on, let's get this done."

Together they grabbed her under each arm. Yvonne was much bigger than her sister. It wasn't too hard to get her off the road. They laid her on the ground, the large scrape just in front of her right ear laying against a tree.

"Go," she ordered. "It'll be light soon."

He left, and she could hear Dick grunting and the tires crunching on the snow. She waited and listened to Eva's ragged breathing.

When Yvonne finally yanked open the passenger door of her own car, Dick was waiting inside for her. Her arms were scratched and bleeding, and strands of her hair were white with ice. She peeled off her sweatshirt, shivering violently. She twisted the temperature control to its highest setting.

"What happened to you?" he asked. "What the hell was that, a gunshot?"

"Get going," she hissed. "Got no time to talk."

Dick showered down on the accelerator and flipped on the lights. The car lurched forward onto the shoulder, and he yanked it back to the center. The tires slid sideways, and Dick over-adjusted a couple of times before it straightened. At the stop sign at the end of the county road, the car slowed to a halt and idled patiently as a snow-covered truck crept by on the state route, likely one of the overnight laborers at the lime quarry up the road. The Volvo inched onto the highway, just like any other early morning commuter in an Alabama snowstorm.

Thirty-five

"You find that boy yet?" Leon had dropped any pretense about calling "that boy" his boy.

"We've got eyes out for him, Leon. He'll turn up. Right now, I need to talk to your daughter."

"What about? The dog? It's about time." Leon left the sheriff in the living room and went to the back door to call out for Teresa. Ben followed him into the den and stopped by the gun cabinet in the corner of the room. Buck's Marlin rifle stood on one side behind the glass. A vintage double-barrel shotgun stood on the other. Two handguns hung in the middle. One appeared to be a Colt .45 and the other a tiny Derringer.

"That's some beautiful pistols. And that 12-gauge reminds me of the shotgun my old man had."

"Gives a helluva kick," said Leon. "I let the boy shoot it one time, and it knocked him flat on his back."

"You keep 'em shined up. Got any other ones?" asked the sheriff.

"You mean like the one that shot the dog? You already seen that one. It's standing right there." Leon pointed to the Marlin.

"Hmmm," said Ben. "I don't know. Got any .25s?"

"Wouldn't have one. They ain't no good except for varmint shootin'."

"Yeah, little critters about the size of a dog."

"You sayin' it was a .25 shot the dog?

"Lab's confirming it. Sure looks like it, though."

"How you tell by looking at a goddamn skull, Sheriff?"

Teresa walked through the back door, huffing from riding her bicycle.

"Hi, Sheriff," she said.

Leon eyed her for the familiar way she addressed the Black man.

"Go ahead and ask your questions," he said. "I'll try to help, too."

"Okay," said Ben, smiling. "Teresa, can you show me exactly where you found Scout?"

"Yes, sir. It was a ways down the road."

Together, the three of them headed down the drive and walked along the road. After they passed the end of the cleared field, past the last fencepost that Buck had put in before he disappeared, Teresa showed no sign of slowing, and Leon spoke up.

"Honey, where you taking us?"

"It was down here some more, Daddy, close to that trail that runs into the woods."

"The old logging road? That's on Caldwell's land. What were you doing way down there?"

Teresa thought a moment before answering. Her dad would be even more upset if she told him she was following a woman through the woods.

"I thought I saw a fawn, and I followed it."

"You stay off other folks' property. You know better 'n that."

"Yes, sir."

The logging road, really just an overgrown path after the years since the timber was last cut, was almost invisible to somebody just passing by. Teresa turned and walked down the path, stepping around blackberry vines and ducking under pine branches. About fifty feet in, she stopped.

"Right there, Sheriff. Where the vines and the weeds are trampled down."

"What the hell?" Leon said.

"Did you move all the bones?" asked Ben.

"Yes, sir, we took him back by the big oak and buried him. I made a little cross to mark the grave."

Ben smiled at the tenderness children show their pets. No beloved pet would go without a proper burial and a cross commending it to God.

"This is important. Show me where you found the bullet and where you found the cartridge."

"You found the bullet?" Leon was astonished. "Why didn't you tell me?"

Ben broke in before she could answer.

"Take your time, Teresa. It's important to see exactly where you found them. Show me exactly where the skeleton was too."

"The bullet was over here in the weeds." She kneeled and pointed to a spot about a foot beyond where she said the skull was found. She got up and stepped back into the logging road.

"The other part was over here." She stood about three feet away and pointed straight down.

"You told me you heard a shot that night, right honey?" Leon stepped up and put an arm around her shoulder. That was all she needed to dissolve into tears, and she leaned into her daddy's embrace.

"I did, Daddy," she stammered through the tears. "I kept the window open waiting on Mama to come home."

"What time was it, Teresa? What time did you hear the shot?" asked Ben.

"It wasn't light just yet. Almost time for the birds to start singing 'cept none of them was singing that day." Her tears flowed even harder, and she stopped to catch her breath.

"Take her home, Leon. I'm going to dig around a little more, if you don't mind."

"Yeah. That's probably a good idea. Let's go, honey."

Ben watched them leave and turned back to the little area that Teresa and Mandalee had trampled in their efforts to find the bullet. They had done well, finding such tiny pieces in the middle of the woods. Ben wondered at the possibility of anybody ever stumbling across the remains of the dog except possibly for a hunter later in the year. Even then, they would have likely just kicked at it and moved on.

He stood at the spot for a moment and reckoned the distance to the creek where Eva's body was found. Teresa heard a shot before dawn, possibly the one killing their dog. Buck found Eva's body only an hour or two later. The two locations were at least a good one hundred yards away from each other. They had gone over the possible crime scene at the creek and searched meticulously for a couple hundred feet in every direction, but they hadn't gone quite this far. Now six months later, he still couldn't classify the incident as a murder. It hadn't rained hardly any since then. Maybe something was still to be found. Maybe whatever it was hadn't degraded yet. He needed to get a technician out here and comb through the woods around this spot and between the two places. It was a long shot, but more than he had before.

He marked a wide area with yellow caution tape and started to head back to his car. Just as he tied the last ribbon, he spied a small piece of white fabric clinging to a briar vine behind a thick misshapen pine. He knelt to examine the cloth closer and thought he could see spots of dark reddish brown. Something registered in his memory, something about the clothes they found Eva wearing the day she died. A white blouse, torn on the sleeve. Not surprising at the time, given the apparent struggle she had made. The questions were obvious. Did the puzzle piece fit? Did it tie the two scenes together even more? Was blood on the cloth? Was it Eva's?

The possibilities spun through his mind. This could all turn out to be nothing. Maybe Teresa had only heard the sound of a backfiring car. Maybe the dog was shot some other time. It all could be a string of coincidences. But then, as he had told himself before, there's no such thing as a coincidence.

BUCK

Thirty-six

"Well, are you going to talk to me or not?" I was tired of waiting. Even a week after arriving back from their trip, Jeannie had not offered anything.

We sat on the front porch, each of us with a plastic plate of peas and turnip greens on our laps. I stirred mine together like some sort of stew, but I didn't feel like eating. Jeannie scooped her peas with a spoon and dashed more pepper sauce on them.

"Better eat," she said. "We got to load up and make another trip tomorrow."

"Work to do," I finished for her.

"Yeah, work to do. That's what pays for the peas."

"I remember the woman," I said.

"Are we going through that shit again? I told you I didn't have nothing to do with it." Jeannie kept spooning her peas.

"I saw her struggling with my mother that morning I found her."

Jeannie put down her spoon and picked up a fork, cutting the greens into bite-sized portions.

"I thought you told everybody you found her dead," she said and shoveled a mouthful.

"It came back to me the other day when we stopped. I remember it clear as day."

"Yeah, why was it we stopped in that little town, right next to a police station? Why was it I found you talking to a cop?"

"I had to see the ghost."

"Yeah, sounds reasonable. Everybody checks out a ghost in a window at the crack of dawn. Whadya tell the cop?"

"I didn't tell him anything. He thought I was drunk."

"You tell him you was kidnapped? Maybe this crazy woman was making you haul drugs against your will?"

"Why are you changing the subject? I saw a woman that morning, and the next time I'm in the woods, I find you."

"Six months later," she said. She shook another few drops of hot sauce on the greens.

"Were you there? Was it you fighting with her that day?"

"I already told you straight out. Why in the hell do you think I would be fighting her? For God's sake, if I wanted to hurt her, it would've been when she stole you in the first place."

"If it wasn't you, then who was it?"

"It don't matter now. She's dead and gone, and you need to move on."

"You sound like fucking Leon. Move on. Move on. Is that all anybody can say? My mother gets murdered, and all anybody can say is move the hell on."

Jeannie finished cleaning her plate and set it down on the table beside her. She picked up the tall glass of sweet tea and gulped a few swallows.

"What do you want me to say, Jamie? I'm glad she raised you good, but she wasn't no friend of mine."

"Tell me this. I've got blonde hair. Had it all my life. You've got a photo of you and your old man grinning in that picture frame in your bedroom. You were both young. No gray back then. Both of you with a head of hair black as midnight. If you're my mother, how did I get blonde hair?"

"Ever hear of hair dye?"

"Fuck you. We don't even have the same color eyes. If you can't answer a simple question, I'm leaving." I got up and threw the peas and greens in the yard.

"Sit down, Jamie. You ain't leaving and wandering out here in the dark."

"Then tell me something. I'm tired of the dark."

Jeannie put down her tea and leaned out to take my hand. I didn't want none of it, but I sat back down.

"I ain't ever told another soul 'bout this," she said. "Kenny wasn't your real daddy." She leaned back in the chair and stared into the deep woods surrounding the little house. "There, I said it."

Everything was quiet. Nothing rained down from the heavens. Nothing changed.

"After all these years," she continued, "I thought it would make me feel better to tell the truth to somebody." She sighed heavily. "I guess the truth is overrated."

"You were raped?"

Jeannie didn't answer, but she looked him in the eye.

"You . . . you slept with another man?" I asked.

Jeannie kept looking him in the eye, but she didn't deny anything.

"So, I'm a bastard child."

"Oh, Jesus, boy, it ain't always about you. It was about keeping Kenny happy."

"Oh, that's rich," I said. "You wanted to keep your old man happy, so you went out and fucked another man. Bet he was ecstatic about that."

"I told you, I never said a word to nobody, especially not Kenny."

"Why?"

Jeannie sighed. "I guess I owe you that," she said. She took another gulp of tea before she went on.

"Kenny wanted a boy," she said. "That's all he ever wanted. He didn't want money. He didn't want a big house. He didn't even want me that much, truth be told. He just wanted a boy."

"So?"

"So, we tried for years, and nothing. I think Kenny was shootin' blanks. I mean, he didn't get cut or nothin' and he was sure good in bed—just I never got pregnant. His swimmers just weren't no good."

"Thanks for the visual. I could have done without that," I said. "How'd you know it wasn't you?"

"I didn't. That's why I had to find out."

"So, you're telling me you just went out and found some horny guy off the streets and fucked him so you could get pregnant and please your sterile husband."

"Sounds better when I say it in my head," she said. "But to be fair, it wasn't just any old horny man. I made sure it was somebody smart, somebody who had made something of his life."

"Somebody with money you could blackmail? Tell me who."

"No. Ain't no use bringing anybody else in this."

"What do you mean no? You feed me lies for a couple weeks about this wonderful music man being my daddy, and now you spring this shit on me?"

"All that matters now is that I'm your real mama."

"So, I have a whore for a mother and a sleazeball for a father."

"You know, it don't matter who your sperm donor daddy was. What really matters is who loved you. Me and Kenny loved you more than you can imagine."

I fell back in the chair, and the dark got deeper. My thoughts drifted to who I knew loved me. My real daddy took me fishing, read me bedtime stories, carried me around on his shoulders. At least, that's what I was told. That daddy was real. That daddy was touchable, huggable. That daddy loved me. Maybe Kenny loved the thought of a son. But he wasn't there, was he? If he really loved me, he would have been the one carrying me around, showing me a chord on a guitar, singing to me. But he wasn't.

This woman telling me wild stories hauled marijuana for a living. She lived in the woods and fucked men she didn't love just to have a baby. Wasn't even for her, it was for her husband. Did she ever really love her baby? If she did, why did she just show up seventeen years later?

"I'm taking a walk," I said.

"Don't wander off too far. If you want to go somewhere tomorrow, I'll take you. I promise."

I walked up the long narrow driveway winding through the woods, heading for the county road a half-mile away. I planned to walk another mile to the state highway. Jeannie had given me fifty dollars for my help. Fair, I thought, considering I was new. If I stayed here, I could make a few dollars as long as they didn't get caught. But I'd demand a bigger cut if my ass was going to be on the line. Right now, though, the money burned in my pocket, and the pang in my heart ached to be quenched. I'd buy two or three six-packs and find a place under a bridge somewhere. Maybe tomorrow I'd go back if I decided the situation was worth it. Maybe I'd move on. Maybe I'd stay right there under a fucking bridge and drink myself to death. Probably need more than a few six-packs, but if you want something bad enough, you can always find a way to make things happen. I just needed to figure out what I wanted.

Thirty-seven

The week was up, and Billy Weisman still wasn't talking. After he lawyered up, the information he might have had stayed locked up with him. Ben suggested trying a little more leverage to loosen him up. Both Schuyler Jenkins and Ben had to call in a few favors. Willie Pearson himself was pulled in by the Fulton County Sheriff's Office and held for a few days. Jenkins made arrangements to transfer Weisman to the federal prison in Atlanta, which just happened to be running behind in its paperwork. Perhaps, if they didn't mind, Fulton County could hold Weisman for a few days while the orders cleared. Sure, they said, anything for a friend and a fellow cop. Fortunately, the Fulton County jail had a cell on the same block as Pearson. Jenkins came by and informed Weisman of the plans the day before he was to be transferred.

"Trying to throw a scare in me, man? I ain't worried about Willie Pearson. I can handle his kind." Weisman puffed himself up every chance he got, but Jenkins wasn't impressed.

"I'll tell him you said so. He'll be glad to see you, I'm sure." Jenkins smiled. "You know, Willie don't ever do his own dirty work. His 'kind' outnumbers your 'kind' four-to-one over there. You won't know who's working for him and who's not. How many eyes you got in the back of that thick skull, Billy? How long can you go without sleeping? Won't be any guard looking out for your ass."

"Yeah, well, I might have a few friends, too."

"You probably got a few in Tierney County, Alabama," said Jenkins. "You don't have any you can count on in Atlanta, Georgia. See you tomorrow. I'll be by around daylight to be sure the transfer goes smooth. Get a good night's sleep. Could be the last you get for a while." Jenkins and Ben left without another word. They didn't see Billy Weisman hang his head or curse under his breath, but they didn't have to. An hour later, Jenkins got a call from Weisman's attorney. Billy was ready to make a deal.

"I want to be there," said Ben. "You can get him first; get what you can. Then I've got some things I need to hear him say." Ben Jefferson knew Weisman's bodyguard, Patch Wilson, was involved in Laura's death. He just couldn't prove anything. Her death was no accident, no matter what the DA said, no matter what the Highway Patrol said. When Wilson wound up in the hospital after the harsh treatment by Ben's hand, the DA demanded the sheriff leave the investigation. Ben wasn't stopped that easily.

Ben knew that the paint found on Laura's car door matched the paint on the passenger side of Wilson's truck. Conveniently, Wilson claimed he was out of town. He even had McDonald's receipts proving he was in Mobile the day before and the evening of Laura's wreck. The closed-circuit camera shots showed his Escalade, including the tag number, in line at the fast food place on both days. Patch Wilson was driving both times.

What Ben knew is that there was plenty of time to get to Stewarton from Mobile and make it back again to get in the McDonald's camera. What the security video didn't show was the passenger side of the truck. Wilson's truck appeared to show new body work on the passenger side when Ben pulled him over, but he couldn't prove when the work was done. Patch Wilson had a habit of going out of his way to hurt people, especially Black people, and especially the families of Black sheriffs who tried to shut down the little operation that Weisman and Wilson had going in their little town.

Patch Wilson was dead now. Ben made sure. He should have been satisfied, but he wasn't. He didn't think Weisman himself had ordered the hit on Laura. That would have been stupid. Just like he didn't think Weisman had ordered the hit on Ben and his deputy. Both incidents had all the earmarks of Patch Wilson's psychopathic mind.

He hated Black people, plain and simple. Always had. So had his father, who had been killed in a bombing attempt, and his grandfather, who once was a grand dragon in the Klan and worked sometimes with the Birmingham klavern. The hate was deep in their blood, as much a part of their upbringing as mother's milk, nurtured with each generation. Yet Ben couldn't fathom why Patch had picked his wife to kill instead of going after Ben. Maybe it wasn't a matter of understanding. Maybe it was more a matter of accepting. Maybe it was more a matter of facing his own failure to keep Laura safe. That failure ate at him from the inside out.

God help him, Ben hated Patch Wilson with an intensity he didn't think he had inside him until he stood over Patch at the bottom of a ditch. He didn't think he was capable of picking up a rock with both hands, raising it high over his head, and crashing the damn thing down on Wilson's temple. But as Ben knelt over him, and Patch Wilson's one good eye fluttered open for just a second, he did it. Goddamn him to hell, he did it and he didn't feel an ounce of remorse. The hate was undeniable, yet Wilson's death was not enough. Ben needed to have the record show that Patch Wilson killed his wife, blew apart an innocent man with a hidden bomb, and tried to finish off the sheriff and the deputy. Laura deserved that much.

Before the interview, Ben Jefferson felt that whatever Weisman fed them about the killings, the dirt on Patch Wilson would be all he'd get. He said Patch actually expressed regret about Laura's death, though he didn't claim responsibility for it. Maybe not exactly regret. What Wilson said was that he didn't like that a woman got killed, but that things worked out because Laura Jefferson was about to fuck him over. Wilson didn't have any qualm about killing a man, though, especially the Black man that took his eye.

"He held that grudge deep, Sheriff. It was my fault, if you really want me to come clean. I shouldn't have trusted him to just scare you. That's all I wanted. A little scare to make you look weak, to make you think twice about running for sheriff again. I never thought he'd try to kill you. I was just wrong."

In exchange for a one-way ticket to a prison in California, where Weisman had family in the same line of business, Billy gave them much more than just Patch Wilson. He gave them names of the men who had looked the other way even as Ben Jefferson had tried to crack down on Weisman and his cohorts. He gave them the name of the man who pledged to protect him when Jefferson was gone, complete with a recording.

Ben and Jenkins both knew Weisman's statement might not be enough. What judge is going to believe a drug dealer? And after listening to the recording, what did they actually have? A shake-down? A crime? Or just a warning to a crime gang from a guy who might be the next sheriff? Besides, Leon and the DA could simply say they were running an undercover sting, and they left the sheriff out because they suspected he was in on the fix. They'd play the good guys. All would come down to his word against theirs. Knowing the judges in this county, Ben didn't like his chances. The information was useful, but the recording wasn't enough on its own. A lot of work lay ahead of them.

Weisman's story was a solid start, Ben thought, as he reviewed his notes afterwards. He had gotten some of what he wanted–testimony on the record that Patch Wilson had something against Laura–but not enough to prove he did it. He clenched his teeth and squeezed his eyes shut each time he imagined what happened. He could see Wilson, possessing two good eyes at the time, running up behind Laura's car and shoving her off the road. He could see the evil grin on the fucking redneck's face. He could feel the terror rising in Laura's chest as she lost control of the car. He slammed the notes down and paced the room. But then he settled in and stared at the words he had written down verbatim in the interview. He underlined them and circled them and cursed silently as he read them over and over.

"Laura Jefferson was about to fuck him over."

Thirty-eight

Before he left the office, Ben unlocked the bottom drawer to his desk and pulled out the thick case file marked "Laura Jefferson—Homicide." This file stayed in his desk because it wasn't the official file. This one wasn't anything like the thin one in the main file room—the one with a few sheets of paper and the coroner's report that listed the cause of death as "vehicular accident." He carried the folder home and spread all of the pages on the living room floor. He sat in the middle of them and read each page, one by one. At four a.m., with still forty or fifty pages still stacked in front of him, he slumped on the carpet and closed his eyes.

Laura played the classics. That was how she had earned her fame in the symphony circuits on the East Coast. Nobody could play Chopin better than Laura Edwards. Ben's eyes fluttered rapidly, his pupils wide under the dark cover of closed lids, scanning the internal wide-screen movie playing out before him. He sat in the front row, just behind the orchestra. A white-haired gentleman with a whiter face stood with his thin baton ready in front of rows of highly trained musicians. Laura stood in front of a gorgeous grand piano, the two of them dominating the stage, towering over the orchestra and the audience. She wore a bright red evening dress that sparkled as she moved. A string of white pearls gleamed against her vibrant, glowing ebony skin.

The audience applauded loudly, and Ben turned to take in their faces, all adoring, all beaming, all elegant, all White. She settled on the piano bench and stretched her long graceful fingers. The crowd grew quiet in anticipation. She pushed a single black key, B flat, and held the note until it almost died in the silence. Then with breath-taking speed, her fingers danced along the keyboard with the precise agility of a ballet dancer and the soul of a gospel singer.

He sat, enthralled, until the last note rang out and reverberated through the auditorium.

He stood, clapping furiously, yet no sound echoed around him. He turned, but the adoring faces were gone, replaced with broken trees. A smell of burned oil filled his nostrils. He whirled to find Laura. A crumpled pile of metal lay center stage. Red and blue spotlights flashed in strobe. He held his hand over his eyes to calm the jarring effect. A siren rose behind him, its awful wavering noise crashing over him like a tsunami, rushing through him, and stealing his soul.

A persistently ringing phone finally pierced his consciousness, and he bolted upright, gasping. He didn't know how long he had been out, and for a moment he didn't know where he was. His heart raced wildly. His eyes darted around the room until he found the photograph he kept on the mantle, him and Laura holding onto each other when they had whirled through the streets of New Orleans behind a Mardi Gras float carrying a jazz band in full tilt.

He remembered Laura, in a long red dress held up with one hand, showing her long legs and sneakered feet flying beneath her while strings of multicolored beads flew in rainbow circles around her neck. His heartbeat found its rhythm and pounded along for a minute, keeping time to the dancing feet. Finally, his heart slowed, and he caught his breath and he cried out in a voice so deep, he could not find the bottom. For two long minutes he sat in silence, until his eyes crept upwards and caught the gaze of Laura's deep brown eyes smiling at him. And he laughed—a thundering laugh he could not control that rushed out of him in great sobs until he grabbed the pile of papers still on the floor in front of him and threw them to the ceiling. He lay back and let them fall like confetti all around him.

The phone rang again. He picked it up. A Montgomery number. He slid his finger across the screen. A female voice called his name twice before he grunted.

"Sorry to disturb you so early, Sheriff. I got some answers last night on the blood sample you sent me. I worked through till this morning to confirm it. You might want to sit down for this one." Mary Lawson was on the phone. The lab manager at the State Department of Forensic

Sciences was an old friend of Laura's and was willing to go the extra mile for Ben.

"Go on," Ben said. He got to his feet and headed to the kitchen for something to clear his brain.

"You have two distinct blood types on the cloth you sent in. One of them matches the sample of Eva Bustard. The other one doesn't match anybody else in the database."

"Shit. Well, okay, we've already matched the cloth to the blouse Eva was wearing that day, so that means a second person was there the day Eva Bustard died. We just don't know who."

"Not exactly, Ben."

"Go on," he said.

Mary briefly outlined the things you could tell from DNA and the things you can't.

"So, first off, no Y chromosome is in the unknown sample."

"Which means the sample belonged to a woman."

"That's right."

"Which means someone got blood on Eva Bustard's clothes before Buck found her. Pretty strong evidence to clear the boy."

"That's not all. The second sample is a close relative of Eva's. They appear to share the same parents."

"Well damn, Mary, you sure know how to bury the lede."

"Yeah, figured I would get you good and awake before springing it on you."

"The only female sibling of Eva Bustard that I know about is Yvonne Morrison."

"That's the judge's wife, isn't it? Better go careful on this one, Ben."

"Yeah, can you give me a little time before you release the report, Mary?"

"I can bury it on my desk for a few days, maybe a week. I got a boss to answer to, though. That's about as long as I can afford."

"Thanks, Mary. You've always been a friend, ever since Laura introduced us."

"If she thought enough of you to marry you, the least I can do is respect her judgement of character."

"She could have married any man she wanted, and she chose me."

"You're a lucky man, Ben, and she was a lucky gal."

"Yeah, lucky," he said.

"I'll call you when the report is about to go out. Be careful."

When they hung up, the coffee was ready. He poured an extra-large cup and stumbled back to the living room. Fifty pages of notes lay scattered around the room.

"Shit," he muttered and took a sip. He leaned down and grabbed several pages and placed them on the coffee table. The top page was a blurry photocopy with a hand-written title: "Laura's Whereabouts."

He sat down on the couch and leaned in, tracing his finger down the copy taken of Laura's calendar book. When he got to the four p.m. item, he stopped.

"Tierney Academy—Lessons, August 29."

In parentheses underneath was a sublist of initials and names: C. Breckinridge, D. Thomas, M. Kingsbury, F. Cassidy. Laura had contact information on all of them except Cassidy, and he had interviewed the first three, two ladies and a young teenaged girl. None of them knew the last one on the list although the Kingsbury kid said a large-chested woman of about 30 was waiting for a lesson when she left. Nobody she knew. Just another White lady looking for something new to do.

"Well, if you took lessons from Laura Jefferson, she would give you her soul. I hope you all learned well. You had the best."

Ben spent a few minutes thinking through his options while he cleaned up the rest of the room and put everything back into the file. Mary Lawson's boss was Sam Nowicki. The man was brilliant. Held a law degree and biochemical engineering degree. What's more, he was a political animal. He knew every DA in the state, and it was no secret that Frank Stone had cultivated a particularly close relationship with the man. Nowicki would get his hands on the report before the week was out, no matter how hard Mary tried to be discreet. He would know what it meant almost immediately. Ben had a couple days. Any extra time after that would be pure luck.

First things first. He had to be sure Yvonne was the only person that could fit the bill. He didn't remember any other sibling, but he couldn't rule anything out.

Second, he needed a DNA sample from Yvonne. Normally, the test results he already had should be enough to get a warrant for collection of a sample. But this wasn't a normal circumstance. He could surreptitiously collect a sample from a discarded bottle or tissue. How long would that take and how risky would it be for him to do the surveillance? Tom wasn't back on duty yet, and he wasn't quite sure about his other deputies. Tailing the wife of a powerful judge isn't exactly a good way to ensure career success.

He could just show up at Yvonne's house one day and ask her for a sample. That would be a lot quicker. Once the sample was collected and sent to the lab and properly documented, of course, the information would be hard to pull back, and even more difficult to bury. She probably wouldn't accede to the request, but he couldn't think of a better way. He had to try, and it had to be done quickly. No later than tomorrow.

That gave him one day to do some genealogical research.

The good thing about small towns is that they usually have a town historian, somebody that's been around for a long time, and even more likely, someone whose family has been around forever. Nancy Stewart was the keeper of the past in this town. History was her passion. She had no children herself, having never married. She was pushing 90 now, so a lot of what she knew she was around to witness. Plus her great-great grandfather founded the town. A plaque to the founding father was displayed prominently in the library where Nancy still presided. The plaque wasn't complete, though.

The historical plaque didn't mention the man's slaves who laid out and cleared the town streets, though that fact was known to every Black family in the county, some of whom were descended from those slaves and had just as much a claim on the title of town founder as the Stewarts. That's not the way things work in small-town Alabama. None of the Black families had anybody who belonged to the United Daughters of the Confederacy. Miss Nancy Stewart was almost a charter member, her mother having founded the local chapter.

Ben Jefferson, a Black sheriff in a mostly White town, had managed to win the seat because of the corrupt nature of the previous sheriff, Leon's father. He was also a beneficiary of the times, when White folks were willing to vote for a Black man just to prove to themselves they weren't the racist crackers everybody outside the South thought they were. He had applied justice evenly. He was polite without being obsequious. Until the last two years, he had solved most of the major crimes that cropped up in the county.

Lately, the ambitions of Leon Bustard, the continued rise of drug-related crimes and activities, particularly the crank factories and pot fields in and around the refuge, and the high-profile death of Leon's wife had combined to drag his reputation down. He hated to think of it this way, but his own wife's death and the recent attack on Ben and his deputy rallied the decent folk behind him. This respite wouldn't last, though. If he went after a judge's wife, he better have something strong enough to stand up to any questions.

He needed an ally. One who wouldn't be suspected of digging into things that shouldn't be disturbed. Sarah Covington wasn't exactly from a prominent White family. But she was White, and she was non-threatening. He grabbed the phone and dialed. She answered right away.

"Sarah, I need a favor."

SARAH COVINGTON

Thirty-nine

Sarah wasn't sure how to address the librarian when she stepped in the door. Nancy Stewart was old-money or at least once upon a time she was. So she decided on Miz Stewart. It was more formal and more respectful, especially coming from someone who had always been no-moneyed. Sarah didn't need to worry. The librarian was happy to talk, particularly about one of her favorite topics, which was the goings-on of past townspeople.

"You know, dear," she said, settling at her desk and pulling out a thick hard-bound book from one of the drawers, "nobody cares about history anymore. And if they do, they take too many shortcuts. Do you know how many flat-out wrong genealogical charts are on the internet these days?"

Sarah looked at the portrait of Robert E. Lee behind the desk. The general sat calmly on his horse Traveller surrounded by Confederate soldiers charging into battle. The print was displayed in a gold-leaf frame with the name of the general and his horse proudly printed on a brass nameplate. On one side of the front door, an American flag stood on a pole. The first Confederate flag was afforded nearly equal status on the other side of the door. Better than equal actually, because the Stars and Bars was the first thing a visitor saw as they entered. The U.S. flag was hidden behind the door when it was open.

While Sarah surveyed the surroundings, she allowed that she knew just how Miz Stewart felt. She had heard the same thing about trying to chase your family history. Judge Morrison had told her that Nancy Stewart was the definitive source of genealogy in Tierney County.

"You must know everyone in the whole county," Sarah exclaimed.

"Well, maybe not everyone, but everyone who is someone, at least by name."

"You mean like the judge's family. I've worked for him for a long time, and he's a pretty important someone."

"Oh, I suppose the Morrisons have been here for a few generations. Don't tell him I said this, but the judge is probably the first one in his family to really make a name for himself."

"I just assumed his family was big around here, you know, him being a judge and all."

"Oh dear, you don't have to get your money from your own family. That's what a good marriage will do for you." Miz Nancy Stewart was onto her truly favorite subject now, the status and goings-on of current townspeople.

"I see. Kind of like arranged marriages, huh? Keep a good bloodline going?"

"Something like that, I suppose. Look dearie, you don't have to be so formal," she said as a reward to Sarah for bringing up such a juicy story. "Call me Miss Nancy."

"Miss Nancy," repeated Sarah.

"Now I really shouldn't say this, but Dick didn't exactly represent a good bloodline. His father was..." Miss Nancy lowered her voice and leaned toward Sarah. "Well, he was the town scoundrel, if you know what I mean."

"Oh," said Sarah. "But the judge is such an upstanding man."

"Well, he married well. That's what I'm trying to tell you. A good marriage can make up for a lot of sins." Miss Nancy looked around her to make sure no one else was listening, even though Sarah was nearly a stranger to her except for the few times she had done research at the courthouse. But surely Sarah could be trusted. Such a nice, polite lady, and always very helpful when she needed to find a particular land record.

"Yvonne. Yes, I've met her. A nice Christian woman," said Sarah.

"Good family name, active in the Baptist church. Her father was a deacon there."

"I didn't know that. What was his name again?"

"Everett Pickens. You know, dear, one of his ancestors was governor of the state, way back after it was just founded."

"This is all so fascinating. Who knew our town was so interesting?"

"Such a sad thing about his daughters. The scandal with the youngest one was what killed him. I'm glad he passed before the middle daughter died."

"The youngest one? I thought Eva was the youngest one. Do you mean Yvonne?"

"Oh, dearie," said Miss Nancy, "Yvonne's always been the stable one. Marie was the wild one. It was an absolute scandal the things that girl put the deacon through."

"What happened?"

"Oh, I've already said too much. It's just nobody ever comes to talk to me about history things anymore. I should just leave it there, honey. You'll think I'm just an old gossip."

"Nobody thinks that about you, Miss Nancy. Every town has to have someone to hold it together. Somebody has to be the keeper of the facts."

"That's right, dear."

"You want scandalous?" asked Sarah. "My mother ran off with a vacuum cleaner salesman."

"I know, honey," said Miss Nancy, and Sarah's eyes shot up. "But you weathered that pretty good, didn't you?"

"Uh, it took me a while, I suppose."

"Is that why you're here? To find out more about your mother?"

"Well, that's part of it, I guess. I'm sure it's nothing like what happened to the Pickens family, though. I mean one daughter killed and one daughter . . ." she trailed off, hoping Miss Nancy would fill in the blank.

Miss Nancy did not disappoint.

"She got herself pregnant when she was a young teenager. At least that was the rumor. Officially, she just left town one day and never came back. Betty, the deacon's wife, she was a lot stronger than Mr. Pickens. Only time I ever heard either one mention her was when I asked Betty if she ever heard from Marie. You know what she said? She told me Marie might as well be dead to her. That was after the deacon died—just pined away."

"Wow, that seems a little harsh. I mean, I'd love to see my mother again, if just to get her side of the story."

"You have to understand, dear. The Pickens were a prominent family. That kind of stuff happens to ordinary families all the time, but it's enough to destroy a family like the Pickens."

"Yeah, ordinary."

"Oh dear, I didn't mean it that way." Miz Stewart put on her glasses and opened the heavy book in front of her. "What did you say your mother's maiden name was?"

"It doesn't matter. I don't think I'm ready to find out more yet. Maybe you can help me another day." Sarah rose and walked briskly to the door, her hand quickly brushing her face.

"Don't go away. I didn't mean to offend you," said Miz Nancy Stewart, but it was too late, the door to the library was already closing. She sighed and closed the book, brushing the dust off the leather cover before safely tucking it away.

"People just don't care about history anymore," she said to herself. "What are you going to do?"

BEN JEFFERSON

Forty

Nothing's ever simple. Just when you think the suspect list narrowed, something, somebody else comes up. Instead of one sister, turns out Eva Bustard had two. Either one could be the one he was looking for. He needed Yvonne's DNA sample, and he needed it now.

He waited until Sarah called him and told him the judge was in his chambers. Then he headed to the Morrison house in Highlands Estates. A guard met him at the gate.

"Morning, Nate," he called to the Black man in the security uniform. "Looks like another beautiful day."

"Hey, Sheriff, I'd as soon it be raining or I'm gonna lose my beans and squash, too."

"Yeah, I missed your tomatoes this year. You tell Glenda I appreciate that apple pie she made. I believe she might be about the best cook in the county."

"You can tell that from looking at me," said Nate, patting his belly.

"How's that daughter of yours? She 'bout finished at A&M?"

"One more year, Sheriff. One more year."

"You tell her I said, 'Hi,' and that we're proud of her," said Ben as he looked towards the gate, which raised with no further question. "Good to see you, Nate."

Funny thing about White folks. They'll choose to live behind fences to keep out the Brown and Black folks yet hire them to watch the gates.

Ben was one of the few who moved in both worlds, but even he had his limits. He could come and go in Highlands Estates, but he'd never be able to buy a house here, even if he had the money. Sheriffing was a respectable job, but it wasn't a country club type of occupation. All but one of the houses were owned by Whites, the token offering to colored folk going to the Birmingham surgeon who decided to retire to the countryside. Nobody could say these people discriminated.

The surgeon lived in the five-acre lot section. Judge Morrison and Yvonne lived in the twenty-five-acre estates near the large lake. Ben took note of the lush green lawn in front of the 10,000 square-foot house and the five horses grazing in the pasture. The vibrant-colored grass stood in stark contrast to most every lawn in town, where a watering ban had been imposed the month before. Two Hispanic gardeners were tending the flowerbeds ringing the house. Ben nodded to them as he mounted the stairs to the wide veranda that wrapped halfway around the structure. He glanced over to the garage where one of the doors was open. A freshly waxed black Volvo was visible inside. The car had one of those school-related license tags—crimson and white with a large cursive A.

He rang the bell, half-expecting a maid to answer. A few seconds later, Yvonne Morrison herself opened the door.

"Mrs. Morrison," said Ben, tipping his brown cap but not removing it.

"Sheriff," said Yvonne with surprise in her voice. "What brings you way out here?" She got a worried look on her face and quickly asked, "Is this about the judge? Is everything okay?"

"Oh yes, ma'am, everything is fine. I was just hoping you might be able to help me out with something."

"I don't know how someone like me could possibly help you. I'm just a housewife. What would I know about police matters?"

Ben's eyes couldn't help but fix on the crystal chandelier hanging from the vaulted ceiling behind her when Yvonne said she was a housewife.

"Well, it's kind of a sensitive matter. I really wanted to keep it quiet until I had a chance to talk to you. It's about your sister."

"Eva? You're finally going to do something about her murder?" Her tone carried more than a hint of sarcasm.

Ben moved on. "We found some blood near the scene where Eva died, and it isn't hers."

"The boy's blood? I hope you lock him up now."

"No, ma'am, that's the thing. It doesn't belong to him."

Yvonne looked past Ben's shoulder at one of the gardeners who was kneeling at the flowers near the bottom of the stairs.

"Let's go inside, Sheriff. I'll make you a cup of coffee."

"Thank you, Mrs. Morrison. That would be nice."

Ben followed her in and shut the door behind him. The hardwood floors glistened under his dusty boots, and for a second, he thought about removing them. Instead, he followed Yvonne to the kitchen where she pointed to a barstool. He took his hat off and laid it on the counter while she opened a cabinet and reached for a coffee mug. Hesitating for a second, she closed the cabinet and walked to the pantry where she retrieved two Styrofoam cups and placed one in the single-cup coffee machine.

Ben marveled at how white everything was in the kitchen. White cabinets. White floors. White counters, White chairs. An overpowering sense of whiteness. He felt uneasy and out of place, but he was used to that. Yvonne had not asked more questions, which was a bit strange, so he dove in again.

"Wasn't much blood. Just enough to get a sample."

"Uh-huh," she said, pulling out a carton of cream from the white refrigerator.

"The thing is, it doesn't match anybody we have on file."

Yvonne pulled out the full cup and set it in front of Ben, who had taken a middle seat at the kitchen bar.

"Cream or sugar?" she asked.

"No, thank you. Black's fine."

She placed the second cup under the machine's spout and started it. She retrieved a plastic spoon and napkins from the pantry and reached for a packet of sweetener from a canister on the counter. Ben sipped his coffee while Yvonne studied the slowly-filling cup in the machine. Nobody spoke.

When her cup was ready, she said, "I like mine with lots of cream. Something about black coffee I can't take, even with sugar. Don't have the stomach, I guess."

"It's an acquired taste," said Ben.

Yvonne came around the kitchen bar, stirring her coffee with the plastic spoon. She placed a napkin down, handed one to Ben, and sat down. She dipped the spoon in the cup and lifted it to her lips, blowing slightly.

"This coffeemaker puts out a cup that's a little too hot for my taste." She took a sip from the spoon and laid it beside the cup. A smudge of red lipstick rimmed the edge of the spoon. "Yours okay?" she asked.

"It's fine," he said and turned his stool to face hers. "Well, maybe a little something to take out the bitterness." He reached in front of Yvonne to retrieve a sweetener packet and poured it into his cup.

"Do you mind?" he said, laying his hand on the spoon by her cup. "I can just use this one. No need for another."

She looked at his hand on the spoon and leaned backwards slightly, almost imperceptibly.

"Uh, sure," she said. "Take it."

"Do you have another sister, Mrs. Morrison?"

Yvonne coughed.

"What?"

"Another sister. Besides Eva."

"Besides Eva?"

"Yes, ma'am, besides Eva. I understand you have another sister named Marie. Is that right?"

"Marie. My God, I haven't seen Marie in nearly twenty years." Yvonne stood up abruptly and walked to the kitchen window. She stared out at the pasture. One of the horses was running, apparently frightened by a sudden wind or a shadow in the trees. "You think Marie had something to do with Eva's death?"

"I have reason to believe she could have been at the scene."

"It was her blood? That's not possible. Marie hasn't contacted anybody in the family since she left."

"Why did she leave town, Mrs. Morrison?"

"Marie was a spoiled little daddy's girl. She got away with everything."

"I see."

"You have brothers or sisters, Sheriff?"

"I had two brothers."

"Had?"

"One died in Vietnam. The other one was killed in Chicago."

"Were you close?"

"Very close."

"Must be nice. I never got along with my two sisters. Marie was the surprise baby—six years younger than Eva. I was the oldest. Neither one of them listened to me. Marie was the wild one. Eva was the pretty one. I was just the bitch."

"That's too bad. You probably could have taught them a thing or two."

Yvonne walked around the room, studying the walls. A painting of a flowered field adorned one wall, the only color in the room. The other walls were bare except for the window and the white cabinets. Ben stood and stepped toward the window. The horse danced in the far corner of the pasture, by itself.

"So, you said the blood doesn't match anybody on file. So, how do you know it's Marie's blood?"

"I know it belongs to a female, and I know it belongs to a close relative, probably a sibling."

"Then, it could be mine, couldn't it?"

"Was it, Mrs. Morrison?"

"I think you'd better leave."

"If you drop by the office, I could get one of the techs to collect a swab. Clear things up."

"I'm going to call my husband, Sheriff. I suggest you leave now."

Ben picked up his hat and poured out his cup in the spotless sink. He scooped up the spoon and napkin from the counter and dropped the cup in the white-capped trashcan at the end of the counter.

"Thank you for the coffee, Mrs. Morrison."

Yvonne followed him to the front door without a word. He put his cap back on and tipped it again. "If you change your mind, I'll be around. Just call me." He placed a card on the small table by the door and stepped out. The door slammed behind him. He patted his jacket pocket to make sure the spoon, wrapped in the napkin, was still there.

At the bottom of the stairs, he tipped his hat to the gardener, who was trimming the large shrubs.

"Nice day, isn't it?"

FRANK STONE

Forty-one

The next morning, the pictures waited in a non-descript manila envelope on the desk of the district attorney's office. When Frank Stone settled in with a hot cup of coffee and pulled them out, he nearly spit out the brown liquid all over the case files stacked up for the morning meeting of assistant prosecutors. He canceled the meeting immediately and yelled for his secretary to get the sheriff on the phone.

"Jefferson," he plunged in without a greeting, "get your ass over here now. I think you might have some explaining to do."

Ben allowed a good hour to go by before stepping into the DA's office. He kept his hat on and didn't sit down.

"You want to see me?" he asked.

"Jefferson, I've got all kinds of complaints about you lately. A fight in a bar."

"Wasn't much of a fight," Ben interrupted.

"Bustard's boy still running loose."

"Leon never filed a missing person report. He come squawking to you?"

"A man blown apart."

"And my deputy nearly killed. Don't forget that."

"And the suspect dead with a smashed-in face."

"He got hit by a truck. Remember?"

"And now you're beating up women."

"What the hell are you talking about, Frank?"

"I get an anonymous complaint that you've been hurting women. One of our own, as it turns out," The DA tossed the photos onto the desk in front of Ben.

"Sarah's been in the courthouse for twenty years, Sheriff. We take care of our own."

Ben examined the photos. One clearly showed him shoving Sarah Covington, a surprised look on her face. Another showed her struggling to get up off the ground, her blouse torn, and her face scratched and bloodied.

"We fell off her porch."

"Her porch? You fell? That's how you got those scratches on your face? Or did Sarah fight back a little too hard?

"Let's go ask her. The fall was an accident."

Frank leaned over the desk, his weight on the incriminating photos, and stared into Ben's face.

"You aren't going anywhere near Sarah Covington. Give me your badge."

"You can't do that."

"The hell I can't. I'll have a judge's order before you can say, 'Oh shit, what did I do?'"

"I didn't do anything," Ben protested.

"Your gun, too." Frank straightened up and held out his hand.

Ben stared at the man until he lowered his arm. He unholstered his service revolver and laid the gun on the desk. He placed the badge next to it.

"You listed five sins I supposedly committed, but it wasn't until you got a picture of me with a White woman that you did anything about it. I guess the more things change, the more they stay the same."

Then he turned and headed out the door.

"Hope you got a ride because don't even think about driving a county vehicle."

Ben kept walking and slammed the door behind him.

Frank Stone picked up the phone and dialed Leon Bustard's number.

"Get over here, Leon. Looks like the vote came in early. Judge Morrison's appointing you acting sheriff today."

Forty-two

S arah Covington knocked on Ben Jefferson's door at three-thirty that afternoon. Tom Walters let her in. The guitar twang and driving beat of rock and roll blasted from the living room.

"Thought you'd be over watching your new boss get swore in," she said.

"My boss is right here. Besides, I'm still on leave," said Tom.

"How's he taking it?" she asked.

"Better than I thought. He's still sheriffing, even if he don't have a badge. And I'm still his deputy, even if I don't have a badge either, at least until someone runs me off."

"Whadya mean, sheriffing?"

"Let him tell you himself."

The speakers at each corner of the wall vibrated with "Don't be cruel to a heart that's true." Ben stood over a map spread on a table dragged into the middle of the room, bouncing from side to side with the beat.

"I didn't know you're an Elvis fan," Sarah shouted.

"You would think that," he said and tossed an album cover her way. "Elvis wouldn't be nothing without this man. Otis Blackwell, greatest rock 'n roller never known."

"Huh, never heard of him," said Tom, rubbing the side of his face where the bandages had just come off a couple days before.

"Yeah, you're too young," said Ben. "And you're too white," he said pointing to Sarah. "But enough music lessons. Turn down the volume. We got work to do."

"Look, Ben. I think this is all my fault. When I heard what the DA was showing around, I went straight to the judge. I told him it was all just a funny accident. He said I shouldn't have been out with you in the first place, and he was thinking about firing me. I told him it wasn't any of his business."

"Sarah, save your breath. They aren't going to listen. It don't matter what you say. Only matters what people think."

"Nobody cares what color their sheriff is, long as he's doing his job," Tom offered.

"Uh-huh, you keep thinking that. Anyway, that's what I'm going to do, my job. Come here and look at this." Ben leaned over the map again. He pointed to the red-circled area on the lower left corner of the map. "This is Leon's place. This creek on the east side, that's where Eva Bustard's body was found and the last place anybody saw Buck Thompson."

"You think something bad's happened to the boy?" asked Sarah.

"No, other than running away from home. But if Leon Bustard owns the home, who am I to say running away is bad? Anyway, that was the last place Buck was seen…until a few days ago. I got a call from the chief down in Carrollton. Said one of his cops almost picked up a boy matching Buck's description. He got into a white van and drove off with a woman who claimed to be his mother. He got the plate number. It's registered to Jeannine Roberts at this address right here." He pointed to another red circle on the right side of the map.

"Out in the middle of nowhere," said Tom.

"Yeah, five miles of wilderness between her place and Leon's place. That's the wildlife refuge. Only poachers, fishermen, and pot growers in there," said Ben.

"Which one is Jeannine Roberts?" asked Sarah.

"We already know Jeannine and suspect her of being mixed up in the pot trade. But here's the surprising thing. Her maiden name is Wilson. She's Stevie Wilson's sister."

"Patch Wilson? The one who tried to kill us?" asked Tom, his voice rising.

"The same," said Ben. "And that's not all." He pulled some papers from a yellow official-looking envelope. "The woman who gave up the boy for adoption—the boy that Eva adopted? Jeannine Roberts."

Tom whistled.

"Well, that's some coincidence," said Sarah.

"Isn't it now?" said Ben. "So now we've got three high-profile murders in less than two years, and Buck's family, one or the other, is linked to all three."

"What do you mean three, Sheriff? There's Eva Bustard, who we can't say for sure was murdered. And there's the bomb that killed the young man and nearly got us killed a coupla weeks ago. That's two, maybe." Tom was rubbing his jaw again.

"And Laura," said Ben, not looking up from the map.

"I thought Laura's death was ruled an accident," said Tom.

"That's what the DA said. Bad weather, slick road, sharp curve, an unfortunate accident. So he said."

"You don't believe them?" asked Sarah.

"I believe the black paint I found on the driver-side door on Laura's silver car. I believe that Wilson's Escalade was repainted around the same time. I believe Billy Weisman's statement about Laura when we were interrogating him after the bomb. Laura didn't die in an accident. Wilson killed her as sure as I'm standing here."

"So Patch Wilson kills Laura…uh, sorry Ben. The main suspect in Eva Bustard's death, her own son, is seen with Wilson's sister. And Wilson plants a bomb to try to kill us but gets himself killed trying to finish the job." Tom sat down, thinking. Nobody else spoke for a minute.

"So the murderer is dead now," said Sarah finally. "At least the one that ties them all together."

"He murdered two of them—my wife and the young man in the bombing. He didn't have any reason to murder Eva Bustard, though. But another man stands to gain from all three incidents," said Ben.

"Sorry, Boss. I don't follow," said Tom.

"I do," said Sarah. "Laura could have been killed to scare Ben out of law enforcement. That didn't work so he placed the bomb to get rid of him directly, the old-fashioned tried-and-true way."

"Could be," said Ben. "I'm not sure now why Wilson did what he did to Laura, but it's the best working theory we have now."

"I still don't get it," said Tom. "Who's behind it?"

"If I'm gone, who stands to gain, Tom?" asked Ben.

"Well, the word's out that Stone is going to appoint Leon Bustard as sheriff. But why would Leon kill his own wife? Sure she had money, but it wouldn't be his when she died. The money would go to the boy. Leon's name isn't even on the policy. Besides, Weisman ratted on Leon. He gave you a tape."

"The tape. Yeah, the one in the DA's desk drawer. Even the feds can't bust Leon on that evidence. It's too vague. They'll just turn it on me. And the million-dollar policy? You're right, Leon's name isn't on it. Take it one more step. Who else's name is on it, besides Buck? And whose wife appears to have been at the scene of Eva's murder? And guess who will be the one swearing in Leon?" asked Ben.

"The judge," said Sarah. She looked at Ben. "And when Leon is sheriff and the only suspect in the murder of his wife is on the loose, the boy he hates..."

Ben nodded. "Yeah, we got to find Buck Thompson before Leon does."

BUCK

Forty-three

"**G**et this place in shape, boy. While you're at it, clean yourself up. You look like a sack of smashed asshole." I barked out the orders with my best Leon voice. Almost a week had passed since I left Jeannie's place, and I was in rough shape, subsisting on nothing but cheap beer and stolen snacks. On my last trip to the store, the manager chased and nearly caught me; so, time on my own looked like it might be coming to an end. I still had a few cans left, though.

"Yes, sir, awesome stepfather, sir," I replied to myself. "I'm right on it. Plan to cut my hair and learn to march and shape up. Be the best I can be. Yes, sir!" I snapped a salute and fell against the concrete bridge piling. In the dark, I almost lost my balance and slid down the embankment to the muddy flats below the bridge.

I stood up quick-like and saluted again. "I'll work on that, sir. A man like you deserves respect, right? I'll clean everything up…right after I finish this six-pack."

I crushed the can in my hand, spewing several ounces out the top, and threw it down on the pile. When I leaned down to look for another, I fell. My head bounced off the concrete, and I rolled onto my back.

"Oh shit, Leon," I said, rubbing my forehead. "Now look what you made me do."

"Who are you talking to?" A female voice drifted out of the darkness from the corner where the bridge span met the abutment.

I sat up, dizzy, and shook my head. "Goddammit. Go away."

"I don't think so. You're too entertaining," said the voice. I couldn't see through the gloom to make out a figure, but I knew my friend was back.

"What do you want with me anyway? It's not like you're real. Even I can figure out that much."

"Yet here I am again. Maybe it's not me who wants something."

"Oh, I see. You're some figment of my subconscious; so, it's me who wants something."

"You're very perceptive, for a drunk teenage boy."

"Middle of my class in high school. Yep, the smartest kid at County High."

"Imagine what you could do sober."

"Oh, Jesus, I get enough grief from Leon. I don't need it from you, too."

"I'm just not sure how much you remember when you're...not sober."

"You can say it. You mean when I'm stinking drunk?"

"It's important you remember."

"Yeah, I remembered a woman was there. So fucking what? Who was she? You forgot to make me remember that."

"You have to be ready."

"I can barely see, I'm so fucking drunk. How'm I gonna remember anything?"

"Look harder, what do you see?"

"I don't even see you." I gulped a half can of beer and threw the rest in the direction of the voice. "Cause you're not real," I screamed.

A truck rumbled over the bridge, and a second later the empty beer can rolled out of the dark, stopping at his feet.

"Impressive. You can throw a beer can," said the disembodied voice.

"What do you want from me?" The sound of the truck faded in the distance, but my voice echoed in my ears.

"I want to know what you saw. More precisely, I want *you* to know what you saw."

I slumped to the ground, facing the muddy riverbed. I could just make out the tracks of some wandering animal. I picked up a rock and threw it towards where the water used to run. The stone plunked into the mud with a sickening squish.

"I was drunk."

"I figured that much."

"Passed out against the big oak. Something woke me. A yell. A curse. A woman's voice. '*You fucking bitch. You took him away from me.*'"

"Your mother?"

"No. Deeper. Angry. Footsteps crashing through the bushes, running towards me."

"You see them."

"I see Mama. She's running. One arm's out in front of her, the other one's hanging by her side. She's looking back. She falls."

"What else, Buck?"

"I try to yell but nothing comes out. I try to get up but nothing moves. Everything's hazy, I don't know how long I'm watching. A woman's on top of her, grabbing her, yanking her up. Pushing her. They fall. I hear the splash. '*Fucking bitch, you took him.*' I try to get up— but I can't. I hear gurgling and splashing and cursing."

"What did you do, Buck?"

"That's just it. Nothing. I listened to somebody kill my mother. And I did nothing."

The darkness was thick. The riverbed was silent. No voice drifted from above. Even the night creatures had gone quiet.

I fell on my face and cried, but nobody was around to hear me.

Forty-four

Her finger traced the outline of her lover's face and paused, resting tenderly along his strong jawline. Her body trembled slightly. The man in the photo, the only man she had ever loved, ignored her caress and continued to strum the guitar that was always in his hands.

She sighed, kissed her fingertips, and touched his lips.

"I was never enough, was I?" she whispered to the man, who unblinkingly gazed back into her eyes whenever she talked to him like this. This was her favorite photograph of him, the only one in which he wasn't looking at his boy or his guitar or anywhere else, the only one in which he met her eyes and looked at her.

"It's alright, Kenny. I know you didn't have any love for me, but I had enough for both of us."

Kenny held his guitar in mid-strum and smiled back, unaware as always of the depth of Jeannie's love, of the things she did to satisfy him, to keep him around.

"I thought I could find you in him. Lord knows, I tried, Kenny. I thought some of you might have rubbed off on him. But you ain't in him. He ain't sweet like you. He was always cryin'. Couldn't get him to stop. Now he's all growed up and still cryin' 'bout shit. Runned away without even a 'thank you, ma'am.'"

The phone buzzed in her pocket. Jeannie let it ring twice more before she set the photo frame back down on the chest.

"Don't wet your panties, I'm coming," she shouted and dug it out.

"Yeah, I called. We got business to take care of, and I'm gonna need your help. Get over here so's we can work it out today."

She paused, listening to Russell explain something on the other end.

"The boy's more trouble than he's worth, Russell. This is twice he's run out on me.

Another pause while she rolled her eyes.

"Yeah, yeah, whatever. What you know about good kids? Look, we'll take care of him later. Right now, we have an opportunity, and I ain't gonna mess it up. Bring the notebook. See you in an hour."

Jeannie hung up, stalked into the kitchen and put on a pot of coffee. She reached behind the coffee cups, slid open the panel at the back of the cupboard, and pulled out a green hardback ledger. She thumbed through, adding the latest numbers at the bottom of the column on each page.

"Lots of supply. I know there's lots of demand. Just nobody in the middle to hook up the two," she said to herself.

She hit the contact button on her phone and typed in "Flowers." Three numbers came up: one for "Adolf," one for "Bubba," and one for "Red." She erased the first two numbers—they were no longer any use—and hit the text button for the third.

"Time we talked. You need a job, and I need some help. We can meet tomorrow. I'll tell you where. Text me IN or OUT."

The thought bubbles appeared and disappeared. She poured herself a coffee and sipped it, hot and strong, just as she liked. When she finished the cup, she strode to the bedroom with purpose and pulled out the Beretta pistol tucked in the top drawer of the chest.

"Oh, don't give me that look. I know you don't like guns. What the hell did a guitar player need with a gun, anyway? I'm in a different line of work now, baby. Only used this thing once before. Never needed it much 'cause I know everybody on my side. Good people, every one. But tomorrow's a new day. New people, new problems. If Red's on our side, we'll be alright. He knows how to handle things. But you never know; I might just need this thing again."

The phone dinged, and she looked at the screen. One word. "IN."

Forty-five

They took Tom's blue pickup. Sarah went to the courthouse to keep tabs on the new man in charge, Leon Bustard.

Neither Ben nor the deputy wore an official uniform although both wore unmarked khaki shirts. This was not official business. Still, Tom carried his service revolver and kept his badge in his pocket, just in case. Ben placed his twelve-gauge in the back floorboard. Tom asked how they would approach Jeannie Roberts.

"She doesn't know anything about my...situation; so, we don't tell her anything. We're just looking for a missing person last seen headed towards this road. We're canvassing all the residents."

"If she's Patch Wilson's sister, she might be carrying a grudge," said Tom.

"Part of being a lawman; you get used to it."

"But you aren't a . . . " Tom stopped before he finished the words.

"Like I said, she don't know that. Van's registered at 12071 Scotts Mill Road. We ought to be close. Check this mailbox up here." The nearby box was one of only a few scattered along the road.

"No number, boss. Want to try it anyway?"

"Yeah, but go slow. People out here aren't used to folks driving up to the house if they don't recognize the vehicle."

The gravel drive wound nearly a half-mile through the dense woods before a small house made of logs, the kind from a cheap commercial kit, appeared around the last bend. They didn't see any light on, but an unmarked white van and a pickup were parked in the gravel yard in front.

"Looks like the right place," said Tom, "except no florist sign on the truck."

"Magnetic signs. Easy to change. Easy to remove," said Ben.

They parked behind the van and shut off the engine. Still, no movement from the house. But once they got out and reached the steps, the front door opened. A woman stepped out with her hands on her hips. A small pistol was visible tucked in her belt.

"You can just get off my property. My daddy showed me how to hunt coons."

"Listen, lady…" Tom began to object.

Ben spoke up. "I'm a hunter, too, ma'am. Ben Jefferson. Hunting a boy that run away from home. His name's Buck Thompson. You seen him?"

"I know who you are, Sheriff. What you want with a White boy? Go home and mind your own business."

"I didn't say he was White, ma'am. I just want to make sure he's okay."

"Wouldn't be no Black boys around here. He in some kind of trouble?"

"No trouble I know of, ma'am," said Ben. "He's eighteen. Just under six feet. Kind of skinny. And he is White. Long blonde hair and blue eyes."

"Why you think he'd be at my place?" asked Jeannie. Her hands had not left her hips, and she leaned against the doorframe. An older man showed his face over her shoulder.

"Russell? That you? Why don't you come out and talk to us a bit?" asked Ben.

"Come on out and say goodbye, Russell. These fellows were just fixin' to leave." Jeannie stepped forward, and Russell followed her out but stayed behind her. Tom could see the glint of metal from the long gun he held by his side.

"No need for any gun, Russell Lee," said Tom, and he took a step back while placing his hand on the handle of his revolver.

"No need for talking, Deputy. I told you, y'all can leave. Ain't nobody here you need to see." Jeannie's voice was a little louder.

"Buck Thompson. You in there?" yelled Tom.

Both Jeannie and Russell stayed quiet for a few seconds.

"See? Ain't nobody here," said Jeannie finally.

"Yes, ma'am. I guess you're right." Ben took a step back, still facing the woman. "Oh, my condolences about your brother, Miz Roberts."

Russell stepped out from behind Jeannie, but he didn't raise his gun. Tom drew his pistol but kept it by his side.

"Easy, Tom," said Ben. "You got something to say, Russell?"

"Whadya do to Patch's face, Sheriff?" demanded Russell. "Nobody could even recognize him. Didja beat him to death?"

"Russell Lee, you put down the gun, and we can talk," demanded Tom. He raised the pistol and pointed it toward the man who still held the rifle down by his side.

"Russell." Ben tipped his hat. "Ma'am." He nodded Jeannie's way. "We're leaving. You tell Buck he's not in trouble. I just need to see he's okay. I'm going to leave my card on your step here. You tell him to call me." Ben laid the card on the top step.

"He won't need your card, Sheriff, 'cause he ain't been here. Y'all leave now. Russell ain't going to do nothing."

"Like I said, Miz Roberts. You too, Russell. I'm sorry Patch ended up dead. He could have answered a lot of questions." Ben turned and strode confidently back to the truck and opened both the front passenger door and the rear door as if he was about to get something.

Tom waited until Ben was at the truck, then he backed to the driver's side, not lowering his gun until he was behind his door. They both got in and backed out slowly, turning around at the far end of the yard. Not until they were a quarter mile down the road did Ben speak.

"Well, Buck's been here," said Ben. "Probably been here a while. If he's not in trouble now, he will be if he hangs out with those two for much longer." Ben took off his hat and wiped his brow with his shirt sleeve. "I'm getting too old for this shit, Tom. Seems like anybody'll pull a gun on a lawman nowadays. Thanks for having my back."

"I'm just glad you didn't try to come out here alone."

"Something's up with those two. We've suspected them for years for running pot in the refuge. Maybe it's time we shake a few trees out there."

"You know I go back on duty next week, Ben. I'm not going to be able to help you while I'm a deputy for Leon."

"You've done enough already. You're a good friend. Go back to work and be a good deputy. That's all anybody can ask."

They drove on in silence until they reached the paved road. After they turned onto the asphalt, a black Escalade topped the hill in front of them and passed. The driver's window was open, and Tom could see someone with a bald head and thick red moustache at the wheel. Ben whirled in the seat and watched as the SUV slowed and turned into Jeannie Roberts' drive.

"More trouble," said Ben. "That's Red Turner. Weisman's other bodyguard. I've met him a few times. He's not bright enough to run the operation without the Mexican and Patch, especially with the other toughs that backed up Weisman, some of his pals that spoke the same language. You don't suppose the lady's up to something? I always heard she was as smart as Patch and a whole lot more cool-headed."

Just then, Ben's phone rang. Sarah Covington was calling.

"Ben? It's supposed to be secret, but you can't keep this kind of thing quiet," she said. "Leon's going to announce he's bringing you in for questioning."

"About those photos? I'm not worried about that."

"No, not that. It's about the murder of Patch Wilson."

BUCK

Forty-six

Life without a cell phone in the twenty-first century must be like life on a desert island. When I woke up after that long night under the bridge, it didn't take me long to figure out I needed a friend. Mandalee was the only one who might still be willing to help me. But when I left Leon's place, I left everything. Phone, high-tops, music, what was left of my family. All I had now were a pair of worn boots and hand-me-down clothes from a dead man who once claimed to be my father. Jeannie flat-out admitted that was a lie. How could I have possibly swallowed the whopper that she was my mother? I believed nothing she said, but I was convinced that Jeannie killed my real mother, the one who raised me.

This was fucked up, as if my life could get any more screwed up than before. At least now I remembered what happened. My failure to save my own mother tore at me, but it gave me clarity, too. I knew what I had to do. I would make the impostor mother pay for what she did. But I needed a plan. I needed someone to talk to. I needed Mandalee. Question was: would she want me anywhere around?

I counted out the last few coins in my pocket. After the binge of the last few days, I had less than two dollars left. Enough for a phone call. Nothing left for food, and I couldn't go back to the store anyway. Did they even have a pay phone? I only remembered ever seeing a couple of them. One of them might be at Tierney Falls Park, but that was a good five miles by road.

A thought crossed my mind. I knew where Jeannie's pot fields were. I knew where she stored the stuff. I knew where she delivered it to. I had been gone for a few days now. Would she be looking for me? Would she let me just walk away now that I knew her secrets? If I was going to call Mandalee, I'd have to get to the falls. But to make it there, I'd have to stay out of Jeannie's sight, maybe follow the river upstream. When I got there, I'd have to hope Mandalee would talk to me, would still agree to see me.

I hadn't figured out what to do next. Call the law? The sheriff hadn't found anybody but me to look at for the murder, and I didn't have a shred of evidence to show him. Who was going to believe a murder suspect? No, I'd recruit Mandalee into my plans. She would get my cell phone somehow and bring it to me. I'd go back to Jeannie's place. I'd apologize for running off. Fall on my knees and beg if I had to— whatever I needed to do to make her trust me again. I'd take photos on the sly and text them to Mandalee. When I had enough evidence to prove she was the murderer, or at least enough to put her away for drug-running, I'd get Mandalee to take the pictures to the sheriff. That is if I could take it long enough. If I could stand to kiss up to my mother's killer. I didn't trust myself to be up to the job. I needed a weapon—to defend myself in case I got caught, or if I had to take things in my own hands.

I thought about the act of killing someone. I wasn't a good hunter. No killer instinct, according to Leon. Could I really pull a trigger and end somebody's life? The memory of a hooded woman throwing my mother into the creek and jumping in to drown her with her bare hands was fixed firmly in my mind now, drug out of the depths of my subconscious by some weird ghost that kept visiting me, kept prodding me. To do what? Kill the woman who killed my mother? Yes, I decided. If things came to that, I could kill.

The plan, vaguely bumping around in my mind, was still rough-edged, but it had the effect of exciting me. A plan, I thought, is so much better than floating along. Action is so much better than waiting for what's going to happen to you. Now was time to take my future in my own hands. No order from Leon. No expectation from my sister. No waiting on the law. No accounting to anybody but me. This soldier was finally on my own, just like Leon wanted. This soldier had a purpose.

A vague memory of something my mother, my real mother Eva, told me skittered across my mind.

"You have no purpose, Buck. You'll never amount to anything without a purpose."

"I have one now, Mama," I whispered to myself.

The conviction in my belly was the fire I always feared, the anger and hate I tried so desperately to keep bottled up. The belief burned deep in my soul. I feared it, but now, this slow burn felt good. It felt right. I set my jaw, stepped out from the dark underside of the bridge, and finally faced the light.

Forty-seven

DA Stone watched from the side of the room as the county manager announced the decision of the highly unusual Saturday morning meeting of the county commission. A day passed to get everybody together, but this kind of thing couldn't wait. The vote was closer than expected, two to two, divided along racial lines, with one abstaining member. The manager, a cousin of Stone's, cast the tie-breaking vote. Ben Jefferson was stripped of his badge until a complete investigation could be performed, an investigation that included sexual assault and potential murder, an investigation that might take quite some time. Leon Bustard, who was the only other candidate in the upcoming election, would take over as acting sheriff. The election was less than two months away; so, Leon would likely carry the badge until the polls closed and the people had their say. Of course, if the investigation led to charges and the charges stuck, Leon would be the only man on the ballot.

Sarah watched the announcement, too, standing behind the reporters and photographers from two of the Birmingham TV stations who were there with their lights on and microphones thrust out. Stone had made sure he called them before doing anything else. The flashes lit up the room when Judge Morrison asked Leon to repeat his oath of office with hand on Bible. Acting sheriff Bustard kept his Stetson hat on during the ceremony.

When the words were said and Leon lowered his hand, the reporters shouted a few questions. Before he answered, he pinned on a badge and leaned into a deputy, who whispered a message in his ear. A frown crossed his face, and he instructed the deputy what to do. The deputy immediately left the room. Leon must have decided there wouldn't be a better time to take advantage of the cameras. He stepped to the podium.

"I won't be taking any questions today, but I would like to make a short announcement." He pulled out a scrap of paper from his pocket and spread it before him.

"Today, a man we thought we knew, a man we thought we trusted, is being relieved of his duties. This is a serious matter with serious accusations. Enough evidence has come to light that we would be derelict in our duties if we did not act now to protect the community. We have a witness who has indicated that Ben Jefferson may have assaulted a suspect, as he lay incapacitated and defenseless. That suspect is dead, possibly as a result of Jefferson's actions. As the primary police protection for the good citizens of this county, I will not stand by and let corruption and violence permeate our force. Most cops are good people who work hard at a thankless job, but every once in a while, a rogue cop comes around and tries to take the law into his own hands. The law is nothing unless we police our own. That's all. I'll let you know more when we can."

The reporters shouted after him as he left the room. When he didn't respond, they turned their attention to the DA and Judge Morrison.

"Is this the same person who tried to kill the sheriff during a drug bust?" one of them called out.

Frank Stone stated that the details would be presented in due time. He pledged to follow the law and prosecute to his full authority if it was necessary. The judge spoke next. He claimed that government had strayed so far from Christian principles that the time had come for the people to take it back. He reminded the press of the Ten Commandments plaque he kept in his office and said he looked forward to the time when man's law allowed God's law to be displayed in a courtroom again.

Sarah left the room before he could say anything else. She felt sick to her stomach.

"What the hell have I done, Ben?" she mumbled under her breath. She retrieved the key from her locked desk and made her way to the sealed file room. That space was the only place she knew where she could find some privacy. She was already dialing Ben's number before she closed the door.

"Pick up, dammit," she muttered. The phone rang six times and went to voice mail, but when she started to talk, the call dropped.

"Shit, what am I doing? They'll check my phone for sure," she said to herself out loud, apparently trying to convince herself it wasn't worth getting in too deep. She didn't think long, though. A minute later, she typed out a short text and pushed send.

"Remember the rose bushes? I'm picking up another one but don't expect me to take it by your place."

The blue bar crept across the top and stopped halfway, where it stayed.

"Damn."

After a minute, "message failed" appeared. She pushed "retry." Again, the blue bar stopped. Sarah opened the door and peeked into the larger file room. One of her clerks was across the room with her back turned. She slipped out and walked into the hall. Out of the corner of her eye, she thought she saw the clerk turn. Hiding the phone in her skirt pocket, she went back to her office. Another clerk met her there.

"Judge Dick wants to see you. He's in his office," she said. "Are you alright?"

"Tell him I'm sick," replied Sarah, dropping the key in her desk and relocking it. She left without another word. On the way, she peeked at the phone and saw the message had turned green. No way to know if Ben had read the text. She quickly deleted the words and dropped the phone back into her pocket. Ten minutes later, she was on her way to Cat's Nursery. She and Ben had laughed over the ironic name after they both pulled themselves out of the thorns that scratched them worse than any cat could. Hopefully, he remembered. Hopefully, he would understand. Hopefully, she pulled in the parking lot and waited.

Forty-eight

"How did it get to this point?" Sarah's success in meeting up with Ben was more than tempered by her worry.

"How does anything get to a bad place?" he said. "In my business, you find out quick. Everything's about money, power, or love. This is a power play, pure and simple."

"But I've made you lose your job," she said. "It's all my fault."

"Those photos aren't enough, Sarah. You didn't make me lose my job. Stone and Leon just needed something to turn public opinion against me before making the other charge."

"Did you do it, Ben?" she asked, already wishing she had not said the words. "That night, when you were drunk, you said… " She couldn't go further. "No, I have no right to ask you something like that."

"I wouldn't answer it anyway, but I don't hold the question against you. Emotions run extreme under those conditions—a man bent on killing you."

"A man you believe killed Laura," she said.

Ben didn't respond. Instead, he directed her to drive out of town, towards the bombing scene.

"I need to talk to somebody."

Twenty-five minutes later, they pulled into a long gravel drive and headed up the hill towards a modest but respectable house. The grounds were well kept, the last of the hay cut and stored for the winter. The cows looked up from their shady spot under the trees at the far end of the pasture, trying to find refuge from the still-hot September sun. A large, red-painted barn with white trim stood at the top of the hill.

Earl Hanks stood at the barn door, a large straw cowboy hat shading his dark face, and eyed the visitors.

Sarah pulled up to the gate, and Ben stepped out.

"Been expecting you, Sheriff. I don't believe you're supposed to be here."

"You know me, Earl. Come straight to the horse's mouth if you want to get the story."

"Got nothing to say. Might as well leave."

"You don't have to talk. Just listen."

"I'm in enough trouble right now. I'd rather you just leave me alone."

"I'm mighty grateful for what you did that day. I wouldn't be standing here if you hadn't come along. If you hadn't done something."

Earl nodded. "No good deed goes unpunished. Ain't that what they say?" Earl took off his work gloves and walked toward his house, turning his back on the sheriff.

"What they threatening you with, Earl? They can't do nothing to you as long as I'm the law."

The man whirled; his eyes narrowed. "You ain't the law, Ben. You just another Black man dancing around with a White man pulling your strings."

"That ain't how it works anymore."

"You expect me to believe that? While a White man threatens to call in my loan? While a White judge threatens to take away my custody rights? While a White DA threatens to charge me with manslaughter? You been sitting up there in your office with your White deputies. Riding around with your White woman. I expect under that skin, you're as White as they are."

Sarah stepped out of the car. "Earl," she said. Earl simply stared at her.

Ben broke the silence.

"Have I ever treated you or your family with anything but respect, Earl? I'm the sheriff, not the Black sheriff, not the White sheriff. Just the sheriff."

"You was the sheriff. You ain't shit anymore, Ben. You're just another out-of-work Black man they fixing to throw in jail."

"Did you see me kill that man? Did you see me take a rock to Stevie Wilson? I know you didn't leave your truck till the ambulance came. You couldn't see me from there, Earl. You know it, and I know it."

"I saw the blood. That man was staring at me when I hit him, face first, right into the windshield. I'll never forget that. It wasn't the side of his head hit my windshield, but that's where his skull was cracked open when they brought him out."

"But you didn't see me hit him. Did you, Earl?"

"I tell them I saw you, I get to keep my kids. I get to keep my farm. I worked thirty years to make this place. I ain't giving it all up on account of you."

Ben didn't answer for a while. He had no easy answer. Not for him. Not for Earl. He walked back to the car.

"Not but two things we got to fight crooked men," Ben said. "The law and the truth. I ain't asking you to lie. I'm asking you to tell the truth. The law will take care of the rest."

Ben and Sarah got in, and she turned the car around. Ben rolled down his window. Just before they drove away, Earl stepped forward.

"Tell me something, Sheriff. Did the law and the truth save your wife?"

The drive back to town was in silence. Ben had done all he could at Earl's place. Now he had more work ahead of him. If the connections of Jeannie Roberts were going to be investigated, it was up to Ben Jefferson to do the work. He checked his rifle he had put into the back seat. He checked the extra ammunition he had placed into his backpack. He checked the water bottles and crackers they had stopped for. He checked the night-vision binoculars he had packed. He plugged in his phone to make sure it was fully charged. He checked the camo jacket he had grabbed at the last minute.

Then he closed his eyes and rested.

MANDALEE ST. JAMES

Forty-nine

Mandalee slipped down the staircase and grabbed the keys in the bowl by the front door. The canned television audience in the next room laughed through another sitcom while her mother snored in the recliner. Her father, sorting bills on the dining room table, would be furious whenever she returned home, but right now, she didn't care. She would deal with the consequences later.

She backed her mom's Civic down the driveway and into the cul-de-sac, taking care to leave the lights off. Buck hadn't called her until late afternoon, and darkness had fallen now. He was planning something stupid. Now she was going to have to find him and hope he had not already gone through with it.

"I have a huge favor to ask," he had said on the phone. "I know you have no reason to trust me."

"What is it you want me to do?" she asked.

"Once you have everything, meet me at the gas station on the state highway at Scotts Mill Road. Wait with your lights off by the air pump." Those were his instructions. He had asked her the time, and when she told him, he said give him six hours. That would be ten p.m. "If I don't show up by midnight, find the sheriff. I'll be at the end of the long dirt road that turns off Scotts Mill Road one mile from the gas station."

"What are you doing, Buck? Just let me pick you up and take you home now," she said.

"I'm doing what I should have done a long time ago. I've been waiting on things to happen to me. It's time I made my own fate."

"What does that mean, Buck? What are you going to do?"

"I know who killed my mother, and it wasn't me."

"Of course, it wasn't you. I never thought you were capable of hurting her or anybody else."

"I'm capable, Mandalee. Believe me, I'm capable."

Mandalee protested, but whatever Buck had planned, he had made up his mind.

"One more thing, Mandalee. This might be dangerous. I have no right to ask you to help me, but I didn't know anybody else to call."

Mandalee stayed quiet.

For a minute, so did Buck.

"Look, if you don't come, I understand. I've done nothing but cause you pain, and now I'm asking for more."

Still Mandalee stayed quiet.

"I want you to know I'm sorry for hurting you. I never meant to. I just wasn't thinking about anybody but myself. If you decide not to come, I understand. I'll be okay."

"You better be there," she said.

"I will." Just before he hung up, he blurted it out. In all their time together, ever since they were small kids, they had often expressed how much they liked each other, how much they enjoyed each other's company, how much alike they were. This was the first time Buck had said his real feelings out loud.

"I love you, Mandalee."

Then the receiver clicked and went dead.

First, she met Teresa out front of her house and picked up Buck's phone and some clothes. Teresa was so happy that her brother was okay. Now, here Mandalee was, flying blind through the dark into who knew what.

She knew the gas station, at least. It was the one her family always stopped at to load up on snacks on the way to the river. She thought of how many times she and Buck had climbed up the rocks on the side of the falls and how many times they dove into the cold water below. She couldn't remember a happier time in her life.

What did he mean he knew who killed his mother? What was he going to do? The thoughts and fears trampled through her mind, nearly stamping out the good memories. She fought to push the fear away.

"It'll be our great adventure, nobody but you and me."

Buck was eleven and showing her the map with the trail he had picked out around the swamps of the refuge. He had traced the route with a yellow highlighter so he would be sure not to get lost.

"You can't go straight through the swamp," he explained. "You have to stick to the high ground, so the water moccasins and the alligators don't get you."

"Aren't any alligators this far north, silly," she said.

"Oh yeah there are," he said. "I've seen the muddy marks where they come up out of the water and wait on the bank, just for some little girl like you to come along." He extended his arms out slowly to each side.

"I'm not a little girl, and I'm not scared of alligators that don't exist."

"And then," he slapped his hands together, and Mandalee jumped. "They grab you and drag you into the water. Once they get you there, they do their death roll. They take you to the bottom and lay there till you drown. Then they chomp on you and swallow you down."

She remembered he grabbed her and tried to throw her to the ground. At that age, she was a little bigger and a lot more agile than Buck. She easily leveraged his weight backward, and they both tumbled to the grass. Then she kissed him, right on the lips. He looked so surprised, almost as if he had been bitten by a gator. She jumped back up and took off. Neither one mentioned it until their next kiss five years later at the Pipeline.

"Oh God, Buck. What are you planning on doing?" she yelled inside the car, and a few tears trickled down her face before she composed herself.

She reached in the dark and felt in the passenger seat for what she threw there. Buck had asked for it, and she didn't protest. She knew they might need it, just in case the alligators—or their human equivalents— were real, just in case the one that killed Buck's mother came for him too. She felt it with her fingertips. Cold and hard. She had seen her mother slide it under her mattress where her father, who hated violence, wouldn't find it. Mandalee had no idea how to check it. All she knew was to point it at what was trying to hurt you—and pull the trigger.

BUCK

Fifty

All the possible scenarios kept playing through my mind in a continuous loop—worm my way back into her life and sneak out evidence against her, or confront her, or do what I had always done in one way or another, run away. The creatures of the river bottom avoided me like the mad animal that I was, crashing through the brush, slogging through the few remaining puddles, climbing over the jumble of debris that matched my thoughts. At times, I called out to the ragged girl that visited me in my darkest thoughts. Cursing her. Begging her. Reasoning with her. Confessing my deepest fears.

What if I have no purpose? Tell me what to do.

She didn't answer.

Free fucking will? What a joke. We're programmed and set down in the world like a fucking wind-up doll, a toy soldier marching along to someone else's orders—Leon, the sheriff, even Jeannie. By the time I drew near to Jeannie's place, the world around me had darkened to match my thoughts. A lonely car whined along the road. I climbed out of the deep woods and stood straddling the center line. A pair of headlights peered through the distance. I waited.

A fingernail moon peeked from behind a cloud, and I leaned back to look at it. The little moon made me angry.

"Is that all you can give me? A worthless sliver of light?"

I stared, desperately trying to see what was in full view, yet hidden by shadow. I heard the steady thrum of tires growing louder. I reached my arms to heaven, clenched my fists, and extended the middle finger on each hand.

"Fuck you," I shouted.

I never heard a horn. A hot wind enveloped me and swayed me backwards. Tires crunched on gravel, and the car jerked back onto the asphalt, looking for traction. The smell of burning rubber mixed with my own stink filled my nostrils. The tires shrieked, spinning sideways on the road. I continued to stare into the sky.

"Fucking asshole! Get out of the road, you fucking idiot."

I lowered my arms and turned. The car's headlights pointed crazily into the woods. The door was open, and a man stared at me through the cloud of dust and smoke. I began walking towards him, slowly, silently. I could almost smell the fear in the man's voice.

"What the hell's wrong with you?" the voice yelled.

For once in your life, quit running and make something happen.

As I approached, the man climbed back into the car and spun his tires frantically, trying to pull the car back onto the asphalt. When I was within ten feet, the tires finally found the traction to move the car. The automobile whipsawed across both lanes, straightened out and sped away. By the time the car disappeared, I decided. The hell with groveling. The hell with waiting, taking sneaky photographs. It was time to take action now.

March up to the house, throw open the door, grab her by the neck, and scream in her face: *You killed my mother.*

No need to think about what comes next. No, I didn't know what would happen after I confronted the evil bitch. I just knew, this time, I would start things in motion. This time, the beast would be freed.

The rest of the walk was down the center of the road, my road. No car showed up to challenge me. I found the dirt drive leading to Jeannie's place and walked toward the house with more determination than I had ever had in my life. Nothing could stop me now. I began humming, so loudly I didn't hear the footsteps behind me until too late. I turned just in time to glimpse the butt end of a gun crashing down on my head.

Fifty-one

R ed Turner flung the door open and threw an unconscious body onto the floor.

"Your security sucks," he said. "Good thing I like to piss outside."

Jeannie knelt quickly beside Buck and lifted his head gingerly. "What the hell did you do?"

"You know this asshole?"

"He's my son." Buck rolled his head side to side and moaned. "You could have killed him."

"The son-of-a-bitch was humming, goddammit. I don't like happy idiots walking in on me when I'm not expecting it."

By this time, Buck had come to and was trying to sit up. A nasty bump on his forehead was already blue and an inordinate amount of blood was streaming down the side of his face. Jeannie dabbed with her shirt and asked Russell to fetch a wet washcloth. She peered into both of his eyes to gauge the pupils. The right one was abnormally large.

"Bring some ice too, Russell," she hollered. To Red she said, "He needs to go to a hospital."

Red rubbed the top of his head and walked out onto the porch while Jeannie tended to the boy's injury. After a few minutes, Buck stood with Jeannie and Russell on each arm while they guided him to the door.

Red stopped them. "Can't let you do that, Jeannie."

"You gave him a concussion, maybe worse. He needs to see a doctor."

"I ain't letting this boy accuse me of nothing. He stays here."

Russell, up to then, quietly following Jeannie's lead, finally spoke up.

"We're taking the boy to a hospital, Red. Get out of the way."

"Well, look who's talking big all of a sudden? What's this boy to you?" Red eyed him carefully. "You got a thing for Jeannie, don't you? You can forget it. Ain't nobody going nowhere."

"We ain't saying nothing about you or even how he got hurt," said Jeannie. "You gotta let us go."

"No, he's right," said Russell. "Lay him on the couch, Jeannie. He'll be alright."

"Russell, you weasel-faced coward. You sit on the couch, and I'll take him myself." She pushed Russell out of the way and pulled Buck forward.

Red pulled a pistol from his belt. Buck's blood was still drying on the handle. He pointed the gun at Jeannie.

"You fucking call me over here to be your goddamn partner like you're some big shot. I didn't need Weisman, and I can handle his Mexican buddies. But I don't need you. I'll let you stay. Hell, I'll even cut you in some, but we do things my way. We don't risk getting the law involved."

He leaned into her face, nearly spitting. "Now sit down."

"Fuck you, asshole," said Jeannie, calmly and clearly.

Red exploded, grabbing Jeannie by the hair and throwing her backward. Buck stumbled but held onto the door jamb, frozen. His mind was scrambled, but he could remember he was here to confront the woman who had killed his mother. Now a man was violently attacking that woman. Later, he couldn't say why he did what he did next. Was it to protect her or so he would have the chance to kill her instead? He grabbed a lamp from the nearest table and swung with all his might at the tall man. The blow glanced off the man's back, who then turned his pistol on the boy, now sprawled on the floor. He aimed the pistol slowly.

"Not too smart, you son-of-a-bitch," he said.

The shot rang out, and Jeannie jerked around to see where the sound came from. Russell stood with his rifle, wispy smoke still streaming from the barrel.

Red looked surprised and dropped to his knees. His pistol tumbled onto the floor by Buck, who was still too dazed to grab it.

"Get out of here, Jeannie. Take your boy with you," said Russell, still pointing his rifle at Red's back.

"You shouldn't have done that, old man," said Red weakly.

Jeannie helped Buck to his feet again and pulled him quickly out the door. At the steps, she turned back and said, "I didn't mean it, Russell. You always had my back."

Jeannie got Buck loaded into the van and cranked the engine, quickly backing out. As she took a last glance at the house, two blasts cracked the night. She showered down on the accelerator, slinging gravel and dust. A third shot crashed through the rear door window and shattered the windshield. Instinctively trying to duck, Jeannie nearly lost control but managed to whip the vehicle back on the road.

"Russell," she yelled. "Oh shit, Russell, what did we do to you?

Buck's mind was slowly clearing. He remembered.

"My girlfriend's waiting up here at the store. He won't know to look for her car."

In spite of the danger that would soon be gunning for her and Buck, Jeannie processed the information for what it meant.

"Why is your girlfriend waiting on you? What the hell was you planning, boy?"

"I was going to kill you," he mumbled.

"Looks like you'll have to get in line now, boy."

The silver compact was parked right where Buck had told her. Jeannie pulled the van all the way behind the building, so the vehicle couldn't be seen from the highway.

"You got some explaining to do, boy," she said. "Right now, we got to get the hell out of here. Can you do a little walking? We're gonna have to lay low for a while."

"Why are you helping me? I told you I was going to kill you. I'll just go with Mandalee after we drop you off."

"You don't want that animal chasing your girlfriend. You stay with me. I know how to stay out of sight. Red don't know about her. She'll be alright."

They hurried, as fast as Buck could, to Mandalee's car. She unlocked the doors when she saw them, and they tumbled in.

"Girl, if you have feelings for this boy, you best get us out of here."

She pointed up the highway, away from town. Mandalee complied, afraid to talk back. As they pulled out, Jeannie could see a pair of headlights weaving up the county road toward the gas station.

"Not too fast, honey. He don't know this car and I don't want him to notice it."

She watched through the rear window until the Escalade pulled out onto the highway. It headed the other way.

Fifty-two

Ben had no more found a place to settle in to watch the cabin when the shots rang out. Through his binoculars, he could see two figures stumbling to the white van parked out front—a woman and a boy. One or both of them were hurt. In a few seconds, a third figure fired at the fleeing couple.

Ben dialed 911 and identified himself.

"Multiple gunshots at 12071 Scotts Mill Road. Two vehicles fleeing the scene. White Econovan without markings and a black late-model Escalade. The man in the Escalade armed and dangerous. I'm moving towards the house. Need backup immediately. Send an ambulance, too. I don't know who's inside."

The door stood open, but the house was quiet when Ben made it to the front porch. A puddle of blood dripped from the top step. One of the people fleeing was hurt badly.

He slipped to the front door and readied his rifle before stepping inside, pointing in each direction, looking for any movement. He heard a slight moan and followed the sound behind the couch. Russell Lee was sprawled on the floor, one arm above his head as if thrown there. A rifle lay a few feet away.

Ben took a quick check of the rest of the house, assuring himself the place was clear. He knelt by Russell, laboring through ragged breaths, desperately clinging to what was left of his life.

"What the hell did you get yourself into, Russell Lee?" said Ben. He pulled his shirt off and used it to apply pressure to the gaping wound in Russell's chest.

"Jeannie and her boy. They make it?" Russell gasped through the blood filling his mouth.

"Stay still, Russell. I got help coming."

Russell lifted his hand weakly and wrapped it around Ben's wrist. "Did they get out?"

"Yes, Russell, they made it out."

"Good," he said, and his hand slipped to the floor. Ben listened until the rattling stopped.

In spite of the blood, in spite of the obvious chest injury, Ben began heart compressions and CPR breaths. Fifteen minutes later the medics arrived. After only a quick check, they stopped him.

"No use, Sheriff," one of them said. "You can't save him."

Ben's dedication to life was legendary among the paramedics of the area. They had arrived many times at a crime scene to find the sheriff working feverishly to revive somebody who had just been trying to shoot somebody else. He had earned their respect if not that of all the cops, most of whom wouldn't touch an injured suspect unless it was to continue to incapacitate him. The only time they could remember him not helping a suspect was after the bombing. He made sure they took care of Tom before he pointed to where to find Patch Wilson.

When Leon arrived, sporting the same cowboy hat he always wore along with a shiny star pinned on his chest, his first order was to place Ben in the back seat of a deputy's cruiser, hands cuffed. Leon was kind enough to place the cuffs in front. Ben stayed there for the next four hours until Tom Walters arrived. Still off-duty, he heard about the shooting from a buddy on the force. He immediately took off the cuffs and let Ben out of the car.

"Anybody say you could do that, son?" hollered Leon from his command position on the front porch. Tom ignored him.

"I'll be good, Tom," said Ben.

"Anybody take your statement yet?" asked the deputy.

"Leon asked what the hell happened and why I was here. I told him but he didn't write anything down."

Tom pulled out his witness forms and took down all the details.

Ben asked, "Anybody looking for that van and SUV?"

"Leon shut that down."

"The boy's out there, and the man that did this is chasing him. Somebody's got to find him before he does."

"You still got friends on the force, Sheriff. Most of us don't believe all that crap the DA put out. Far as I'm concerned, you're still my boss."

"He and Jeannie Roberts are running in that white van we saw here. I've seen the SUV before. I think it's Red Turner."

"Weisman's goon."

"Yep."

"On it," and Tom was gone, enlisting one other deputy to take with him.

Ben managed to take a piss before Leon had him thrown back into the cruiser. This time he left the cuffs off.

JEANNIE ROBERTS

Fifty-three

One of Jeannie's lean-to shelters was the perfect place for Buck to cocoon himself from the scrambled world around him. He closed his eyes and slept for nearly three days straight. Jeannie moistened his lips with wet rags, but they cracked and bled even as his forehead began to heal. Each night, as Jeannie sat outside the shelter, she listened as Buck rambled in his unconsciousness.

It was like eavesdropping on half of a phone conversation. Even so, she recognized who the boy was talking to.

"Why do you keep showing me?" he yelled, his voice ragged and raspy.

After a few moments, "I was a fucking coward."

"No," he pleaded, "it's too late."

He curled into a ball, and sobbed, tearless, until he finally grew quiet.

On the third night, in the midst of one of his one-sided arguments, Jeannie burst into the shelter and shook him hard.

"Tell her to leave you alone. You hear me?" She shook him again and he woke, scrambling backwards, peering into the dark. "Tell her to leave," she whispered again.

"I keep seeing her," he gasped.

"Tell her to leave."

"The woman that killed my mother. I keep seeing her do it, and I can't do anything to stop it." Buck could hardly talk through the sobs.

Jeannie waited, stroking his back. Finally, he raised his head from his arms and looked her in the eye.

"I thought you did it," he said.

"No, not me."

"I thought it was you. I mean, she stole your baby. You told me so. I thought she stole your boy and you killed her for it."

No," she said. "Think about it Buck. Eva was the mother what raised you. Why would I do that to my baby?

Buck looked confused and lay back, his eyes darting around the space.

"Drink some water, Buck. You've been out for days, and you're not thinking straight. I'll tell you everything, but you got to believe me. I didn't hurt your mother."

Over the next hour, the truth poured out, the real truth, a relief to Jeannie. Buck listened.

The desperate search for a man to get her pregnant. The judge, always judging, always condemning. But always ready to lay with you. The chase lasted for several months, and yet she stayed barren, even though she always made sure to sabotage his protection. Each month, the blood flowed and washed out her hopes. Each month she found a looser dress to wear and stuffed it with padding. She would do anything, anything to keep Kenny's love. Without a child, he would not stay, because that's all he ever truly wanted.

Finally, she developed her plan. If the judge could not give her a child one way, she would make him do it another. He knew which babies need a place to go because their mothers were too wicked or too weak to be trusted with a child's life.

She hid her phone and took secret videos. She worked him until he got tired of her. Until he found another desperate woman to fill his needs.

She took the videos to his wife. She didn't trust the judge. He was too powerful to trust.

But a wife, a wife in her position, would protect that position, even if she had to convince her cheating husband to find a baby.

It worked. The next month, she discarded the padding for a real infant. Yvonne Morrison met her one night. She gave up her phone with the incriminating videos and took the baby—tiny, the umbilical cord scar still fresh. He had a thin fresh cut on his back, dressed with a bloody bandage. Yvonne explained the mother had tried to hurt the baby and that's why he was taken away from her. Jeannie didn't ask questions.

A man will see what he wants to see. The baby boy Kenny longed for lay in his wife's arms. She spun a story of going into labor while Kenny was off at work. Said she went to the creek behind the lot where they parked their car and pushed the baby right out into the cool water, just the way she had heard an old woman at the mission describe how babies were birthed up in the mountains where no doctor or midwife was around to help.

He didn't care how it happened. The child was a miracle, and he would accept a miracle with an open heart.

He had a son.

She had Kenny.

They were both happy.

Happiness lasted about a year, until they picked up Kenny and threw him into jail. The judge gave her a choice. Keep your man and your freedom or give up both. Either way, she was no longer fit to keep the baby.

"I tried to love you like you was my own, Buck. I did," she cried to him. The tears flowed freely, so heavy he almost believed her.

"I understand. I wasn't yours to begin with. Why would you fight for me?" he asked.

"I didn't have a choice," she said.

"Mama told me that Dad, my real one, said we always have a choice."

"No, you have to believe me. I didn't have no choice at all."

"No, maybe you thought you didn't. It seemed I never had a choice. Somebody always told me what to do. Leon, or whoever pulled the strings, had their own plans. It didn't matter what I wanted. But I'm finally beginning to realize. If I don't do something, things will always be the same. Now it's time for me to make the choice."

"It's God who has the plan. He has a plan for everybody," said Jeannie. "I remember a preacher saying that one time."

"Fuck that. What kind of God steals a baby? What kind of God gives him to a whore like you, who just throws him away when it gets too hard? What kind of God puts a man like Leon in your life, kills the one that raised you, and leaves you to take the blame? What kind of plan is that? Tell me, who would do that to a person?"

"The preacher said we can't understand God's ways."

"I understand," cried Buck. "I don't need anybody else's plan for my life. It's just what I decide to make it, what I decide to do. Not some old man in the sky. Just me."

"You came back to kill me because you thought I killed your mother. But I told you the truth, all of it. You were better off with your mother what raised you. I didn't want to take you away from her. I just wanted to see you every once in a while, just to make sure you were okay."

"You're right," he said. "I was going to kill you."

"I didn't hurt your mother, Buck."

"No, you only look out for yourself, don't you? You didn't want me back then, why would you want to take me away now."

"I wanted what's best for you."

"Yeah, best for me," he said. "You said you were my real mother. Now, you've taken that away from me, too. I don't know who I belong to."

"I saved you from Red, didn't I? I still love you."

After a long while, Buck spoke.

"If you really love me," he said, "this is what you're going to do."

Fifty-four

When Tom Walters reported to the sheriff's office on Monday morning, his suspension over from shooting the unarmed man, the hammer dropped. Leon Bustard met him at the door and threatened to take his badge, this time permanently. The investigation into the bombing incident had cleared him, and now Tom was somewhat of a local hero. No, Leon couldn't afford to take his job, but Tom had to pay for his insubordination at the Russell Lee crime scene.

Leon had already officially reprimanded the other deputy who accompanied Tom away from Jeannie's cabin. This was in spite of the two deputies finding Red Turner dead inside his SUV in a ravine off Highway 25 and identifying the owner of the Honda Civic they saw on the convenience store security video. Two other deputies, at Tom's request, were on the way to Mandalee's house at that very moment to question her. Leon did not call them back but swore to Tom that they also would be punished. Nine other deputies had called in with a case of the blue flu earlier in the day. The five remaining deputies and three sergeants were all summoned to a meeting in Leon's office at eleven o'clock. In the meantime, Leon took one of the deputies, the son of a second cousin, and headed to Earl Hanks's place. Their intent was to bring him in for further questioning about the death of Patch Wilson.

Earl was in the barn, replacing the clutch in his tractor when Leon arrived. The acting sheriff strode to the house and yelled for Earl twice outside.

"I ain't telling you one more time, Hanks. Come on out before we come in."

"No need busting into somebody's house, Sheriff," Earl yelled from the barn.

"You're going with me to the office, Hanks. I need a further statement from you."

"I got nothing to say to you, Sheriff."

"You're a witness. Get in the vehicle."

"You have a warrant for me, Sheriff? 'Cause that's the only way I'm coming with you."

"I don't need a warrant to take you in for disorderly and suspicion of theft. My discretion. You want to add resisting arrest?"

"Ask me your questions here, Sheriff. I ain't going nowhere unless you arrest me."

A sedan pulled into the gravel drive and Earl's ex-wife stepped out from the driver's side. Their thirteen-year-old daughter stepped out, too, and went to stand behind her mother.

"You stay out of this," said Leon to the woman. "My business is with Earl."

"If you got business with him, you got business with me, too."

Two Black men stepped out of the barn and stood behind Earl.

Two more cars pulled into the driveway, each carrying three more Black men. They all got out and stood facing the sheriff, saying nothing. Each person kept his hands down by his side.

"You all family of this man?" hollered Leon. "I can run you all in if you want."

Nobody moved. Nobody spoke. Leon looked at his deputy and nodded toward Earl. The deputy drew his pistol and began walking towards the barn. The two men with Earl stepped in front of him but said nothing. The deputy hesitated and glanced back at Leon.

"Go on. Do your job," said Leon.

"Step aside, fellows, we got no beef with you. We just need Earl to come to town and answer a few more questions." The deputy's pistol stayed pointed towards the ground. All three men in front of him sat down. The deputy stopped, figuring his next step.

Mary Hanks, with her daughter Kecia only a step behind, marched up the driveway, passing by Leon, whose face grew a deep red.

"Stay out of this, bitch," he snarled.

Mary kept walking, and Leon grabbed her daughter by the arm, throwing her to the side. She fell onto the gravel with a thud. Mary whirled, the anger flashing in her eyes. Leon had his gun out and pointed it at Mary.

"Get out of the way before somebody gets hurt," said Leon.

Mary stood her ground.

"Get up, Kecia," she said, extending her hand slowly to the girl, who was whimpering softly. A trickle of blood traced down her arm.

"Get off the ground and up on your feet."

"Yes, Mama," said Kecia.

By this time, five more vehicles had pulled along the roadside, and twenty more faces watched the unfolding drama with determined and rising righteousness. Eighteen of the faces were black or brown. A White man and his wife who lived across the road joined them, standing shoulder to shoulder, blocking the drive.

Kecia began crawling to her mother, but the woman rebuked her quickly.

"Get off your knees, girl. We don't crawl no more," she said. The girl stood and together, hand in hand, she and her mother walked to join Earl. Confused, the deputy placed his pistol back into its holster.

"Earl," called Leon, "you told this deputy the other day you thought Ben Jefferson killed that man you hit. Now you got a choice to make; so, listen and listen good. Either Jefferson killed that man or you killed him. Which is it?"

"I couldn't see the sheriff when he went down to the man. I stayed in the truck the whole time."

"So you gonna take the rap for it?"

"I was minding my own business, and that man stepped out in front of me. Wasn't a thing I could do about it."

"What you want me to do, Sheriff?" asked the deputy.

"I want you to do your job and arrest the Black son-of-a-bitch," Leon shouted, but as he was talking, the crowd behind him kept growing. Five of the men, giving a wide berth to the acting sheriff, began walking toward the barn. A few seconds later they were joined by another five, circling in a different direction. Then, another two or three. Finally, most of the crowd fell in line and formed a large circle around Earl. The last one, an elderly Black man in overalls, took a place a foot in front of the deputy.

"You one of the Bustard boys, ain't you?" he said, not averting his gaze.

The deputy nodded, almost imperceptibly.

"Well, you do what you gotta do, son."

"Jake, you don't do like you're ordered, and you won't ever work in law enforcement again," shouted Leon.

"The man said he didn't see anything, sir," yelled Jake Bustard over his shoulder. He and the old man kept their eyes locked.

"That ain't what he told you the other day, Deputy."

Jake nodded to the old man and turned around. He snapped the guard on his holster and pulled his cap low over his face.

"I heard wrong, sir," he said, and got into the cruiser.

The rest of the crowd in the driveway parted when Leon backed onto the road. No dramatic spinning of tires, no throwing rocks and dust, and frustrated rage over the people watching. He simply drove off and didn't say a word on the way back to town.

A week of protests roiled the town. Marchers came from Huntsville and Birmingham, and even a few came from Atlanta. A few carried signs saying, "We want OUR sheriff back." A few others said, "Justice for All." The town had a Black population of approximately forty percent. About half of the protestors, according to most counts, were White.

The county commission met in another emergency session at the end of the week and talked to the DA behind closed doors. The mayor personally told Ben the investigation into Patch Wilson's death was closed. However, until the sexual assault questions were settled, Leon would keep the badge. Leon accepted the decision but not before venting his frustrations with the county's weak leadership.

BEN JEFFERSON

Fifty-five

The next morning Ben received a call from the forensics lab in Montgomery. Mary Lawson was on the other end.

"I've got something else for you, Ben, and you're not going to believe it. The DNA sample you procured from Yvonne Morrison matches the second blood sample on the cloth."

"So now we can tie Yvonne to the scene," said Ben. "Still not enough to arrest her. The coroner won't even say it was homicide. Is there more? You said I wouldn't believe it."

"Yep. Ever heard of the DNA Doe Project?"

"Something about figuring out who unidentified dead people are, right?"

"I got a wild hair and asked them to compare Yvonne's DNA with their database."

"And?"

"Police in Charlotte had an unsolved murder from nearly two decades ago—the Valentine Murder they called it. The case got a lot of press but none of the leads panned out. The cops took another look at it last year and asked the Doe Project for help."

"Are you saying…?"

"Turns out, they had a partial hit when they got to the Charlotte Jane Doe. She's a close relative to Yvonne."

"How close?"

"Same parents."

"Jeez, it's Marie Pickens," said Ben. "Yvonne's long-lost sister."

"In a couple of days, the cops are going to call and ask the sheriff to notify the next of kin. I understand you're not the sheriff anymore. You're all over the news. I figured I could at least give you a heads up."

"You said the case got a lot of press. Why?"

"Lots of reasons. White woman found dead on a day meant for lovers. Mainly because there was a baby involved, too." Mary paused. "They never found the child."

"Oh, my God. Can't be. Could it?"

"Could what?"

"Exactly how many years ago was the girl murdered?" asked Ben.

"It would have been eighteen years last Valentine's Day."

"The thought never crossed my mind until just now. Eva Bustard's boy was adopted a little over a year after that. The adoption papers listed his date of birth as February 14, eighteen years ago."

"You think...?"

"It's a crazy idea, I'll admit."

"...Buck Thompson is the baby?"

"Look, Mary. I took a sample of Buck Thompson's DNA even though he wasn't arrested. Never submitted it because we never charged him with anything. I'll get Tom to send it to you. How fast can you have something back to me?"

"Look, first of all, you don't have authorization to run a test on anything right now. Second, if I understand the situation, that's an illegally obtained sample"

"He didn't object."

"Look, Ben. You know the law. Unless he was charged or you got consent from his parent, that sample isn't legal."

"Nobody's charging the kid with anything. If it shows he's not Marie's son, then just file it away. No harm, no foul."

"And if he is her son? Pretty big motive to kill somebody you thought might have been involved in the murder of your real mother. We go way back. I knew Laura as a kid. I would do anything legal to help. You know that."

Mary was right, legally. He would never be able to use the information against anyone. On the other hand, what trouble was the kid in if his aunt was involved in Marie's murder?

"We can't wait, Mary," said Ben. "I can't get another DNA sample from the kid right now. He's missing. I need to know if he's in danger or not."

"Dammit, Ben. Why do I have to like you? It'd be so much easier to tell you to go to hell if you were an asshole." She mulled it over for only a few seconds before agreeing. "Okay, but not because I like you. It's only because I loved Laura, and Laura loved you. Got it?"

Ben grinned. "Thank you. You'll have the sample tomorrow. In the meantime, I'll keep an eye on the only living Pickens sister. And you can still call me an asshole if you want."

"I probably will," said Mary, "but there's more you need to know." She told him all she had learned about the unfortunate fate of Marie Pickens. When she was finished, he let out an audible breath.

"Ben," she said. "Be careful with this one."

"Always, Mary. Always."

Fifty-six

Tuesday morning, an official request from the Charlotte Police Department dinged into the sheriff's general email inbox. The dispatcher was charged with forwarding new emails to Leon until the IT guys worked out the addresses. Tom had already asked her to be on the lookout for this particular notice. Fortunately, she liked Tom, a lot. She didn't like Leon, but she didn't want to lose her job either. She gave Tom a printout of the message and told him she wouldn't be able to keep it from the acting sheriff for long.

"You owe me," she said, knowing Tom was already spoken for. Still, a drink with the best-looking deputy in the department wasn't too bad of a consolation. Who knows what the future holds?

"I owe you," Tom replied. She offered her cheek and Tom kissed her.

A few minutes later, Tom was at Ben's place, holding the message to notify Marie's next of kin. Ben took these notifications very seriously, to the point that the shroud of despair inherent in the visits nearly always threatened to envelop him in a sadness that was difficult to escape. Notification of next-of-kin was among his most sacred duties, and one he always attended to with utmost respect. Except this time.

Yvonne and her sister, Marie, had no love lost between them. Once the black sheep of the family was gone and out of sight, the elder sister moved on with no regret. No one inquired of Marie's whereabouts. No missing person report was ever filed. Her broken parents pined or hid in shame until they died. Marie was simply forgotten in the way that the pain from a severed limb was sublimated below your consciousness, capable of being dredged up but best left buried.

Except Marie was not left buried. She was left in a swamp, off a gravel road, a feast for the scavengers. When she was found by hunters a couple of weeks later, what was left of her was barely recognizable as female.

She lay in the morgue cooler for over a month after the autopsy, until the county needed room and finally assigned her a date to be cremated. Just before her remains were scheduled to be transported to the crematorium, a local AME Church offered to give her a place in their graveyard. An inexpensive tombstone was purchased, simply inscribed with the words "Mother Doe" and "God Will Always Love You," for it was apparent that no one else did.

Tom Walters, in his uniform, drove his cruiser to the Morrison residence. Ben rode along in his civilian clothes. The ride was somber, as these trips usually were. On the way, Ben remarked that he was glad Tom had gotten his job back.

"I'm thinking about leaving," said Tom. "I don't belong there."

"Whadya mean leaving? You're the best deputy on the force."

"No, I can't do it, Ben. Leon was right about one thing. I shot an unarmed man. A deputy's not supposed to do that."

"How did you know what he had in his hand? If it had been a gun, you'd be dead now."

"But it wasn't a gun, was it? And maybe it didn't register with me because I wasn't looking hard enough, or I was too amped up, or there wasn't time, but you knew it wasn't a gun. You tried to stop me."

"Look, Tom, I understand. You're going through hell right now, doubting yourself. Wondering if you would have done something different."

"I shot a man, Ben. An innocent man. I don't know if I can live with that. What happens the next time? What if I freeze up, scared I'll do it again, but it turns out to be a real gun? Who will be dead then? Me? You?"

"Tom, no; it ain't right."

"Maybe not, I don't know. I've made up my mind though."

"I understand," sighed Ben. He looked out the window at the pastures and trees rolling by, collecting his thoughts, figuring out how to tell Tom what he needed of him. He faced his deputy.

"It's a selfish thing I'm gonna ask. You're the only one I can depend on. This boy we're looking for is going through some hell of his own, and he needs our help before he hurts himself or somebody else. Stick with me a while, Tom."

"You know, we all heard it since we were kids. *Thou shalt not steal. Thou shalt not bear false witness. Thou shalt not kill.* I'm an officer of the law. I'm supposed to protect people. Not send them to heaven or hell."

"I heard a preacher one time," Ben said quietly. "Half singing, half shouting, stomping back and forth, pulled his tie off and wiped the sweat off his head with it, you know the way a preacher does when he's got the spirit and he's just got to testify. He points to me, like I was the only one in the congregation, and he says 'Sinner, believe on the Lord while you got the chance. When God calls your soul, you'll find out your fate: your everlasting just rewards or your well-deserved eternal punishment. Heed the call, sinner, because when you die, it'll be too late.' I waited till after the service and I come up to him, you know. Looked him straight in the eye. I said 'Preacher, I don't have to die to see what's on the other side. I done seen it all.' I never went back to that church. He didn't have nothing to tell me I didn't already know."

"If you're saying this life is hell, right here on earth, I'm about there with you." Tom's words carried an edge of desperation.

"What I'm saying, is this life, well, I can't make neither heaven nor hell of it. It's bits and pieces of both and everything in between, all mashed together into one big tangled mess. All you can do is find a rope to hang onto and keep following it. See, you're always gonna feel the pain. It don't go away, but sooner or later, you learn to deal with it. Sooner or later, you get through the hell and find another small piece of heaven somewhere down the line." Ben looked out the window again. "Least that's what I believe. It's what I gotta believe."

The rest of the ride was in silence, until they reached Yvonne's place. Tom pulled into the drive and shut off the engine. He picked up his hat and stared at the insignia on the front. It was a six-pointed star with the outline of the state in the center and the words 'Tierney County Deputy Sheriff' emblazoned in gold above and below the star.

"I'll stick with it until we find the boy," he said, brushing the brim of the already spotless hat. "I'll help you any way I can. I owe you that. I love this hat and this badge and everything they stand for, but when the smoke clears, I'll hand them in."

"Just till the smoke clears," said Ben. "I can live with that."

Tom stepped out of the car, stood shoulders back and head high. He tucked the hat firmly under his arm and together the two walked to the door.

Fifty-seven

Ben had not told Tom of his suspicions about Buck's relationship to Yvonne yet; so, the opening of the conversation when they arrived took Tom by surprise.

"Yvonne," said Ben, touching the bill of his unmarked brown cap still firmly in place and pulled low.

"I thought I told you to leave me be," she said. "Besides, you got fired, didn't you? She didn't close the door, probably because she recognized that this must be official business with the deputy along.

Tom stood behind Ben a couple of feet and nodded. "Mrs. Morrison," he said crisply.

"I have some news to deliver. Thought it best that it come from me. Can we go inside?" Ben asked.

"Is it about Dick?"

"No, ma'am, but maybe it's best we go inside and sit."

"Okay," she said, leading them to the formal living room. An unused piano, judging by the closed keyboard cover and lack of sheet music, sat in a dark corner.

Ben motioned to it. "Do you play?"

"No, it was a family piece."

"One of your sisters, maybe?"

"You didn't come here to talk about pianos, Sheriff. Get to the point."

"It's just my wife played piano. I love a well-played classical piece."

"Hmm," said Yvonne. "I wouldn't have taken you for a classical music fan. Maybe more R&B."

"Oh, you'd be surprised. I could listen to all types of music. I guess somebody in the family played the piano. Maybe Marie?"

Tom couldn't figure out Ben's line of talk here. He usually got to the point quickly, said his goodbyes, and left the family to grieve in private.

"Yes, I suppose Mother sent Marie for lessons for a while. I even remember her taking some lessons on her own when she got older. Never thought she was very good. Didn't your wife teach piano, Sheriff?"

Ben ignored the insult. "Maybe she didn't have the talent. Maybe she was just an annoying younger sister, always making noise. You were probably glad when she disappeared."

"That's enough, Ben. What's your business here? If you have none, then leave, please."

"It's about Marie."

"What about her?"

"She's dead."

"Dead?" repeated Yvonne.

"Yes, ma'am. Dead."

"I'm shocked but not surprised," said Yvonne. "She was always in trouble. Had to catch up to her sooner or later."

"Yes, ma'am," said Ben. "It catches up with all of us, I suppose."

"Well, thank you for coming out to tell me. Does my husband know yet?"

"No, ma'am, you're the only one who knows."

"Okay," she said. "I'd appreciate it if you kept it quiet. I'll tell him tonight when he comes home."

"I'll do that." Ben stayed seated until Yvonne stood up first to walk them to the door.

"If you like, I can get you the name of the church where she's buried," Ben offered.

"Yes, that would be nice, Sheriff. Thank you."

Just before they got to the door, Ben stopped to admire a photograph of a young family of three. The father, his arm around his wife, beamed with pride. The buxom mother held a child of about six months. The woman appeared to be several years older than the husband. She wore a blank expression, her closed mouth a straight line. Looking into her eyes, though, Ben felt a pang of something sorrowful.

"What a lovely photograph. Dick's nephew, isn't it?" asked Ben. "The wedding was only last month, right?"

"That's right," she said and opened the door.

"I'm getting bad at remembering names, I guess. His name is Bobby, but I can't recall hers. Is it Fay, maybe?"

"Francine," said Yvonne with a roll of her eyes.

"Francine, that's right. Tell them congratulations for me."

Yvonne did not reply. When the two men stepped out, Ben turned.

"Just one more thing, Mrs. Morrison. When did you say was the last time you saw Marie?"

"Oh, uh, I don't really remember. It's been so long. Almost twenty years I guess," she said.

"About the time she died, then," said Ben.

Yvonne stayed quiet with no visible reaction.

"Good day, Mrs. Morrison. I'm sorry for your loss."

Tom nodded his condolences, too, but the door was already closing.

When they settled into the car, Tom remarked how well she took the news.

"Yeah, almost like she knew it already, wasn't it?" said Ben, staring at the house. "You'd think someone might ask some questions. How did she die? Where's the body? What do I need to do? None of that."

"You said she died about twenty years ago?" asked Tom. "What happened?"

"See, even you asked questions. But not Yvonne. It was eighteen and a half years ago. She wasn't the least bit surprised or interested, except maybe that the body was actually identified all these years later."

"Wait, you're saying this girl was murdered?"

"More than that. I'm saying Yvonne might have had something to do with it," said Ben.

"That's a long time ago. How're you gonna prove it?"

"I don't know yet. Travel records maybe," said Ben. "Won't find any video or phone records from that far back, but if Yvonne was there, she would have had to either drive or fly or take a bus. Probably drove if she had to get the baby back home."

"What baby, boss? None of this makes sense."

"Not yet, Tom. Not yet," mused Ben, his mind working even as he spoke. "So Marie took piano lessons?"

"Yeah. So?"

"Not many in town gave lessons back then. Maybe Miz Webster at First Baptist."

"Oh God, she was awful, God bless her soul," said Tom.

"Yeah, that's why most students went after hours to Tierney Academy where the only good teacher in town gave lessons."

"Who was that, Boss?"

"Laura. They couldn't come to our house to take lessons, but the good White folks didn't mind going to the Christian private school to get lessons from a Black lady," said Ben. "Laura taught there for years and years. I bet Laura taught Marie way back then."

"What's that got to do with Marie's murder?"

"Maybe nothing about Marie. When I saw the piano in there, it reminded me that's where Laura was coming from the day she got killed. One of the names on the list of Laura's students the day she died. F. Cassidy."

"And?"

"And I never interviewed her because I didn't have a number and I didn't think it was important."

"But you do now?"

"I don't know, maybe. That photograph reminded me about Estelle at the diner saying the judge's nephew got married recently. She said the bride was from up around Muscle Shoals."

"Estelle told you her first name was Fay?"

"No, that was just a wild guess, but Yvonne corrected me like I figured she would. She can't help herself. Estelle only told me the bride's last name. Cassidy."

"F. Cassidy. Wait, we think Laura's death and the bombing murder are related. Are you saying that Laura's death and Eva's death might be related too?"

"I don't know. Like I told you, all I know is to find something and keep following it." Ben shook his head violently to clear his thoughts and sighed. "Let's go, Tom."

Fifty-eight

Mandalee looked and felt a wreck. Her hair sprayed wildly in every direction, so much so that her scars were prominently visible—leathery splotches behind her ear. She had not changed from her pajamas and only left her room to grab an apple or go to the bathroom since her father grounded her. She did get online, following the news to see if Buck had been found yet.

She had not told the deputies anything except that Buck and Jeannie told her to drive to some gravel road in the middle of nowhere and let them out. She didn't know where, she swore to them. To get home, Jeannie told her to keep driving until she came to a paved road, then turn right and drive until she recognized something. She told the deputies that she had been too upset at the time to remember how to get back. She could barely see through her tears.

After all the news about Ben Jefferson, she didn't know who she could trust. Not Leon Bustard, that was for sure. Probably not any of his deputies, either. Leon would just as soon Buck die or wind up in jail. She was sure of that, too. No, if Buck needed help, and the more she thought about it, the more she was convinced he did, then only Ben Jefferson could help. When the news said the investigation into Ben's conduct at the bombing site was dropped, Mandalee found the card Ben had given her. She hoped the number on it was his personal phone and not the sheriff's office.

"Sheriff?" she whispered when Ben picked up.

"I'm not the sheriff anymore. Who is this?" asked Ben.

Mandalee lowered the phone, her finger trembling as it hovered over the end button.

"Don't hang up. I can still help you," said Ben in a softer tone.

Mandalee brought the phone back to her ear. "I don't know if you can," she said.

"If I can't, I'll find the person who can. Let's start with this. What's your name?"

"It's Mandalee, Mandalee St. James."

"Are you in trouble, Mandalee?"

"No, sir, but Buck might be. I'm worried about him. I think he might be hurt pretty bad."

A half-hour later, Ben was parked in his truck at the end of Mandalee's block. He stared hard at her when she got in the passenger side. Her eyes were sunken and dark, the sclera an angry red. Her mouth drooped on both sides. She looked much older than her eighteen years. She was dressed in jeans and an old flannel shirt. She had a ball cap pulled down over her face.

"Are you alright, Mandalee? You don't have to go with me. Just tell me where you dropped them off."

"I'm alright now that I'm doing something," she said. "I can't tell you. I have to show you."

It took four tries down different dirt roads before she recognized a large dead tree, partially leaning over the road. A branch lay across the ditch, where somebody had pulled it out of the way.

"This is the road," she said. "That tree scared me that night. In the headlights it looked as if it was grabbing at me."

"Good, Mandalee. You did good. Now that we have a starting place, maybe we can find them."

Ben pulled out his phone and looked up the name of an old friend.

"Nate," he said when someone answered. "You still run those hunting dogs of yours?"

BEN JEFFERSON

Fifty-nine

Tuesday evening Ben spread all his files before him and tried to put the pieces together. He suspected Buck was Marie's baby. If he was right, then how did her baby wind up as the adopted child of Eva Thompson Bustard?

Dick Morrison had put the adoption papers under seal, the same papers that Tom Walters photographed, the same papers that Judge Dick Morrison signed. So how did the good judge come to be involved in adopting out his murdered sister-in-law's baby?

The adoption agency listed Jeannie Roberts as Buck's mother. Why would she claim that if Buck actually belonged to Marie? How did she come into possession of the child?

Did Jeannie kill Marie to get the baby, then kill Eva years later to get the boy back again? Suspect Number One.

Only, why travel to North Carolina to murder someone? And why wait so many years to get revenge on Eva? Jeannie was a long shot.

Ben scanned down the list of arrest calls from the two months around Buck's adoption date that Tom had printed out. Ben's number was written on a sticky note attached to the adoption papers. Why was someone trying to reach him on a private number? The list was five pages long, counting the short description that came with each. One hundred twenty-two arrests in sixty days. Most were drunk and disorderlies. A few were more serious. A break-in. Domestic calls. A lot of drug arrests.

One caught his eye. "Kenneth Robertson." Picked up for possession of cocaine along with his wife and child. The mother was not charged; so, her name did not appear. A short sentence at the end noted, "Judge M. directed sheriff's office to request DHS intervention." Bingo. That would explain who was trying to reach Ben and why. Except Morrison didn't want Ben involved. He wanted a deputy who would do what he needed and keep it quiet. Plenty of those willing to go behind Ben's back when quite a few of the previous sheriff's men were still in the department.

Ben dug out the Eva Bustard file one more time and scanned through the folder until he found the notes on Jeannie Roberts that Sarah had put together for him. Jeannie was the widow of Kenneth Roberts, who died in jail. Kenny Roberts not Robertson, a misspelled name. Of course. How could he forget that day? He just hadn't coupled it with Kenneth's name until now. The day Ray Thompson was killed by an inmate was huge news in the county, and Ben's own deputies had to shoot him down.

So Dick Morrison signed Buck's adoption papers to Eva and Ray a few days after Kenny's arrest. Then Dick Morrison's former law partner was murdered by Kenny three years later. And Dick Morrison's name shows up as the second beneficiary on Eva's million-dollar life insurance policy. Did Dick Morrison kill Eva? Suspect Number Two.

Buck was the one person connecting everybody. Ben fit the several possibilities together to see which made the most sense.

Did Leon kill Eva in a fit of rage? Or maybe because he thought she had a life insurance policy, and he could somehow manage to get his hands on the proceeds? Suspect Number Three.

Teresa swore by his alibi that night. Plus, Ben had no evidence Leon even knew of the life insurance, much less figure out how to get the money when his name wasn't on the policy. No, Leon didn't make sense.

Perhaps Yvonne killed Eva. She certainly seemed to despise her sister. But enough to kill her? Dick had a million reasons to get rid of Eva and figure out how to get Buck out of the way. This made the most sense, perhaps with Yvonne's participation. Yvonne's blood was on Eva's shirt but that didn't prove Eva was murdered. He just didn't have enough proof.

Maybe Buck was the lock that bound them all together, but somebody else might have the key. Jeannie. Find her and get her to tell how she got Buck and came to lose him only a year later. That was the only way to move forward on the case. Bring Jeannie in for questioning.

She had a story to tell, and he needed to get that story even if he had to lean on her. Nate Williams and his team of dogs, along with Jake Bustard and another deputy that Ben trusted would be searching the woods first thing in the morning. They had a little time to work with but not long. Tom's friend had "lost" the email about Marie, but she would have to find it and forward it to Leon soon. Once Leon found out about Marie, he would step in with both feet.

Next thing: tail Yvonne. She knew a lot more about Marie than she had allowed. Her reaction to the news told him that much. He didn't have enough reason to bring her in, yet. But she might lead them somewhere. Ben would have to do it. There was nobody left.

Finally, talk to Judge Neighbors about issuing a subpoena for Dick Morrison to bring him in for questioning. Judge Neighbors had already felt the wrath of Dick Morrison after the last subpoena he gave to Ben, but instead of being hesitant this time, the judge was more than happy to help out. Ben would ask Tom to get the paperwork signed tonight.

When the sun rose on Wednesday, the wheels would begin to turn.

Yvonne Morrison

Sixty

Hell has no madness to compare to Yvonne's mood by the time Dick Morrison arrived home. Dick had taken his time leaving the courthouse after he got the furious call from his wife demanding his presence.

When he finally walked in the door late in the evening, the storm was at its peak. Shards of broken crystal ground under his shoe. High-pitched curses, mostly aimed at Yvonne's long-missing sister, Marie, bellowed from the living room. They were joined by a cacophony of piano wires stretched over a broken soundboard. Yvonne uttered a fresh epithet each time she rained down another blow on the keyboard from the iron lampstand she wielded in her hands.

"What the hell, Yvonne? Have you gone crazy?"

"Shut up, Dick, or you're next," she yelled.

Dick stood in the doorway for at least ten more minutes until the piano was completely destroyed. Finally, Yvonne slid down the wall and settled like a mound of melted wax in the corner.

When he thought she had quietened enough, Dick went and stood before her.

"What's this all about?" he demanded.

"Damn you," she said. "Goddamn you to the lowest pit of hell, you worthless whore-chasing bastard."

"Yvonne," he said, raising his voice. "Stop it."

"It's too late for that. I put up with it for years. Every skirt you ran after with your dick hanging out of your pants. Every late-night phone call from some woman asking for you. Every time you left me here at home while you were out fucking some desperate mother who would do anything to keep her child, any fucking thing you asked."

"That's enough."

"Oh, you don't want to hear about your own sins, do you? You self-righteous prick. You pretend to be the judge of the dregs of humanity, looking down from your high and mighty bench. But you never dare to look at yourself. You're lower than any of those men you sent to jail for not paying up so you could go lay with their whore wives. You'd fucking make them watch if you could, wouldn't you?"

"What the hell are you carrying on about, Yvonne?"

"Marie. That's what."

"Marie? Your sister, Marie? What's she got to do with anything?"

"Everything, Dick. She's got something to do with everything. Sit down."

Yvonne made Dick listen to what she had to say, everything she had done for him over all the years of loyalty she had paid to him. It was his fucking time to listen.

"Eva wasn't the first for you," she said, still seething. "I knew who you were already by that time. But I made my bed, and by God, I was going to sleep in it, even if I had to kick out every other woman to do it. God knows why, but I did everything in my power to protect you from your own shortcomings, all the while eating the shitty lies and excuses you served up."

"I've always loved you. You know that," he said.

"You don't know what love is. You have no idea what it takes. You remember the whore that tried to blackmail us?"

"I put all that behind me years ago, Yvonne. Let it go."

"I can't let it go, you bastard. Do you even know why she quit threatening you?"

"She figured it was useless. I protected myself. Besides, nobody was going to believe her."

"She had you on video. Goddamn, you can be so stupid sometimes. You never knew that, did you?" said Yvonne.

"No wife of mine is going to talk to me this way. Shut up, Yvonne. She left us alone, didn't she?"

"But you didn't leave Eva alone, did you? A few months later and suddenly, you find her a baby. You would've done anything for that slut, wouldn't you?"

"I told you, that's all behind us," he said. "Leave it be, Yvonne. Why are you having a nervous breakdown nearly twenty years later?"

"Because they found Marie," she began to cry, but her tears burned. She wiped them quickly so they wouldn't leave scars.

"They found Marie? Is she okay?"

It was time, she told herself. Time to explain just how far she would go for the man she loved. Time to explain the sacrifices she had endured and the pain she had gone through, just for this man. Somebody had to know besides herself. What good is love if you can't tell your lover what you did for him?

So she did.

NATE WILLIAMS

Sixty-one

Thursday morning, dawn
Although the dogs could hunt in the night, the deputies decided to call it off the evening before. Raccoons are one thing but hunting humans in the dark is too dangerous. Nate and the deputies were ready to resume the chase. The dogs were on the leashes and yelping, ready to close in on their quarry. Nate gave them the woman's shirt again, the one Ben retrieved from Jeannie's cabin. They didn't have anything recent of Buck's so all they could hope is that they were still together.

Though a few days had passed, Jeannie's scent was still there. No rain to wash it away. They found the trail yesterday at dusk. Today, the dogs pounced on it, running in and along the riverbed, crossing over and doubling back a few times. With only a few puddles left to hide the scent, and some of the best dogs in Alabama working it, the trail led deeper and deeper into the refuge. The dogs grew more and more excited.

At some point, Nate decided to loose the dogs. They shot through the woods, baying and sniffing and doubling back until the fresh direction was discovered and the process repeated again. The deputies followed Nate, who knew they couldn't stay on the dogs' tails. Finally, just out of sight around the next river bend, the baying took on a deeper, more insistent note. The hunt was over. Guns drawn, the deputies took the lead, spreading out on either side of the hounds. Perched atop a boulder in the middle of the rocky riverbed, Jeannie sat with hands up, waiting. She was alone.

TOM WALTERS

Sixty-two

Thursday, three p.m.
Tom Walters, in his official car, found Dick Morrison in his front yard, directing a crew of Mexican workers where to dig the water line trench for a new fountain. The boss man, the one who spoke the best English, nodded when the judge shouted his orders as if he was deaf. When the boss did not immediately begin pointing to the others, the judge did it for him, yelling even louder. Most of them stared back silently until the foreman came up and calmly directed each one what to do. The judge threw up his hands and turned, just then seeing three lawmen standing in his driveway.

Tom held out a paper.

"Come with me, Judge," he said. "I need to ask you a few questions."

Dick glared at the deputy. "Who put you up to this? Not Leon. He would know better. Now, get out of my yard," yelled Dick. "I have nothing to say to you."

"Maybe, maybe not, but this paper says I have the right to ask. Best you come with me to the office downtown. Or I could get another deputy to come out with his lights and siren on to help me escort you. Your choice."

Yvonne stepped onto the porch but said nothing, as was her custom when she and her husband were together in public.

"What's this all about?" asked Dick angrily. "I knew I shouldn't have put Uncle Ben in office all those years ago. And you? You're just his goddamn lackey."

"Get in, Judge, or I can help you."

Yvonne watched until they were out of sight. The Mexican crew continued working as if nothing had happened. Yvonne pulled out her phone and looked through her contact list for the lawyer who did their last deed work. She thought better of it and put the phone up. No use getting an attorney involved and stir up further suspicions. One of the landscape workers leaned on his shovel for a second and looked at Yvonne. He shook his head. She slammed the door behind her.

BUCK

Sixty-three

Thursday, seven p.m.
I drove the truck in silence. Jeannie had told me where to find the extra set of keys, the spare that Russell Lee kept at Jeannie's house. Even in the dark, I could see the stains on the living room floor, soaked into the pine boards so deep they would never come out. I didn't know Russell very long, but I liked the wiry man who had a ready smile and a likable laugh. I paused to thank the blood stains, the only thing left of Russell, except for his truck still parked outside.

Now I was pulling up to the gates of the high-class subdivision where I knew Yvonne lived. They would never let me in, I realized, so I mumbled a lame excuse about a wrong turn and backed out. The female security guard walked behind me and when I pulled away, she took down the license number as she was trained to do.

Gated communities keep out vehicles, and the really well-patrolled ones keep out the walk-up trespassers. This one was protected by a brick wall along the paved road, but at the point where the property lines turned up into the woods and ran away from the road, the fence turned to barbed wire. Easy to cross. I found an old logging trail to turn into and hide the truck. I hiked through the woods, climbed the fence, stole through a couple of back yards and around a house, then stepped onto Highlands Drive, the well-lit wide boulevard where all the wealthy people of Tierney County came and went, whether they lived there or they simply played golf from time to time.

I took my hoodie down so I wouldn't look out of place and pulled my phone out, just another self-absorbed White rich kid lost in himself and his social media. Soon, I found my destination and made my way to the back yard. I almost fell onto my face when I stumbled into an open shallow trench. I cursed and peered around me. No light came on. Everybody behind gates likes to think they're secure.

The night provided plenty of cover for me to slip over the wooden fence to the back yard. Yvonne was there, on the deck, a phone in one hand and a drink in the other, a lone light keeping her company. Even in late September, the heat was thick. She wore a halter top cinched tight under her breasts, and her artificially blonde hair hung long over her shoulders. I watched for a few moments, thinking she was a handsome woman if not exactly pretty. She reminded me of a somewhat mannish version of my mother. Her face was square and severe, something the enhanced boobs and long hair were intended to divert attention from and to soften, but somehow all fell short of the mark. She didn't notice when I started up the stairs—until it was too late.

BEN JEFFERSON

Sixty-four

Thursday, eight-thirty p.m.
The black Volvo glided through the four-way stop without the "rock-backward, then go" that Ben's deputies always told the drivers to do the next time, as they tore out traffic tickets. Tonight, Ben simply waited a few seconds and followed safely along behind the car. When the Volvo reached the guard house, the gate automatically opened and drove through slowly. The guard peered at the car but could not make out the driver through the tinted glass, even though she knew the vehicle to belong to Yvonne Morrison. She made a note on her pad, even though she was not required to check identities leaving the place. Double-checking was a practice she got into the habit of when Mrs. Morrison first began paying her to log the judge's coming and goings. Just for fair treatment and maybe her own amusement, she did the same when Yvonne passed through the entrance and exit gates. The car turned left, away from town. Ben followed a couple hundred feet behind. For the next two hours, the car seemed to wander slowly down back roads with no apparent purpose or direction. Ben kept it in his sight until the car pulled into a church yard and the lights went out. He debated about stopping but decided against it. He drove slowly by and turned around at the next crossing gravel road. When he came back, the car was gone.

Sixty-five

Thursday, nine p.m.
"Look, Judge, we know you ordered Kenny Roberts arrested. We know you took his baby boy away from him. We interviewed the deputy who did it for you. He confirmed it was at your direction. Now," Tom said, holding up his phone showing a letterhead of the state forensics lab that Ben had forwarded to him earlier, "we know who that baby boy really belonged to."

Leon had railed at Tom when he brought the judge into the station, making sure that Morrison knew he was not involved in it. Tom merely handed the subpoena to Leon, who swore he'd call Judge Neighbors to get to the bottom of this travesty.

Out of Dick's hearing, he growled at Tom. "I don't care if the town loves you enough to marry you. You're fucking gone when this is over."

Tom had let Dick stew for more than an hour while he stood behind the one-way glass watching Dick pace back and forth, like a caged tiger. Finally, Dick settled in a chair with his elbows on his knees and his face in his hands.

Tom returned to the room and apologized for being gone so long. He turned on the recorder and kept his voice low, quiet and respectful while he laid out the evidence one more time. The soft tone belied the harsh accusing words he spoke. Leaning forward, head down, hand almost touching Dick's knee, an observer might even get the impression that Tom was a close friend, ready and willing to take the burden off Dick's heavy conscience.

The judge leaned back in his chair and rubbed both eyes with the heels of his palms. The wheels in his head continued to turn, calculating the outcomes of any word he might utter. The balance had for so long tilted in his wife's direction, but with each piece of new evidence presented to him by the deputy, they inexorably swung the other way. Soon, he had a decision to make. He could stop the questioning until he had an attorney present. That would delay things, but it would also mean he was throwing his lot in with his wife, at least in the law's eyes. Or…

Tom could almost read Dick's thoughts. For all the judge's passionate, Old Testament-laced sermons from the bench, Tom knew him to be cold, analytical, and, most of all, self-serving.

"We have to believe you knew who Buck's real mother was," said Tom, calmly, quietly. "You're involved somehow in the abduction of a baby and the grisly murder of his mother. The only question is this: was your involvement witting or unwitting?"

Finally, Dick sat up in his chair and leaned forward toward his confessor, not seeking absolution but rather protesting his innocence.

"I didn't know," he said.

"What didn't you know, Judge?" asked Tom.

"That the boy was Marie's."

Tom slid his chair back and stood up. The man hunched in front of him—stripped of his ceremonial black robe and his usual lofty position behind a raised bench—seemed so small, so pitiable.

"It sure looks like you knew. Why take this boy? Why give him to Marie's sister, the one you really loved for all those years?" Tom's tone, no longer that of a friend, dramatically changed to the stern voice of the law. He was taking a risk, showing disrespect to the judge, but he needed to push the judge into giving up the details.

"I didn't know, dammit." Dick's eyes narrowed and his chin shot up, like a boxer with a second wind. "Who's putting you up to this?" he demanded. "Like Leon said, you can kiss your badge goodbye when I get through with you."

"Look, Dick, I understand your wife left home this evening. It's late, and she hasn't come back. Buck is missing, too, and I've got a bad feeling that he has nothing good on his mind. If you care anything about your wife, she might be in danger. Time to come clean."

"Whatever that boy does to her, she deserves," said Dick.

Tom sat down and leaned in toward the judge again. "Why's that, Judge?" he asked softly.

The scales tipped once and for all, and Judge Morrison told everything that Yvonne admitted to him. If he was to survive, it was the only way.

BUCK

Sixty-six

Friday morning. Still hours from dawn. No moon. Clouds hid all the stars. Pitch black. Yvonne and me in her fine black car. Made me think of the ride to the cemetery except we were headed down the road towards Leon's house. Funny. I don't think of it as my house anymore. I'm not sure I ever did.

A few hundred yards from his driveway, I had Yvonne pull onto the old logging road. I waved the pistol at the keys in the ignition, and she shut the car off and waited. I took another swallow from the now half-empty vodka bottle. It had been nearly full when I first came up to her.

"What are you doing, Buck?" asked Yvonne. It was her first words since leaving her house. The hard end of the pistol in my hand pressed into her ribs.

"Shut up," I said. My only words to her for the past five hours had been where to drive.

"You're drunk. You're not thinking straight," she said.

"I'm thinking straighter than I ever have," I said, but my words tumbled out like broken beer bottles against the asphalt. "I saw you there."

"You saw me where?"

"A woman. I saw you. It was you, wasn't it?"

"You're not making any sense, Buck. Look, we can go home and forget this ever happened. You just got a little mixed up and carried away. That's all."

"Get out," I said.

"This is close to your place. Why are we here? Are you taking me to see Leon?"

"Shit," I said. "Why would I want to see that bastard?"

"So he can talk some sense into you," she offered. "That's a good idea, Buck. Let's go see Leon. He'll work it out."

"Leon ain't going to fuck with me no more. Buck Thompson is in charge now. Buck Thompson. Captain of my fate. Master of my soul." I took another swallow of courage and shook my head violently to clear my thoughts. "Get out," I said again.

Yvonne complied. She must have thought about running, and I was probably too drunk to catch her. So, before she could firm her resolve, I got around to her side of the car.

"Don't think about trying to get away," I said. "I'll shoot your ass."

"Think about what you're doing, Buck. They'll take you to jail."

"They already think I killed my mother. It won't matter if I kill you, too."

"Don't say that. You're talking out of your mind." She held out her hand. "Give me the gun, and let's go home. No harm."

I grabbed her hand and swung her around face first into the car hood. She yelped and gasped, but I pushed the gun muzzle against her head.

From my pocket, I drew out a cord and wrapped her hands behind her back. I pulled out a bandanna, and pushing all of my weight against her, I used both hands to pull the cloth between her teeth. The gun banged against the side of her head as I held onto it, and she whimpered in pain. Then I secured the knots around her hands and pulled her up by the hair.

"Let's go," I ordered, pushing her into the woods where the briars tore at us and where ghosts hid.

When we pushed into the pine trees, a soft rain began to fall. The dust on the branches slid off in muddy drops that smelled like a fresh grave. I pulled my hoodie back over my head and pushed Yvonne through the trees and down to the creek bottom. She stumbled several times, but each time, I pulled her up and pushed her forward. In the darkness, I couldn't see, but I knew exactly where we were going, even though I had been there only once since the…murder.

That's what it was. Murder. And I had the murderer now. She had to be the woman in my visions. The only woman left who had a reason to murder my mother. The woman who had stolen me as a baby. Had sold me to Jeannie in exchange for her silence. If Jeannie wasn't responsible, and I no longer believed that, then Yvonne had to be the one who attacked my mother that terrible night.

When we reached the creek, I pushed her onto the ground. The rain was harder now, and Yvonne's hair looked like ropy seaweed, thin and slimy. She shivered.

I jerked her around and tugged at the bandanna until it came off.

"Why?" I cried.

"Why what?" she spit back. "What is it you think I did?" She rocked forward and back. The rain came harder, and water streamed down her face. She squeezed her eyes and shook her head to clear them.

"I saw you. Who else could it be?" I raised the pistol and pointed the barrel at her face.

"Buck, you have to believe me, I didn't kill her. It wasn't me you saw."

I slumped my shoulders and dropped my arm. I stared at the creek bed where I had found my mother so many months ago. It seemed like forever.

"Don't believe her."

When I looked up, the girl was standing there, next to Yvonne. She was ragged, and her hair was still as matted as always. Even so, I could see that she was a beautiful young woman. I imagined her with a long, red dress, her hair combed and bright red lipstick contrasting with her pale blue eyes, and as I looked, she changed into my mind's image. She was stunning.

"This is what I looked like before."

"Before what?" I asked.

Yvonne stared at me, apparently unable to comprehend.

"Before her. She made me what I am today," said the girl.

"What are you?" I asked.

"It's me, Buck," said Yvonne. "Look, you've got to come to your senses. Whoever was following us will keep looking. It's just a matter of time before they find us. Let's go home now, and I won't say anything bad. Okay?" She looked around desperately to see if someone, anyone, was coming to help.

"Not you," I yelled. "Her. I'm talking to her." I took another swallow from the bottle and pointed the gun at the vision of a beautiful young woman in an evening dress. Her hair was thick and blonde and flipped up at the ends. One blonde strand hung seductively over one eye.

"I should shoot the both of you."

"Go ahead," said the young woman.

Yvonne whimpered and hid her face. The rain fell even harder, and a few lightning streaks crossed the sky. I could hear water gurgling in the stream bed.

"No, you're not real. You're making me crazy. Go away."

"I can't go away, Buck. I don't have the power to do that anymore. She took it from me," she said, pointing at Yvonne curled at her feet.

"Go away, goddammit," I yelled.

I pointed the pistol at the beautiful young girl and pulled the trigger, over and over and over until the hammer clicked uselessly. Yvonne shrieked. Instantly, the girl changed to the way she was before, ragged and rough. She laughed.

"This is who you've been looking for, Buck. Right here in the mud in front of you. This is the monster that killed your mother. What are you going to do about it?"

I dropped the gun. "I don't know what to do."

"Eva was right," said the girl. "You can't do anything for yourself, can you? All you can do is whine about how hard you have it."

"Eva?" I said.

"Don't you remember that night? Right before you ran off to get drunk, and she ran off to get laid. Don't you remember Eva's words?"

"No," I said "No, no."

The image in front of me morphed into a blonde middle-aged woman with a hard look in her eyes and a razor's edge in her words.

"My God, Buck," said the woman in Eva's voice. "You're just like my sister Marie. You have no purpose. God knows I tried to give you one. Leon's tried his damnedest. But it's just no use. You'll never amount to anything without a purpose."

"No, Mama." I squeezed my eyes shut. When I opened them again, the ragged girl in white stood before me.

"You need a purpose, Buck. Do you want to see what this devil did to your mother?" said the girl, pointing accusingly at Yvonne, still hiding her head in the mud.

"You showed me. I don't want to see it again."

"I didn't show you this."

The girl reached to her waist and gathered up the thin nightgown she was wearing, pulling it up and off over her head. She dropped it by her side and opened her arms wide.

"Look at what she did," she said. Her voice remained steady and clear, even as I fell to my knees.

Her abdomen gaped like a tattered curtain from sternum to crotch. Torn tissue hung from the wound like ghastly, bloody, birthday streamers. She grasped both edges of the gash and pulled it apart. A chunk of gray flesh ripped off and fell onto the ground next to Yvonne.

"Come here, son," said the girl. "Put your hand into my sliced-open womb and tell me you don't believe I'm real. This is what SHE did to me. This is what SHE did to your mother."

"I don't understand. You're . . ."

The girl nodded and stepped toward me. She put out her hand, still bloody, and I took it. I quieted and stood effortlessly, as if I was lifted.

"Touch it," she said, "and you will believe."

I reached my fingers toward her and touched inside her belly. It was cold.

"Feel that? That's the cord that attached you to me. That's the placenta that nourished you. It's all of you I have left. Now do you see your purpose?"

"No," I whispered but my hand stayed where it was. I felt myself being drawn toward her, my hand disappearing inside. It felt good to be back, to be protected. I closed my eyes.

"Buck, let me go," pleaded Yvonne, her voice barely audible over the rain that came down in sheets now. A crack split the night with a blinding light, and Yvonne stared into my eyes. I smiled. A broad smile. I moved with swift purpose to Yvonne and snatched her to her feet.

"It's your turn."

Yvonne screamed, but I grabbed her by the hair and dragged her to the stream. The creek bed, dry for so long, had filled rapidly, washing leaves and old death out, preparing itself for new death. I picked her up and bodily threw her into the creek. She landed with a crack against the branches, and her breath rushed out in one quick release. Her arms came free and she tried to struggle to her feet. I was already on her. I pulled her to the deep end, where the water was rising fast.

"Don't. No. Help me," she tried to yell but only whimpering protests came out.

"You killed me. Yvonne. You tracked me down, pretending to help me, and then sliced me open like a slab of meat." The voice coming from my mouth was strong, steady, as sharp as a butcher's blade.

Yvonne pulled away and fell backwards. "What? No, I... I..." Her words abandoned her, and she stared in horror into my eyes.

"Do you remember, sister?" spoke the cold voice from my own mouth.

Yvonne opened her mouth, but she could not speak.

I grabbed her by the head, one thumb in each eye and pushed her face under water. Yvonne's fighter instincts returned. She would not give up easily. She kicked. Her arms flailed. She managed to get her head to the surface and coughed. My hand slipped off, and she caught my thumb in her teeth. She bit hard.

I yanked my hand away, tearing the skin. Blood oozed from the wound, mixing with the rain, flowing into Yvonne's face.

"Buck, stop it." A familiar female voice yelled out to me.

The voice was distant. I couldn't tell where it came from. I held both my hands to my ears. I didn't want to hear any sound anymore except the pleading cries of an evil woman. I grabbed Yvonne and pushed her head under again.

"No, Buck, this isn't you," cried the familiar voice, someone I knew, someone I loved.

I let go and sat back on my ankles. Yvonne swung an open hand toward my face, and it landed true. I fell backwards. She scrambled out of my way, coughing violently. I rose once more.

A gunshot cracked through the night and slammed into a tree above my head. My mouth fell open and I looked at my hands. My eyes widened into the surprised look of a falling lost child, dropped from the heavens and crashing to earth.

"Buck, don't move or I'll shoot you this time." Ben stood beside Mandalee and pointed his pistol directly at my face. Mandalee held a flashlight shining down into the waters.

I looked down at my bloody hand. "Eva told you," my voice said. The words pierced my chest, and I shook. "She said you were just like me, a drunk with no purpose. She was wrong. You're not like me. I know my purpose. Take control, boy, or nothing good happens."

"No," I screamed.

I threw my face into the water, still barely only a foot deep, and held onto a root at the bottom, held on for dear death. Ben and Mandalee both jumped in. Only the two of them together could pry my hands loose.

Sixty-seven

The metal clanged behind me. I waited until the officer escorting me buzzed the control guard. A second later, the lock on the door in front of me slid open with a metallic snap. The heavy door rolled sideways like a boulder from a burial cave, lumbering on the worn bearings and groaning in protest, not yet ready to release its prisoner. This wasn't release, though. Only two years of my ten-year sentence had passed. In exchange for my plea, the assistant district attorney dropped the attempted murder charge. Judge Neighbors, presiding over my trial, considered the extenuating circumstances and gave me the minimum sentence for first-degree kidnapping under Alabama law. Even so, I would be behind bars for quite some time yet. But in another sense, this was a real release. This was the first time I had been allowed in the visitor's yard.

Mandalee visited me behind glass every month for over a year until I asked her to stop coming. Not because I didn't want to see her. I love her. But she's much too young to waste her life on a felon stuck in prison. She argued, of course, and cried. I stood firm. I remembered my last words to her, written on prison paper, with the ink on the last lines blurred where my wet hand had lingered before I signed it.

"Find your happiness while you can."

Since then, my only other visitor has been Coach Ben, who stopped by every few months to make sure I was being treated well. I was happy that he won re-election. He's a good man that treats people fairly, even the ones that screw up, like me. Each time he came by, I asked about Teresa. How was she? Was Mandalee's family taking good care of her? Could you ask her to write?

"Go on, Thompson," said the officer, pushing me through the opening. "Don't got all day."

I stepped forward into the sunshine. The yard was dotted with steel tables concreted into red dirt. A heavy steel fence topped with razor wire surrounded us. At each table, a gaggle of people—kids and old men in beards and women with cigarettes hanging from their mouths and girls with hopeful looks, gathered around a fellow in an orange jumpsuit. I scanned the yard until my eyes stopped at the far corner where a small teenaged girl with curly brown hair stood, looking back at me. She didn't wave.

I approached until we were only a couple feet apart. I looked her up and down for a minute. She didn't say anything.

"Oh, my God," I finally said. "My sister got boobs."

Teresa flung her arms wide and grinned.

"Finally," she said and threw herself into my arms.

"How did you get here? It's too dangerous—a kid like you traveling alone."

"I'm not a kid anymore. Besides, I know how to take care of myself."

"Yeah, I bet you do." I held her hands and looked her over. "Seems like it's been forever. God, it's good to see you."

We sat and talked for nearly an hour, trying to pack in as much as possible before our time was up. Mostly, I asked questions and let Teresa do the talking.

"Daddy gets out in a few months," she said. "Time off for good behavior, if you can imagine that."

"And Jeannie?" I asked.

"I don't like to talk about her. She's no good. It was her words that put Daddy in jail."

"I heard she got time, though."

"She made a deal. One year," said Teresa. "It isn't right. She was the criminal, and she's already free."

We talked about the boys in middle school.

"They're either children or rednecks," she said. "Maybe there'll be some smarter ones in high school."

"No hurry," I said. "You tell anybody giving you problems that your brother has connections in prison. That'll scare 'em straight."

"Don't talk like that, Buck. I don't know why they have you in here, anyway. What that woman did was unforgivable. You had every right to do what you did, I say."

"No, I didn't. Quit thinking that. A man's gotta pay for what he does, or he isn't really a man."

"Well, at least she'll pay, too," said Teresa, "even if it takes another twenty years for them to execute her."

Neither one of us spoke for several minutes, content just to sit beside each other. Teresa leaned on my shoulder and said, "What really happened to Mama? The sheriff says the case is closed, but I'll always wonder. Did Aunt Yvonne do that too?"

"I thought I knew, but I'm not so sure anymore," I said after thinking about it for a minute. "I really don't know at all."

"Some people still think you did it because of what you tried to do to Yvonne."

"Some things will never change," I said.

"I brought you a surprise, you know," she said, with a sly smile.

"The guards don't like surprises too much," I said. "You're going to get me in trouble."

"I don't think you'll mind." Teresa pointed to the parking lot barely visible through the front gate. A young woman raised her hand and slowly let it fall.

"Mandalee," I whispered. I raised my hand in return and held it there for a long moment.

"She brought me. She said even if you didn't want her to come, friends don't abandon friends."

The buzzer rang and Teresa flinched slightly. All the jumpsuits got up slowly and straggled to the door.

"Got to go, girl. Thank you for coming to see me. It's been a long time."

"Let's don't say it, Buck."

"Say what?"

"Goodbye. Let's don't ever say it and mean it. Okay?"

"Deal, kiddo,"

I looked back when I got to the line of inmates at the door.

"Tell Mandalee…" I yelled but I stopped, not sure what to tell her.

The guards began ushering the visitors out the other side. Teresa was among the last. She waved.

That night, after the buzzer sounded the last warning and all the prisoners were back in their cells and the guard came by to count each one and the lights went out, I stared at the ceiling and listened to the old man ranting curses from the end of the block and a boy two doors down who cried each night and another man just past him who yelled at him to shut up.

I am comfortable here. I've grown used to the noise. I have a schedule to meet every day. Somebody tells me where to go and when to be there, what to do, and how to do it. I don't miss the alcohol.

Someday I'll have to face the world again. I don't know if I can make it on the outside, but I know I won't be alone. Besides, whatever happens, it will be my choice.

Teresa's question lingers in my head, bobbing up through all the unanswered questions still in my mind.

"What really happened to my mother, Marie?" I whisper from time to time.

But Marie isn't talking anymore.

Photo courtesy of PPM Consultants

WB Henley has been a geologist for 45 years. He's read a lot of rocks in his time. Believe it or not, rocks are the books written by Nature using Earth as her paper, Wind and Water as her writing tool, and Fire as the emotion at the heart of every good story. Not different than for us mere mortals.

WB has been a Southerner for even a couple of decades m' that the South holds a lock on good writers. It's just there ar conflicts, contradictions, and customs in the South that a ' pretty much around every turn in a dirt road or smo' skyline. Two of his stories were featured in the Writers' Collection published by the Alabama W' (AWC) including *Vigil*, a flash fiction piece abo' a hospital waiting room, and *Ashes*, a story abo' dreams at a funeral home. He made the short ' Windom Writing Competition with *On t'* *Sea*, a tale of lost chances and second c'

Inescapable won the 2022 prize f' awarded in the AWC writers' comr

WB makes his home in India' wife Shelia. Over his years the' seven grandchildren. Along ι. three horses, numerous dogs, an ι bird or two.

Lightning Source UK Ltd.
Milton Keynes UK
UKHW040615120223
416808UK00004B/447